Memory
of
Water

Memory
of
Water

Emmi Itäranta

HARPER
Voyager

HarperCollins*Publishers*
77–85 Fulham Palace Road,
Hammersmith, London W6 8JB

www.harpercollins.co.uk

Published by Harper*Voyager*
An Imprint of HarperCollins*Publishers* 2014
1

Memory of Water (Teemestarin Kirja)
Copyright © Emmi Itäranta 2012

Original edition published by Teos Publishers 2012, Finland

English edition published by agreement with Emmi Itäranta and
Elina Ahlback Literary Agency, Helsinki, Finland

Emmi Itäranta asserts the moral right to
be identified as the author of this work

A catalogue record for this book
is available from the British Library

ISBN: 9780007529919

Typeset in Sabon LT Std by Palimpsest Book Production Ltd,
Falkirk, Stirlingshire

Printed and bound in Great Britain by
Clays Ltd, St Ives plc

MIX
Paper from
responsible sources
FSC www.fsc.org   FSC C007454

FSC™ is a non-profit international organisation established to promote the
responsible management of the world's forests. Products carrying the FSC
label are independently certified to assure consumers that they come from
forests that are managed to meet the social, economic and ecological needs
of present and future generations, and other controlled sources.

Find out more about HarperCollins and the environment at
www.harpercollins.co.uk/green

PROLOGUE

Everything is ready now.

Each morning for seven weeks I have swept the fallen leaves from the stone slabs that form the path to the teahouse, and forty-nine times I have chosen a handful among them to be scattered on the stones again, so the path wouldn't look too much like it had been swept. That was one of the things my father always insisted on.

Sanja told me once the dead don't need pleasing. Perhaps they don't. Perhaps I do. Sometimes I don't know the difference. How could I, when they are in my blood and bones, when all that is left of them is me?

I haven't dared to go to the spring in seven weeks. Yesterday I turned on the tap in the house and held the mouth of the waterskin to its metal. I spoke to it in pretty words and ugly words, and I may have even screamed and wept, but water doesn't care for human sorrows. It flows without slowing or quickening its pace in the darkness of the earth, where only stones will hear.

The pipe gave a few drops, perhaps a spoonful, into my waterskin.

1

I know what it means.

This morning I emptied the rest of the water from the skin into the cauldron, brought some dried peat from the shed into the teahouse and placed the firestarter next to the hearth. I thought of my father, whose wishes I had violated, and my mother, who didn't see the day I became a tea master.

I thought of Sanja. I hoped she was already where I was going.

A guest whose face is not unfamiliar is walking down the path, offering me a hand I'm ready to take. The world will not spin slower or faster when we have passed through the gate together.

What remains is light on water, or a shifting shadow.

PART ONE

Watchers of Water

'Only what changes can remain.'

Wei Wulong, 'The Path of Tea'
7th century of Old Qian time

CHAPTER ONE

Water is the most versatile of all elements. So my father told me the day he took me to the place that didn't exist. While he was wrong about many things, he was right about this, so I still believe. Water walks with the moon and embraces the earth, and it isn't afraid to die in fire or live in air. When you step into it, it will be as close as your own skin, but if you hit it too hard, it will shatter you. Once, when there were still winters in the world, cold winters, white winters, winters you could wrap yourself in and slip on and come in to warm from, you could have walked on the crystallized water that was called ice. I have seen ice, but only small, man-made lumps. All my life I have dreamed of how it would be to walk on frozen sea.

Death is water's close companion. The two cannot be separated, and neither can be separated from us, for they are what we are ultimately made of: the versatility of water, and the closeness of death. Water has no beginning and no end, but death has both. Death *is* both. Sometimes death travels hidden in water, and sometimes water will chase death away, but they go together always, in the world and in us.

This, too, I learned from my father, but I now believe I would have learned it without him just as well.

I can pick my own beginning.

Perhaps I will pick my own end.

The beginning was the day when my father took me to the place that didn't exist.

It was a few weeks after I had taken my Matriculation Tests, compulsory for all citizens the year they came of age. While I had done well, there was never any question that I would remain in my current apprenticeship with my father instead of continuing my studies in the city. It was a choice I had felt obliged to make, and therefore, perhaps, not really a choice. But it seemed to make my parents happy, and it didn't make me miserable, and those were the things that mattered at the time.

We were in our garden behind the teahouse, where I was helping my father hang empty waterskins to dry. A few of them were still draped on my arm, but most were already hanging upside down from the hooks on the metal rack. Sunlight filtered in veils through their translucent surfaces. Slow drops streaked their insides before eventually falling on the grass.

'A tea master has a special bond with water and death,' my father said to me as he examined one of the skins for cracks. 'Tea isn't tea without water, and without tea a tea master is no tea master. A tea master devotes his life to serving others, but he only attends the tea ceremony as a guest once in his lifetime, when he feels his death approaching. He orders his successor to prepare the last ritual, and after he has been served the tea, he waits alone in the teahouse until death presses a hand on his heart and stops it.'

My father tossed the waterskin on the grass where a couple of others were already waiting. Mending the skins didn't always work out, but they were expensive, like anything made of durable plastic, and it was usually worth a try.

'Has anyone ever made a mistake?' I asked. 'Did anyone think their death was coming, when it wasn't time yet?'

'Not in our family,' he said. 'I've heard of a past-world master who ordered his son to prepare the last ritual, settled to lie down on the teahouse floor and walked into his house two days later. The servants thought he was a ghost and one of them had a heart attack. The tea master had mistaken the servant's death for his own. The servant was cremated and the master lived for another twenty years. But it doesn't happen often.'

I slapped a horsefly that had landed on my arm. It darted off just in time with a loud buzz. The headband of my insect hood felt tight and itchy, but I knew taking it off would attract too many insects.

'How do you know when your death is coming?' I asked.

'You know,' my father said. 'Like you know you love, or like in a dream you know that the other person in the room is familiar, even if you don't know their face.' He took the last skins from me. 'Go and get two blaze lanterns from the teahouse veranda, and fill them for me.'

I wondered what he needed the lanterns for, because it was only early afternoon, and this time of the year even the nights didn't drown the sun in the horizon. I went around the teahouse and took two lanterns from under the bench. A stiff-winged blazefly was stirring at the bottom of one. I shook it into the gooseberry bushes. Blazeflies liked gooseberries best, so I kept shaking the branches above the lanterns until there was a handful of sleepily crawling flies inside each. I closed the lids and took the lanterns to my father.

He had lifted an empty waterskin on his back. His expression was closed behind the insect hood. I handed the lanterns to him, but he only took one of them.

'Noria, it's time I showed you something,' he said. 'Come with me.'

We walked across the dried swamp spreading behind our house to the foot of the fell and then up the slope. It wasn't a long walk, but sticky sweat glued the hair onto my scalp. When we reached the height where the boulder garden began, I took my insect hood off. The wind was so strong that there weren't as many horseflies and midges here as around the house.

The sky was pure and still. The sun felt tight on my skin. My father had stopped, perhaps to choose his route. I turned to look down. The tea master's house with its garden was a speckle of floating green in the faded land-scape of burned-out grass and bare stone. The valley was scattered with the houses of the village, and on the other side rose the Alvinvaara fell. Far beyond its slopes, where the watering areas were, loomed a stretch of dark-green fir forest. Yet further that way was the sea, but it couldn't be seen from here even on bright days. In the other direc-tion was the slowly decaying trunk tangle of the Dead Forest. In my childhood there had still been occasional birches that didn't grow higher than to my waist, and once I had picked a whole handful of lingonberries there.

A path ran along the border of the boulder garden, and

my father turned to it. On this side the slope of the fell was full of caves. I had often come here to play when I was younger. I still remembered when my mother had once found me here playing mountain trolls with Sanja and a couple of other kids. She had yelled at my father, who had forgotten to look after me, and dragged me by the arm all the way home. I wasn't allowed to play with the children from the village for a month. But even after that I had sneaked to the caves with Sanja whenever my mother was on research trips, and we had played explorers and adventurers and secret agents from New Qian in the Mediterranean Desert. There were dozens of caves, if not hundreds, and we had explored them as thoroughly as we thought possible. We had kept looking for secret passage-ways and hidden treasures, the kind you'd read about in old books or pod-stories, but never found anything more than coarse, dry stone.

My father stopped outside the mouth of a cave that was shaped like a cat's head, and then passed through it without a word. The entrance was low. My knees rubbed against the rock through the thin fabric of my trousers, and I had trouble bringing the lantern and the insect hood in with me. Inside the cave the air was cool and still. The lanterns began to glow faintly as the yellowish glint of the blazeflies grew in the twilight.

I recognised the cave. We had fought about it one summer with Sanja, when she had wanted to use it for the headquarters of the Central And Crucially Important Explorers' Society of New Qian. I had insisted that there was too much wasted space, because the cave grew steeply lower towards the back, and that it was too far from home for convenient smuggling of food. Eventually, we had opted for a smaller cave closer to my house.

My father was crawling towards the back of the cave. I saw him stop and push his hand right into the wall – so it seemed to me – and I saw the movement of his arm. The rock above him made a faint screeching sound as a dark hole opened in it. The cave was so low there that when he sat up, his head was already at the level of the hole, and he slipped through it, taking his lantern with him. Then I saw his face, when he looked at me through the hole.

'Are you coming?' he said.

I crawled to the back of the cave and felt the wall where I had seen him open the hatch. All I could see in the wavering light of the blaze lantern was the coarse rock, but then my fingers found a narrow shelf-like formation behind which there was a wide crack, and I discovered a small lever hidden in it. The crack was nearly impossible to see because of the way the rock was formed.

'I'll explain later how it all works,' my father said. 'Now come here.'

I followed him through the hatch.

Above the cave there was another one, or rather a tunnel which seemed to plunge right into the heart of the fell. On the ceiling, right above the hatch, there was a metal pipe and a large hook next to it. I had no idea what they were for. On the wall were two levers. My father turned one of them, and the hatch closed. The glow of the lanterns grew bright in the complete darkness of the tunnel. My father removed his insect hood and the waterskin he had been carrying and placed them on the floor.

'You can leave your hood here,' he said. 'You won't need it further ahead.'

The tunnel descended towards the inside of the fell. I noticed that the metal pipe ran along its length. I had no space to walk with my back straight, and my father's head brushed the ceiling at times. The rock under our feet was unexpectedly smooth. The light of my lantern clung to the creases on the back of my father's jacket and the darkness clung to the dents in the walls. I listened to the silence of the earth around us, different from the silence above the ground: denser, stiller. And slowly I began to distinguish a stretching, growing sound at its core, familiar and yet strange. I had never before heard it flowing free, entirely pushed by its own weight and will. It was akin to sounds like rain knuckling the windows or bathwater poured on the roots of the pine trees, but this sound wasn't tame or narrow, not chained in man-made confines. It wrapped me and pulled me in, until it was close as the walls, close as the dark.

My father stopped and I saw in the lantern light that we had come to an opening between the tunnel and another cave. The sound thrummed loud. He turned to look at me. The light of the blazeflies wavered on his face like on water, and the darkness sang behind him. I expected him to say something, but he simply turned his back on me and went through the opening. I followed.

I tried to see ahead, but the glow of the lanterns did not reach far. The darkness received us with a rumble. It was like the roar of heated water at the bottom of an iron cauldron, but more like the sound of a thousand or ten thousand cauldrons when the water has just begun to boil and the tea master knows it's time to remove it from the fire, or it will vanish as steam where it can no longer be caught. I felt something cool and moist on my face. Then we walked a few steps down, and the light of the blazeflies finally hit the sound, and I saw the hidden spring for the first time.

Water rushed from inside the rock in strings and threads and strands of shimmer, in enormous sheets that shattered the surface of the pond at the bottom of the cave when they hit it. It twisted around the rocks and curled in spirals and whirls around itself, and churned and danced and unravelled again. The surface trembled under the force of the movement. A narrow stream flowed from the pond towards the shelf of stone that the doorway we had come through was on, then disappeared into the ground under it. I could see something that looked like a white stain on the rock wall above the surface of the water, and another lever in the wall further away. My father urged me on, to the edge of the pond.

'Try it,' he said.

I dipped my fingers in the water and felt its strength. It moved against my hand like breathing, like an animal, like another person's skin. It was cold, far colder than anything I was used to. I licked my fingers carefully, like I had been taught to do since I was very young: never drink water you haven't tasted first.

'It's fresh,' I said.

Lantern light folded on his face when he smiled, and then, slowly, the smile ran dry.

'You're seventeen, and of age now, and therefore old enough to understand what I'm going to tell you,' my father said. 'This place doesn't exist. This spring dried a long time ago. So the stories tell, and so believe even those who know other stories, tales of a spring in the fell that once provided water for the whole village. Remember. This spring doesn't exist.'

'I'll remember,' I told him, but didn't realise until later what kind of a promise I had made. Silence is not empty or immaterial, and it is not needed to chain tame things. It often guards powers strong enough to shatter everything.

We returned through the tunnel. When we came to the entrance, my father picked up the waterskin he had left there and hung it from the hook on the ceiling. After making sure that the mouth of the skin was open, he turned one of the levers on the wall. I heard an electric noise, similar to the noises the cooling appliances in our kitchen made, and a roar yet different from before, as if captured in metal. In a moment a strong jet of water burst from the ceiling straight into the waterskin.

'Did you make all this?' I asked. 'Or mother? Did she plan this? Did you build this together?'

'Nobody knows for certain who built this,' my father said. 'But tea masters have always believed it was one of them, perhaps the first one who settled here, before winters disappeared and these wars began. Now only the water remembers.'

He turned both levers. The rush of water slowed down and died little by little, and the hatch opened again.

'You first,' he said.

I dropped myself through the hole. He closed the skin tightly, then lowered it carefully into the cave where I took it from him. When the hatch was closed again, the cave looked like nothing but a cave with no secrets.

The glow of the blazeflies faded swiftly in the daylight. When we walked into the garden, my mother, sitting under the awning, raised her eyes from the notes she was taking from a heavy book on her lap. My father handed his lantern to me. The shadows of leaves swayed on the stone slabs, as he walked towards the teahouse with the water-skin on his back. I was going to follow him, but he said, 'Not now.'

I stood still, a lantern in each hand, and listened to the blazeflies bouncing against their sun-baked glass walls. It was only when my mother spoke that I thought of opening the lids of the lanterns.

'You've burned again in the sun,' she said. 'Where did you go with your father?'

The blazeflies sprang up into the air and vanished into the bushes.

'To a place that doesn't exist,' I said, and at that moment I looked at her, and knew that she knew where we had been, and that she had been there too.

My mother didn't say more, not then, but calm vanished from her face.

Late that night, when I lay in my bed under an insect net and watched the orange light of the night sun on the pine trees, I heard her speaking with my father in the kitchen for a long time. I couldn't make out the words they were saying, yet I discerned a dark edge in them that reached all the way to my dreams.

CHAPTER TWO

The ground was still breathing night-chill when I helped my father load the broken waterskins on the low cart at the back of the helicycle. Their scratched plastic surface glinted in the morning sun. I fastened the thick straps around the skins, and when I was certain they were sufficiently steady, I flung my seagrass bag on my shoulder and got up on the seat of the cycle.

'Use Jukara,' my father said. 'He'll give you a discount.' Jukara was the oldest plasticsmith in the village and my father's friend. I hadn't trusted him since some waterskins he had repaired the year before had broken again after only a few uses, so I said nothing, merely moved my head in a way that could be interpreted as a nod. 'And don't take all day,' my father added. 'We have guests coming in tomorrow. I need your help with cleaning the teahouse.'

I stepped on the pedal to start the helicycle. One of the solar panels was broken and the motor was acting up, so I had to pedal almost all the way along the dusty pathway through trees of wavering gold-green scattered around our house. Only just before the edge of the woods did the cycle settle into a steady, quiet spin. I steered the cycle and the cart carefully to the wider road, locked the pedals and let my feet rest on them as the cycle moved unhurriedly towards the village. The morning air felt crisp on my bare arms and there weren't many horseflies yet. I removed my insect hood, letting the wind and sun wash over my face. The sky was a dry, bare blue, and the earth was still, and I saw small animals moving in the dust of the fields in search of water.

After I had passed a few houses at the edge of the village, the road forked. The way to Jukara's repair shop was to the left. I stopped and hesitated, and then I continued to the right, until I saw the familiar chipped-blue picket fence ahead.

Like most buildings in the village, Sanja's home was one of the past-world houses, a one-storey with multiple rooms, a garden and a garage from the time when most people still owned fast past-tech vehicles. The walls had been repaired repeatedly, and Sanja's parents had told me there had once been a nearly flat roof without solar panels, although it was hard for me to imagine.

When I stopped outside the open gate, she was standing in the front yard, emptying the last of a waterskin into a metal tub and cursing. The front door was open and a barely audible flow of pod-news was drifting from inside the house through the insect curtain covering the doorframe. Sanja wasn't wearing an insect hood, and when she looked at me, I saw that she hadn't slept.

'Bloody sham sold me salt water,' she said, furiously tucking her black hair behind her ears. 'I don't know how he did it. I tasted the water first, like I always do, and it was fresh. His prices were atrocious, so I only bought half a skin, but even that was wasted money.'

'What sort of a container did he have?' I asked as I steered the cycle through the gate to the yard.

'One of those old-fashioned ones,' Sanja said. 'A large transparent container on top of a dais, and a pipe from which he sold the water.'

'A double-pipe fraud,' I said. 'I saw those in the city last year. Inside the dais there's a secret container with salt water in it. The pipe has two settings; the first one takes water from the fresh-water container and the second from the hidden one. The seller offers a taste from the drinkable water, but then changes the pipe setting and sells salt water.'

Sanja stared at me for a moment and said then, 'Stupid idiot.' I knew she was talking about herself. She must have spent most of her budget for the week on the salt water.

'It could have happened to anyone,' I told her. 'You couldn't have known. Might still be a good idea to warn others, though.'

Sanja sighed. 'I saw some other people buying from him at the evening market right before the closing time. He's probably far away by now, looking for the next idiot.'

I didn't say aloud what I was thinking: more than once I had heard my parents talk about how seeing lots of frauds on the move usually meant that the times were getting harsher, no matter how often the pod-news repeated that all unrest was temporary and the war was well under control. In the best of times there was sometimes shortage of water, but mostly people were able to do with their monthly quotas and shams didn't bother to go touring. While travelling water merchants who occasionally stopped in small villages kept high prices, they were also aware of how easily their business could be jeopardised and didn't treat any rivals selling undrinkable water kindly. Shams weren't unheard of, but this was the third one in our village within two months. This kind of sudden increase in numbers usually meant that there were strong rumours in the cities about new and stricter quota plans, perhaps even rationing, and some of the water-shams left the over-crowded markets of the cities in search of less competition and more gullible clients.

'Is your water pipe out of order again?' I asked.

'That old piece of rubbish needs to be dug up and replaced with a new one,' Sanja said. 'I'd do it myself if I had time. Minja fell sick again last week, and I don't dare to give her our tap water even if it's been boiled. Father says it's perfectly fine, but I think he's just grown an iron stomach after drinking dirt water for so many years.'

Minja was Sanja's two-year-old little sister who had been sick constantly since her birth. Lately their mother Kira had also been unwell. I had not told Sanja, but once or twice in the half-light of late evening I had seen a stranger sitting by their door, a dark and narrow figure, not unkind but somehow aware that it wouldn't be welcomed anywhere it went. It had been still and quiet, waiting patiently, not stepping inside, but not moving away, either.

I remembered what my father had told me about death and tea masters, and when I looked at Sanja, at the shadows of unslept hours on her face that wasn't older than my own, the image of the figure waiting by their door suddenly weighed on my bones.

Some things shouldn't be seen. Some things don't need to be said.

'Have you applied for permission to repair the water pipe?'

Sanja gave a snort. 'Do you think we have time to wait through the application process? I have almost all the spare parts that I need. I just haven't figured out how to do it without the water guards noticing.'

She said it casually, as if talking about something trivial and commonplace, not a crime. I thought of the water guards, their unmoving faces behind their blue insect hoods, their evenly paced marching as they patrolled the narrow streets in pairs, checking people's monthly use of their water quotas and carrying out punishments. I had heard of beatings and arrests and fines, and whispers of worse things circulated in the village, but I didn't know if they were true. I thought of the weapons of the guards: long, shiny sabres that I had seen them cut metal with, when they were playing on the street with pieces of an illegal water pipe they had confiscated from an old lady's house.

'I brought you something to repair,' I said and began to unfasten the straps from around my load of waterskins. 'There's no rush with these. How much will you charge?'

Sanja counted the skins by tracing her finger along the pile. 'Half a day's work. Three skinfuls.'

'I'll pay you four.' I knew Jukara would have done the job for two, but I didn't care.

'For four I'll repair one of these for you right away.'

'I brought something else too.' I took a thin book out of my bag. Sanja looked at it and made a little sound of excitement.

'You're the best!' Then her expression went dark again. 'Oh, but I haven't finished the previous one yet.'

'Doesn't matter. I've read them many times.'

Reluctantly Sanja took the book, but I could see she was pleased. Like most families in the village, her family had no books. Pod-stories were cheaper and you could buy them at any market, unlike paper.

We carried the skins around the house into Sanja's

workshop, which she had built in the backyard. The roof was made of seagrass and three of the walls consisted of insect nets stretched between supporting wooden poles. The back wall of the house functioned as the fourth wall of the workshop. Sanja pulled the finely-woven wire mesh door closed behind us and latched it so the draught wouldn't throw it open.

I placed the skins on the wooden planing bench in the middle. Sanja put the rest on top of them and took one to the long table by the solid wall. My father had marked the cut with beetroot colour; it was the shape of an uneven star on the surface of the skin.

Sanja lit the solar burner and its wires began to glow orange-red. She took a box with pieces of patching plastic from under the table and picked one. I watched as she took turns to carefully heat the waterskin and the patch until both surfaces had grown soft and sticky. She fitted the plastic on top of the crack and after making sure that it covered the cut in the skin she began to even the seam out to make it tight.

While I waited, I looked around in the workshop. Sanja had brought in more junk plastic since my last visit a couple of weeks ago. As always, the long tables were filled with tools, brushes, paint jars, wooden racks, empty blaze lanterns and other bits and pieces I didn't even recognise. Yet most of the space was taken up by wooden boxes spilling over with junk plastic and metal. Metal was more difficult to find, because the most useful parts had been taken to cities for the army to melt down decades ago, and after this people had gathered most of what they could put to good use from metal graves. All you could dig up these days in those places were useless random pieces that had nothing to do with each other.

Junk plastic, on the other hand, never seemed to run out, because past-world plastic took centuries to degrade, unlike ours. A lot of it was so poor in quality or so badly damaged that it couldn't be moulded into anything useful, but sometimes, if you dug deeper, you could come across treasures. The best finds were parts of the broken technology of the past-world, metal and plastic intertwined and designed to do things that nothing in our present-world did anymore. Occasionally a piece of abandoned machinery could still be fairly intact or easily repaired, and it puzzled us why it had been thrown away in the first place.

In one of the boxes under the table I found broken plastic dishes: mugs, plates, a water jug. Under them there were two black plastic rectangles about the size and shape of the books I had in my room at home, a few centimetres thick. They were smooth on one side, but on the reverse side there were two white, round wheel-like holes with cogs. One of the edges on one of the rectangles was loose and a shredded length of a dark, shiny-smooth tape had unravelled from the inside. There was small print embossed on the plastic. Most of it was illegible, but I could make out three letters: VHS.

'What are these?' I asked.

Sanja had finished smoothing the seam and turned to look.

'No idea,' she said. 'I dug them up last week. I think they're changeable parts to some past-tech machine, but I can't think of what they were used for.'

She placed the skin on a rack. It would take a while for the plastic to seal completely. She picked up a large rucksack from the table and lifted it on her back.

'Do you want to go scavenging while the skin cools down?' she asked.

*   *   *

21

When we had walked a few blocks, I was going to turn to the road we usually took to the plastic grave. But Sanja stopped and said, 'Let's not go that way.'

The mark caught my attention at once. There was a wooden house by the road. Its faded, chipped paint had once been yellow, and one of the solar panels on the roof was missing a corner. The building was no different from most other houses in the village: constructed in the past-world era and converted later for the present-world circumstances. Yet now it stood out among the washed-out, colourless walls and faded yards, because it was the only house on the street that had fresh paint on its door. A bright blue circle was painted on the worn wooden surface, so shiny it still looked wet. I hadn't seen one before.

'What's that?' I asked.

'Let's not talk here,' Sanja said, pulling me away. I saw a neighbour step out of the house next door. He avoided looking at the marked house and accelerated his steps when he had to walk past it. Apart from him, the street was deserted.

I followed Sanja to a circuitous route. She glanced around, and when there was no one in sight, she whispered, 'The house is being watched. The circle appeared on the door last week. It's the sign of a serious water crime.'

'How do you know?'

'My mother told me. The baker's wife stopped at the gate of the house one day, and two water guards appeared out of the blue to ask what her business was. They said the people living in the house were water criminals. They only let her go after she convinced them that she had only stopped by to sell sunflower seed cakes.'

I knew who lived in the house. A childless couple with

their elderly parents. I had a hard time imagining they were guilty of a water crime.

'What has happened to the residents?' I asked. I thought of their ordinary, worn faces and their modest garments.

'Nobody knows for sure if they're still inside or if they've been taken away,' Sanja replied.

'What do you think they're going to do with them?'

Sanja looked at me and shrugged and was quiet. I remembered what she had said about building an illegal water pipe. I glanced behind me. The house and the street had disappeared from sight, but the blue circle was still flashing in front of my eyes: a sore tattoo on the skin of the village, too inflamed to approach safely, and covered with silence.

We continued along a circuitous route.

We crossed a shallow, muddy brook that trickled through the landscape near the plastic grave. As children we had not been allowed here. My mother had said that the ground around it was toxic and the grave dangerous to walk on, a foot could slip at any time and something sharp tear the clothes and the skin. Back then we used to plan our secret excursions to the plastic grave carefully, usually coming between day and night, when it wasn't dark enough for us to need blaze lanterns yet and not light enough for us to be recognisable from a long way away.

The plastic grave was a large, craggy, pulpy landscape where sharp corners and coarse surfaces, straight edges and jagged splinters rose steep and unpredictable. Its strange, angular valleys of waves and mountain lines kept shifting their shape. People moved piles of rubbish from one place to the next, stomped the plains even more tightly packed, dug big holes and elevated hills next to them in search of serviceable plastic and wood that wasn't too bent out of shape under layers of garbage. The familiar smell and sight of the grave still brought me back the memory of the long boots I had always worn in the fear of scratching my legs, the coarseness of their fabric, how hot and slippery my feet had felt inside them.

Now I was only wearing a pair of wooden-soled summer shoes that didn't even cover my ankles, but I was older and the day was bright. Dead plastic crunched under the weight of our steps and horseflies and other insects were whirring loudly around our hooded heads. I had rolled my sleeves down and tied them tight at the wrists, knowing that any stretch of bare skin would attract more insects. My ankles would be red and swollen by the evening.

I kept an eye on anything worth scavenging, but passed only uninteresting items: crumbled, dirty-white plastic sheets, uncomfortable-looking shoes with broken tall heels, a faded doll's head. I stopped and turned to look behind me, but Sanja wasn't there anymore. I saw her a few metres away, where she had crouched to dig something out of a junk pile. I went closer when she pulled what looked like a lidded box out from a mishmash of split bowls and twisted hangers and long black splinters.

The box was the shape of a rectangle; I had never seen one like it before. The scratched, black surface looked like it had been smooth and shiny once. At each end of the rectangle there was a round dent covered by a tight metal net.

'Loudspeakers,' Sanja said. 'I've seen similar ones on other past-tech things. This was used for listening to something.'

Between the loudspeakers there was a rectangular dent, slightly wider than my hand. It had a broken lid that could be opened from the upper corner. On top of the machine there were some switches, a row of buttons with small arrows pointing at different directions embossed on them, and one larger button. When it was turned, a red pointer moved along a scale marked with numerical combinations that meant nothing: 92, 98, 104 and so on. At the right end of the scale the letters 'Mhz' could be seen. In the middle of the top panel there was a round indentation, slightly larger than the one in the front panel and covered by a partially transparent lid.

I knew without asking that Sanja was going to take the machine home with her. Her face revealed that she was already picturing the inside hidden by the cover in her mind and seeing herself opening the machine, memorising the order of the different parts, conducting electricity from a solar generator into it in order to see what happened.

We wandered on the plastic grave for a while longer, but we only found the usual rubbish – broken toys, unrecognisable shards, useless dishes and the endless mouldy shreds of plastic bags. When we turned to return to the village, I said to Sanja:

'I wish I could dig all the way to the bottom. Perhaps then I'd understand the past-world, and the people who threw all this away.'

'You spend too much time thinking about them,' Sanja said.

'You think about them too,' I told her. 'You wouldn't come here otherwise.'

'It's not them I think about,' Sanja said. 'Only their machines, what they knew and what they left to us.' She stopped and placed her hand on my arm. I could feel the warm outline of her fingers through the fabric of my sleeve and the burn of the sun around it, two different kinds of heat next to each other. 'It's not worth thinking about them, Noria. They didn't think about us, either.'

* * *

I have tried not to think about them, but their past-world bleeds into our present-world, into its sky, into its dust. Did the present-world, the world that is, ever bleed into theirs, the world that was? I imagine one of them standing by the river that is now a dry scar in our landscape, a woman who is not young or old, or perhaps a man, it doesn't matter. Her hair is pale brown and she is looking into the water that rushes by, muddy perhaps, perhaps clear, and something that has not yet been is bleeding into her thoughts.

I would like to think she turns around and goes home and does one thing differently that day because of what she has imagined, and again the day after, and the day after that.

Yet I see another her, who turns away and doesn't do anything differently, and I can't tell which one of them is real and which one is a reflection in clear, still water, almost sharp enough to be mistaken for real.

I look at the sky and I look at the light and I look at the shape of the earth, all the same as theirs, and yet not, and the bleeding never stops.

We spoke little on our way back to Sanja's house.

She stood in the shadow of the veranda when I fastened the repaired waterskin to the cart and stepped on the pedal of my helicycle. The day around us blazed tall and bright, and she was small and narrow and grey-blue in the dark shadow.

'Noria,' she said. 'About the charge.'

'I'll bring you the first two skinfuls later today,' I said. When I started towards the tea master's house, I saw her smile. It was thin and colourless, but a smile nevertheless.

My father would not be pleased.

CHAPTER THREE

Late in the following afternoon I climbed the path from the teahouse towards the gate. I stopped on the way by the rock garden to pick some mint. The pale sand rippled around dark-grey boulders like water surrounding abandoned islands. The three tea plants growing just outside the edge of the sand burst towards the clear sky like green flames. I put the mint leaves in my mouth and continued to the small hillock in the shadow of a pine tree by the gate, from where I could see the road through the shadows of the scattered trees. The most burning heat of the day had already passed and the ceremony outfit felt cool and pleasant against my skin. Yet the hard-soled sandals were uncomfortable under my tired feet, and my arms ached.

My father had risen after a few short hours of sleep in the pale-gold light of a white night turning to morning. He didn't always wake me this early on ceremony days, but this time he knew no mercy. I knew it to be my unspoken punishment for having stayed too late at Sanja's house on the day before. He gave me one task after another, sometimes three at once, and by the time my mother got up for breakfast, I had already raked the rock garden, carried several skinfuls of water into the teahouse, swept the floor twice, hung decorated blaze lanterns inside and outside, aired the ceremony clothing, washed and dried the teacups and pots, placed them on a wooden tray, wiped dust from the stone basin in the garden and moved the bench on the veranda three times before my father was happy with its exact position.

It was with relief, then, that I walked to the gate to wait for our guests, when he finally released me from my preparation duties. I had eaten hardly anything since breakfast, and I chewed on the mint leaves to chase my hunger away. In the weary sunlight of the afternoon I had trouble keeping my eyes open. The faint tinkling of wind chimes in the garden flickered in my ears. The road was deserted and the sky was deep above, and all around me I sensed small shifts in the fabric of the world, the very movement of life as it waxed and waned.

Wind rose and died down again. Hidden waters moved in the silence of the earth. Shadows changed their shapes slowly.

Eventually I saw movement on the road, and little by little I began to make out two blue-clad figures in a helicarriage driven by a third one. When they reached the edge of the trees, I hit the large wind chime hanging from the pine. A moment later I heard three chinks from the direction of the teahouse and knew that my father was ready to receive the guests.

The helicarriage stopped near the gate in the shadow of a seagrass roof built for guest vehicles and two men in the military uniforms of New Qian stepped down from it. I recognised the older one: his name was Bolin, a regular tea guest who came every few months all the way from the city of Kuusamo and always paid well in water and goods. My father appreciated him because he knew the etiquette of tea ceremony and never demanded special treatment despite his status. He was also familiar with the local customs, being originally from our village. He was a high-ranked official and the ruling military governor of New Qian in the occupied areas of the Scandinavian Union. His jacket carried insignia in the shape of a small silver fish.

The other guest I had not seen before. From the two silvery fish tagged on his uniform I understood that he was of even higher rank than Bolin. Even before I saw his face through the thin veil of the insect hood, his posture and movements gave me the impression that he was the younger of the two. I bowed and waited for them to bow back in response. Then I turned to the garden path. I walked ahead of them at a deliberately slow pace in order to give them time to descend into the unhurried silence of the ceremony.

The grass at the front of the teahouse shimmered in the sun: my father had sprinkled it with water as a symbol of purity, as was the custom. I washed my hands in the stone basin which I had filled before, and the guests followed my example. Then they sat down on the bench to wait. A moment later a bell chimed inside the teahouse. I slid the door of the guest entrance to the side and invited the guests to move inside. Bolin kneeled at the low entrance with some difficulty, then crawled through it. The younger officer stopped and looked at me. His eyes seemed black and hard behind the insect hood.

'Is this the only entrance?' he asked.

'There is another one for the tea master, sir, but guests never use it.' I bowed to him.

'In cities one hardly finds tea masters anymore who require their guests to kneel when entering,' he replied.

'This is an old teahouse, sir,' I said. 'It was built to follow the old idea that tea belongs to everyone equally, and therefore everyone equally kneels before the ceremony.' This time I didn't bow, and I thought I saw annoyance on his face before his expression settled into an unmoving polite smile. He said no more, but dropped down on his knees and went through the entrance into the teahouse. I followed him and slid the door closed behind me. My fingers trembled lightly against the wooden frame. I hoped no one would notice it.

The older guest had already settled by the adjacent wall and the younger one sat down next to him. I sat down by the guest entrance. My father was sitting on his knees opposite to the guests, and as soon as we had removed our insect hoods, he bowed.

'Welcome, Major Bolin. This is a long-awaited pleasure. Too much water has flown since you last visited us.' He was keeping strictly to the etiquette, but I could hear a slight warmth in his voice, only reserved for friends and longtime customers.

Major Bolin bowed in response.

'Master Kaitio, I take pleasure in finding myself in your teahouse again. I have brought a guest with me, and I hope he will enjoy your tea as much as I do.' He turned to his companion. 'This is Commander Taro. He has only just moved here from a faraway southern province of New Qian, and I wished to welcome him by treating him to the best tea in the Scandinavian Union.'

Now that he wasn't wearing his insect hood I could see clearly that Taro was younger than Bolin. His face was smooth and there was no grey in his black hair. The expression on his face did not change when he bowed his greeting.

After my father had welcomed Taro with another bow,

he went into the water room and returned shortly carrying a cauldron. He placed it into the hearth in the floor on top of dried peat, which he lit with a firestarter. The flint-stones crackled against each other. I listened to the rustling of his clothes as he went into the water room again and returned with a wooden tray laden with two teacups and two teapots, a large metal one and a small earthenware one. He placed the tray next to the hearth on the floor and chose his own place so that he could see the water in the cauldron. I knew Major Bolin to favour green tea that required the water not to be too hot. 'When you can count ten small bubbles at the bottom of the cauldron, it is time to raise the water into the teapot,' my father had taught me. 'Five is too few and twenty is too many.'

When the water had reached the right temperature, my father scooped some of it from the cauldron into the large teapot. As a child I had followed his movements and tried to imitate them in front of a mirror until my arms, neck and back ached. I never reached the same smooth, un-restrained flow that I saw in him: he was like a tree bending in wind or a strand of hair floating in water. My own movements seemed clumsy and rigid compared to his. 'You're trying to copy the external movement,' he would say then. 'The flow must come from the inside and pass through you relentlessly, unstopping, like breathing or life.'

It was only after I began to think about water that I began to understand what he meant.

Water has no beginning and no end, and the tea master's movement as he prepares the tea doesn't have them, either. Every silence, every stillness is a part of the current, and if it seems to cease, it's only because human senses aren't sufficient to perceive it. The flow merely grows and fades and changes, like water in the iron cauldron, like life.

When I realised this, my movements began to shift, leaving the surface of my skin and my tense muscles for a deeper place inside.

My father poured water from the large teapot into the smaller one, which held the tea leaves. Then he poured this mild, swiftly brewed tea from the smaller pot into the cups in order to warm them up. As a final step of preparation, he filled the small teapot again and drenched it with the tea from the cups, soaking the earthenware sides of the pot while the leaves inside were releasing their flavour. The blaze lanterns hanging from the ceiling sprinkled softly flickering light on the water as it spread on the tray. Breath by breath I let myself sink into the ceremony and took in the sensations around me: the flare of the yellowish light, the sweet, grassy scent of the tea, the crinkle in the fabric of my trousers pressing at my leg, the wet clank of the metal teapot when my father placed it on the tray. They all entwined and merged into one stream that breathed through me, chasing the blood in my veins, drawing me closer and deeper into the moment, until I felt as if I wasn't the one breathing anymore, but life itself was breathing through me, connecting me to the sky above and earth below.

And then the flow was cut short.

'Some might say that is quite a waste of water.' The words were spoken by Commander Taro. His voice was low and surprisingly soft. I had trouble imagining anyone commanding armies with such a voice. 'It's rare to find anyone these days who can afford to spend water on a complete, unabridged tea ceremony,' Taro continued.

Although I wasn't looking at my father, I could sense that he had frozen, as if an invisible web had tightened under his skin.

One of the unwritten rules of the tea ceremony was that during it conversation was limited to remarks about the quality of the water and tea, the year's crop in the watering areas, weather, the origins and skilled craftsmanship of the teaware or the decoration of the teahouse. Personal matters were not discussed, and critical remarks were never made.

Bolin shifted as if a blazefly had crawled inside his uniform.

'As I told you, Taro, Master Kaitio is a most distinguished professional. It's a matter of honour that he has kept the tea ceremony unchanged for those of us who have the privilege of enjoying it,' he said without turning to look at Taro. Instead he was staring at my father intently.

'I understand,' said Taro. 'But I couldn't help expressing my surprise about the fact that a tea master of such a remote village can afford to spend water so openhandedly. And you must know, Major Bolin, that the tea ceremony in all its present-world forms is no more than an impure, confused relic of the original past-world forms that have been long forgotten. Therefore it would be mindless to claim that conserving the tradition requires wasting water.'

My father's face seemed made of unmoving stone that hides forceful underground currents. He spoke very quietly.

'Sir,' he said, 'I assure you that I practise tea ceremony exactly as it has been passed on through ten generations since the first tea master moved into this house. Not the slightest detail in it has been altered.'

'Not the slightest detail?' Taro asked. 'Has it always been customary, then, for tea masters to accept women as apprentices?' He nodded towards me and I felt the heat of blood colouring my face, as often happened when strangers paid attention to me.

'It has always been customary for fathers to pass their skill on to their children, and my daughter here will make a fine tea master that I can be proud of,' my father said. 'Noria, why don't you serve the sweets with the First Tea?'

The first cup of the brewed tea, or the First Tea, as it was known, was regarded as the most important part of the ceremony, and any inappropriate conversation at that point would have been a serious offence not only against the tea master, but against other guests as well. Taro remained silent as I held out a seagrass bowl of small tea sweets I had prepared that morning using honey and amaranth flour. My father's face remained mute and unreadable as he apportioned the tea into the cups and offered the first one to Major Bolin, then the second one to Commander Taro. Bolin breathed in the scent of the tea for a long moment before tasting it and closing his eyes while he let the tea remain in his mouth in order to sense its full flavour. Taro, for his part, lifted the cup to his lips, drank a long sip and then raised his gaze. A strange smile was on his face.

'Bolin was right,' he said. 'Your skill is truly amazing, Master Kaitio. Not even the tea masters of the capital, who are regularly provided with natural fresh water from outside the city, are able to prepare such pure-tasting tea. If I didn't know better, I'd think that this tea was made with spring water instead of purified, desalinated sea water.'

The air in the room seemed not to stir when my father put the tray down, and something cold and heavy shifted below my heart. I thought of the secret waters running deep inside the still stone of the fells.

I didn't know who this man was or what was the real reason for his visit; and yet I felt as if in his footsteps, where his shoes had worn the stones of the path and moved grass stalks so subtly that only the air knew, a dark and narrow figure had fitted its feet into his steps and followed him through the garden, all the way to the veranda of the teahouse. It was patient and tireless, and I did not want to look towards it, or open the sliding door and see it under the trees or by the stone basin, waiting. I didn't know if my father had felt the same, because he wouldn't let his thoughts show on his face.

Major Bolin drank from his cup and said, 'I'm glad your tea has impressed Commander Taro. He has been transferred to supervise the local government and is now working in close association with me.'

Taro wiped his mouth.

'I'm particularly invested in bringing water crime under control,' he said. 'You may have heard that it has increased lately in the Scandinavian Union.' He took a pause that filled the room. 'I feel certain that we will see each other often in the future.'

'How delightful,' my father said and bowed. I followed his example.

'He is highly regarded in the capital,' Bolin continued. 'I would say that anyone who has his protection is privileged, but I don't wish to suggest that New Qian isn't an equal place to live for everyone.' He gave a laugh at his own statement, and my father and I smiled obediently.

My father served another round of tea. I offered more sweets, and Bolin and Taro took one each. Taro spoke to my father again.

'I couldn't help but admire your garden, Master. It's highly unusual to see such verdancy so far away from the watering areas. How do you stretch your water quota to suffice not only for your family, but for all your plants too?'

'Due to professional reasons, the tea master's water

quota is naturally somewhat larger than that of most citizens,' Bolin remarked.

'Naturally,' said Taro, 'but I still must wonder what kind of sacrifices keeping such a garden requires. Do tell me, Master Kaitio, what is your secret?'

Before my father had a chance to say anything, Bolin spoke.

'Haven't we spent enough time on superfluous chitchat, when we could be enjoying the tea in silence and forget about the sorrows of the world outside for a short while?' He was looking at Taro, and although his voice was not sharp, I could hear a hidden edge within it. Taro gazed at him for a brief mute moment, then slowly turned to look at my father and didn't take his eyes off him while he spoke.

'Perhaps you're right, Major Bolin. Perhaps I will spare my questions for another visit, which I hope to be able to make soon.' And then he was quiet.

After that, only a few superficial sentences were exchanged, and none of them had anything to do with water, the taste of the tea or the garden. For most of the time silence spread through the teahouse and wrapped us like slow smoke from hidden fires.

The sweets were finished.

The large teapot ran empty, then the cauldron.

The ceremony is over when there is no more water.

Eventually the guests bowed in order to take their leave and placed the insect hoods over their heads. I led the way through the same low sliding door we had used to enter. Outside, the thin web of the summer evening had grown between the day and the night. Blazeflies glowed faintly in their lanterns hanging from the eaves. Major Bolin and Commander Taro followed me to the gate where the helicarriage driver raised his gaze from his portable mahjong solitaire, took a swig from a small waterskin, straightened his back and prepared to leave. The guests stepped into the carriage and spoke their formal goodbyes.

I returned to the teahouse. Around the burn of the late-evening sun the sky was the colour of the small bellflowers growing by the house. The air was still and the grass stalks were turning towards the night.

I carefully wiped and stored the cups, pots and other utensils, then helped my father clean the teahouse. My limbs were heavy, when I finally began to empty the lanterns. The blazeflies disappeared into the bushes, where I saw their glow flittering among the leaves. My father came out of the teahouse in his master's outfit, carrying his insect hood in his hand. The molten light of the night-sky drew lines across his face.

'I think you've learned enough to become a tea master this Moonfeast.' That was all he said before he started towards the house, and while I was surprised at his statement, the following silence made me far more uneasy than any words might have.

I took the empty blaze lanterns back into the teahouse, wrapped them in fabric one by one and packed them inside the wooden chest in which they were kept. I poured the blazeflies from the last one into an undecorated lantern for my own night light.

I walked around the teahouse, among the trees and on the grass for a long time. The night dew soothed the burning, stinging insect bites on my ankles. I did not see the dark and narrow figure under the pine trees, crossing the rock garden or sitting on the tearoom veranda, but I couldn't tell if this was only because I wasn't looking in the right direction.

CHAPTER FOUR

I lay on my bed and listened to the occasional slow clicking of the blazeflies against the glass walls of the lantern. There was no real need for the lantern, for the sun was still an orange-gold globe hanging in the horizon, heavy with late evening. The sky around it was translucent, and light trickled into my room through the insect net on the window. At the other end of the house I could hear my parents' faint voices, their words hidden, stifled; obscured by the distance. I had heard them speak like this nearly every night since Major Bolin and Commander Taro had visited us, and afterwards my mother stayed up much later than she usually did. She tried to be quiet, but I heard her movements as she wandered between her study and the kitchen, and I saw the soft glow of her lantern through the crack under my door when she passed back and forth.

I was holding in my hand one of the old books that remained in the house, a tale of a journey through winter. I knew it by heart, and the words flowed elusive across the pages before my eyes, evading the grip of my thoughts.

I wasn't thinking of the story. I was thinking of the world in which it had been written.

I had often tried to imagine how winters had been in the past-world.

I knew the darkness: every autumn around Moonfeast, night met day in order to swap places and the year turned towards winter. During the six twilight months, large blaze lanterns burned in each room of the house at all hours, and solar lamps were lit beside them in the ink-deep black of the evening. From the top of the fell one could see the glow of the cities in the dark skies: the distant but clear halo of Kuoloyarvi in the east, where the watering areas and the sea lay, and the near-invisible spark of Kuusamo far in the southern horizon. The ground lost its scant greenness. The garden waited for the return of the sun, mute and bare.

Imagining the coldness, on the other hand, was hard. I was used to wearing more layers of clothing during the dark season and carrying peat from the drained swamp for the fireplaces and braziers once the solar power ran out, usually soon after the Midwinter celebrations. But even then the temperature outside rarely dropped below ten degrees, and on warm days I walked in sandals, just like in summer.

When I'd been six years old, I had read in a past-world book about snow and ice, and asked my mother what they were. She had picked one of her thick and serious-looking volumes from a shelf that was too tall for me at the time, shown me the pictures – white, shimmering, round and sharp shapes in strange landscapes, luminous like crystallised light – and told me that they were water that had taken a different form in low temperatures, in circumstances that could only be artificially produced in our world but that had once been a natural part of seasons and people's lives.

'What happened to them?' I had asked. 'Why don't we have snow and ice anymore?'

My mother had looked at me and yet through me, as if trying to see across thoughts and words and centuries, into winters long gone.

'The world changed,' she had said. 'Most believe that it changed on its own, simply claimed its due. But a lot of knowledge was lost during the Twilight Century, and there are those who think that people changed the world, unintentionally or on purpose.'

'What do you believe?' I had asked.

She had remained quiet for a long time and said then, 'I believe the world wouldn't be what it is today if it wasn't for people.'

In my imagination snow glowed with faint, white light, as if billions of blazeflies had dropped their wings, covering the ground with them. The darkness turned more transparent and lighter to bear in my mind when I thought of it against the silvery-white shimmer, and I longed for the past-world I had never known. I pictured fishfires flashing on the sky above radiant snow, and sometimes in my dreams lost winters shone brighter than summer.

I once did an experiment. I filled a bucket with water and emptied all the ice I found in the freezer into it, sneaked it into my room and locked the door. I pushed my hand into the icy wrap of water, closed my eyes and summoned the feel of past-world winters about which I had read so many stories. I called for white sheets of snow falling from the sky and covering the paths my feet knew, covering the house that held the memory of cold in its walls and foundations. I imagined the snowfall coating

40

the fells, changing their craggy surfaces into landscapes as soft as sleep and as ready to drown you. I called for a glass-clear crust of ice to enclose the garden, to stay the greenness of the blades of grass and stall the water in barrels and pipes. I imagined the sound frozen branches of trees would make, or stiff waterskins hanging from the rack, when wind beat them against each other.

I thought of water, ever-changing, and I thought of the suspended moment, the movement stopped in a snow crystal or a shard of ice. Stillness, silence. An end, or perhaps a beginning.

The blunt, heavy blade of the chilled slush cut into my bones. I opened my eyes. The day outside the window burned with a tall, bright flame, turning the earth slowly into dust and ashes. I pulled my hand out of the water. My skin was red and numb, and my fingers ached, but the rest of my body felt warm, and I was no closer to past-world winters. I couldn't imagine a cold so comprehensive, so all-encompassing. Yet it had once existed, perhaps existed somewhere still. My mother had told me that in the midst of the Northern Ocean, where the day lasted six months and the night governed the other half of the year, where the bloodiest battles of the oil wars had taken place, there might still be small islets of ice, floating across the deserted sea, quiet and lifeless, carrying the memories of the past-world locked within, slowly giving in to water and melting into its embrace. They were the last remnants of the enormous ice cap that had once rested on the topmost peak of the world, like a large, unmoving animal guarding the continents.

As I grew older, I often sought more books on the tall shelves in my mother's study, hungry for anything that might help me understand and imagine the lost winters. I spent days and weeks studying their unfamiliar maps and pictures and strange old calendars that measured time by the cycles of the sun, rather than by the moon. Many of them spoke of temperatures and seasons and weather, drowned land and oceans that had pushed their shorelines inland, and all of them spoke of water, but the books didn't always agree on everything. I asked my mother once what this meant. She called herself a scientist. If scientists didn't agree with each other, I asked, did this mean that nobody really knew? She thought about this for a while and then said that there were different ways of knowing, and sometimes it was impossible to say which way was the most reliable.

Little by little I learned that for all their diagrams and strange words and detailed explanations, my mother's books did not tell everything. I wondered how snow would feel on my palm just before melting into water, or what ice would look like on a winter's day in a sun-glazed landscape where the outlines of shadows are sharp-drawn, but those stories I had to seek in other books. I was disappointed with the tall bookshelf and its contents, which promised so much and yet ignored what was most important. What good was it to know the composition of a snow crystal, if one couldn't resurrect the sensation of its coldness against one's skin and the sight of its glimmer?

The conversation of my parents drifted into my ears louder than before. My mother was using her sensible voice and my father's answers were concise. I got up to close the door. The wooden floor creaked under my footsteps. I could smell the scent of pines in the cooling air streaming through the window. A large horsefly was buzzing between the glass and the insect net.

Just as I was pulling the door closed, I heard the message-pod beep my own identification sound further down the hallway. I walked to the entrance, where the light of the pod was flashing red. *To: Noria*, the text on the screen read. I lifted the message-pod from the wall rack and placed my finger on the screen in order to log in. Sanja's family name appeared: *Valama*. I was slightly surprised. Sanja seldom used the message-pod. Her family had only one shared account, and their pod had been bought second-hand. It was out of order more often than not despite Sanja's persistent tuning attempts, or possibly partly as their result. I chose the *Read* option on the screen and waited for the message written in Sanja's bouncy hand-writing to appear. *Come tomorrow*, she wrote, *and bring all the TDKs with you. Possible DISCOVERY!!*

'Discovery' was one of the most important expressions in Sanja's vocabulary. It usually meant she had come up with a use for something looted from the plastic grave. I wasn't always entirely convinced that the uses she invented were in accord with the original purposes of the things, but I was nevertheless curious to see what she had discovered. I picked the pod-pen up from the wall rack, wrote *Before noon* in reply on the screen and sent the message.

I was closer to my parents' voices now. They rattled behind the gap of the kitchen door. A faint smell of seaweed stew floated in the air. As I was turning to go back into my room, my mother's words caught my attention.

'. . . If you told them now, when it's not late yet?'

I couldn't make out my father's murmured reply.

'He'd see to it that we'd be left alone,' my mother continued. 'If the military learns about—' She lowered her voice and the end of the sentence faded away.

I heard my father pacing back and forth in the kitchen. When he replied, his voice was tight and unflinching.

'I only trust Bolin as much as one can trust a soldier.'

This was not unexpected. My father believed most army officers were thieves, and I didn't think he was wrong. Yet my mother's reply surprised me.

'You trusted him more once,' she said.

My father was quiet for a moment before answering, 'That was a long time ago.'

I only had an instant to wonder about the meaning of those words before my mother said something in a soft voice, and then I caught my own name.

'It is her I'm thinking about,' my father replied. 'Would you rather she became one of the tea masters of the cities? They're nothing more than sell-outs, pets of the military. Besides, many still believe it's against the teachings to let women practise as tea masters. She belongs here.'

'She could learn another profession,' my mother said.

What about me, is anybody asking what I want?

'Are you suggesting that I break our family line of tea masters?' My father's voice was sharp with disbelief.

I couldn't hear the words in my mother's response, but her tone was harsher.

'This isn't really about Noria, or even the spring.' My father sounded angry now. 'This is about your research. You need their funding.'

I took a slow step closer to the kitchen door, taking care not to make a sound. This was getting interesting.

'I'm not on their side. But perhaps I need them to believe that I am,' my mother said. 'The water resources of the Lost Lands haven't been properly investigated since the disaster. This project, if it were to be successful—' The words lost their shape again as she lowered her voice, and I only heard the end of the sentence: '. . . less important than your age-old beliefs and empty customs?'

My breathing sounded so loud in my ears that I was

44

afraid they might hear it. I tried to exhale slowly and soundlessly.

'They may seem empty to you, because you are not a tea master,' my father said quietly, and every word fell heavy through the air. 'Yet some things run so deep we can't stop their flow. It's ignorance to think that earth and water can be owned. Water belongs to no one. The military must not make it theirs, and therefore the secret must be kept.'

The silence stretched through the still, dusky air, between the two of them and me standing on the other side of the door. When my mother spoke again, there was no crack in her glass-clear voice.

'If water belongs to no one,' she said, 'what right do you have to make the hidden waters yours exclusively, while whole families in the village risk building illegal water pipes in order to survive? What makes you different from the officers of New Qian, if you do what they would?'

My father said nothing. I heard my mother's footsteps and turned hastily towards the message-pod as she walked through the kitchen door. When she saw me, she stopped in her tracks.

'I was just reading my message and some pod-news,' I said. Without looking back I turned, walked through the house into my room and closed the door behind me. Outside the sun was brushing the horizon among golden shreds of light on the smoke-blue sky. I had barely made it back to bed when the floorboards creaked in the hallway, and then there was a knock on my door. My mother peeked in, a questioning look on her face. I nodded to her and she stepped into the room.

'There's no need to pretend you didn't hear us talking, Noria,' she said and sighed. 'Perhaps it's a conversation we should have had with you in the first place. I sometimes don't know.' She seemed weary. 'You know what we were talking about, don't you?' She pulled a wooden stool for herself from under my desk and sat down on it.

'It was about the hidden spring,' I said. She nodded.

'The times are getting harsher,' she said. 'But whatever happens, whatever decisions we take with your father, you must always remember that we're doing everything with your best interests in mind.' I wasn't looking at her. I pretended to be searching in my book for the paragraph I had been reading. The pages felt stiff and reluctant.

'How would you feel about living in one of the cities?' asked my mother. 'In a place like New Piterburg, or Mos Qua, or even as far as Xinjing?'

I thought of the only two cities I had seen: Kuoloyarvi in the east, and Kuusamo in the south. I remembered my initial excitement at the crowded streets, vault-shaped, large buildings covered with solar panels and whole building tops turned to giant blaze lanterns with transparent glass walls and greenery inside. I had been fascinated by the Qianese market stalls on the narrow alleys selling strange foods and drinks, their strong, spicy and sometimes unpleasant scents perceptible from several blocks away. I had wandered with my mother through the Danish quarters of Kuusamo, buying small bags of coloured sweets to take home with me, and the day I had taken my Matriculation Test I had been treated by my father to a meal in an expensive restaurant with a selection of imported natural waters from around the world.

Excitement flared in me again, but then I remembered the high walls and checkpoints dividing the streets, the ever-present soldiers and curfews. I remembered the exhaustion that had settled on me after only a couple of days, the pressing need to get away from the crowds, the longing for space and silence and emptiness. I could see myself loving visiting the cities, and I could see myself loathing living in one.

'I don't know,' I said. My mother was looking at me intently.

'And how would you feel about not becoming a tea master?' she asked. 'You could study languages, or mathematics, or assist me with my research.'

I thought about it, but not for long, and answered truthfully.

'I know the tea ceremony; I've studied it all my life. I wouldn't know what else to be.'

My mother remained quiet for a long time, and I could tell that her thoughts were running restless; she was much worse at concealing her feelings than my father. Eventually I broke the silence.

'You know that house in the village, the one with the mark of water crime on the door?'

'The blue circle?' Something stirred in her. It took me a moment to understand it was fear. 'What about it?'

'What happened to the people who lived there?'

My mother looked at me. I saw her searching for words.

'Nobody knows.' She stepped to me and squeezed my hand. 'My dear Noria,' she said, and then paused, as if changing her mind and not saying what she had been about to say. 'I wish we could have given you a different world.' She stroked my hair. 'Try to sleep now. The time for decisions will come later.'

'Good night,' I said. With that, she smiled. It was a quick smile, and not at all happy.

'Good night, Noria,' she said, and left.

*   *   *

After she had gone, I got up, kneeled in front of the book cabinet and took a wooden box from the bottom shelf. Through the thin layer of lacquer I could feel the grain of the undecorated wood against my fingertips. I turned the key in the lock and lifted the lid.

Inside the box was a random collection of past-world things excavated from the plastic grave. A handful of smooth-polished, multicoloured stones and a small, twisted metal key with almost no teeth left lay on top. Under them were three partially translucent plastic rectangles with slightly rounded edges and two wheel-shaped holes in the middle. The same three letters were visible on each one: TDK. Dark, thin tape that was broken had unravelled from inside the rectangles. I had always liked the feeling of TDK tape between my fingers: it was light and smooth as a strand of hair, as air, as water. I had no idea what Sanja wanted with the TDKs. Neither of us had any inkling what they had been used for in the past-world, and I had only kept them because I liked to stroke the tape every now and then.

At the bottom of the box glinted a silver-coloured, thin disc that I had once brought home because I found it beautiful. I picked it up in order to admire it once again. The shiny side was slightly scratched, but still so bright that I could see my own reflection in it. When it caught the light of the blaze lantern, it reflected all colours of the rainbow. On the matte side were traces of the text that had once run across it, and a few combinations of letters still remained: COM CT DISC.

I placed the disc and the TDKs back in the box, locked it and stuffed it into my seagrass bag that was hanging from the hook on the wall next to the cabinet, ready for the morning.

When I closed my eyes, I saw the distance that separated our house from the village and from another house, more weather-worn than ours. On its door a blue circle stared into the white night with outlines sharp enough to wound. The distance was not great, and if I looked at it long enough, it would grow narrower, until I'd be able to touch the door of the other house, to listen to the movements behind it.

Or the silence.

I wrapped the image away and pushed it from my mind, but I knew it did not disappear.

CHAPTER FIVE

I passed through the open gate of Sanja's house and stopped the helicycle by the fence. Sanja's mother Kira was standing in the middle of a patch of tall sunflowers, cutting a heavy flower head off the thick stem. At her feet there was a large basket, into which she had already gathered several flower heads, ripe with chubby seeds. Sanja's little sister Minja was sitting on the sandy ground, trying to make a flat stone stay on top of three wooden blocks piled upon each other. The insect hood she had inherited from Sanja swayed on her head, oversized, and the stone kept slipping off her fingers time after time.

'Noria!' Minja said when she saw me. 'Look!' The flat stone rested forgotten in her hand for a moment as she pointed towards her construction site with her other hand. 'A well.'

'Pretty,' I said, although the assembly did not resemble a well in any shape or form that I knew.

Kira turned around. The dust-coloured front of her dress was scattered with the yellow of dry sunflower petals. Her face was weary and pale in the frame of black hair that looked unwashed under the insect hood, and the clothes hung loose on her narrow figure, but she was smiling. At that moment she looked a lot like Sanja.

'Hi, Noria,' she said. 'Sanja's been waiting for you all morning.'

'My mother baked a pile of amaranth cakes yesterday,' I said and pulled a seagrass box out of my bag. It felt heavy in my hand. 'She sent these. There's no rush with returning the box.'

I caught the momentary stiffness on Kira's face before her smile returned.

'Thank you,' she said and took the box. 'Send my best to your mother. I'm afraid we don't have anything to give back.' She dropped the freshly-cut flower head on top of the pile in the basket. The lush, dark-green scent of the stems wafted in the air.

'It doesn't matter.'

Kira didn't look at me when she took Minja's hand. I felt awkward.

'Sponge-bath time, Minjuska,' she said. 'You'll get to play with the pirate ship if you're good.'

Minja squealed, got up to her feet and dropped the flat stone on top of her well construction site. The blocks crashed to the ground, sending dust flying around them. Kira started towards the house, holding the cake box in one hand and Minja's hand in the other.

'See you later, Noria,' she said. I waved goodbye to Minja, but she was only interested in the promise of the pirate ship.

I walked around the house. Through the insect-net walls of the workshop I saw Sanja sitting on a stool at the table and fiddling with something. When I knocked on one of the pillars supporting the roof, she looked up and waved her hand. I stepped inside, closed the door behind me and took off my insect hood.

The machine on the table in front of Sanja was the same she had found in the plastic grave a few weeks earlier. I recognised its angular shape, the dent embedded in the front panel, the strange numerical combinations and another dent on top. Two power cables ran from the machine to the solar generator sitting at the corner of the table.

'Did you bring them?' she asked. She had pulled hair back from her face with a worn scarf and two red spots were burning on her cheeks. I thought she must have woken early out of sheer excitement and fluttered restlessly around the workshop all morning. I placed my bag on the table and dug out my wooden box, from which I produced the TDKs.

'I don't understand what you want these for,' I said.

Sanja disappeared under the table to rummage around. She emerged a moment later, holding a black plastic rectangle. I remembered seeing it a few weeks earlier when I had come to get the waterskins repaired. When she picked up a TDK from the table, I realised how much the objects resembled each other. The biggest difference was in their size.

'I tried to think of what on earth this thing had been used for,' she said. 'I knew it must have been for listening to something, because it had loudspeakers, just like a message-pod – completely different size and much older, of course, but the basic principle is the same. As I was fashioning a new lid for that rectangular dent in the front, I noticed that there were two spindles inside it, and one of them turned. Those plastic blocks,' she pointed at the larger rectangle, 'were lying about next to it, and as I kept looking at them, it occurred to me that it was as if the dent was made for such a piece, with the spindles fitting in the cogged wheels in the middle. Even the shape was right . . . but the size wasn't.' She tapped with her finger the plastic block that bore the letters 'VHS'. 'It's as if these were made for a similar but far bigger machine. Bloody bad luck: the right machine and the right changeable part, but wrong scale. But then I remembered you tend to keep all sorts of peculiar things, and I realised you had the TDKs!'

I began to understand what she was getting at. She smoothed one creased TDK tape as much as she could, knotted the shredded ends together and rolled the tape back inside the plastic shell until it no longer hung loose.

Then she tried the TDK in the dent of the loudspeaker machine.

'It doesn't fit,' I said, disappointed, but Sanja turned the TDK upside down and it clicked into place.

'Ha!' she said, and I, too, felt a smile growing on my face.

Sanja closed the lid and turned the switch on the solar generator. A small, yellow-green light that made me think of glow-worms was lit on the top panel of the machine, next to the numerical combinations.

'Now we just need to figure out what to do with all these switches,' she said and pressed a button with a square on it. The lid on the front panel opened. Nothing else happened. Sanja closed the lid again and tried a button with two arrowheads on it. The machine began to rustle. Sanja brought her face close to the rectangular dent and her eyes narrowed as she stared at it, alert.

'It's rolling!' she said. 'Look!'

I peeked and saw that she was right: the machine was spinning the tape inside the plastic TDK so fast it was difficult to tell its direction. After a while it clicked and churned in place for a moment before clicking again and turning mute.

'Did it break?' I enquired cautiously. Sanja creased her brow.

'I don't think so,' she said. 'Maybe there's just no more tape left.' She pressed another button with only one arrowhead on it. The machine began to buzz faintly. Then the loudspeakers crackled. Sanja jumped and turned to look at me.

'Listen!' she said.

The speakers rustled and hummed and then continued to hum.

And hummed some more.

The smile peeled off Sanja's face like paint chipping in the sun while time stretched on between us, and the humming reached further, into another age and world whose secrets it wasn't ready to reveal. Eventually Sanja pressed the square button again and the tape stopped. She opened the lid, took the TDK out and replaced it with another one after tying the broken ends of the tape together.

There was still nothing but warbled whirring from the loudspeakers.

She tried all three TDKs several times, spinning the tapes back and forth and turning the TDKs from one side to the other, but all we heard were ghosts of sounds sunken in time and distance, a near-silence that was more frustrating than complete soundlessness. If the tapes had once held something comprehensible, earth, air, rain and sun had worn the past-world echoes thin a long time ago.

Sanja stared at the machine and turned one of the TDKs in her hands.

'I'm sure I'm right,' she said. 'These parts fit in the machine, and it translates sounds from them into the loudspeakers. The device and the TDKs must have been used exactly like this. If only we could find a TDK that still had sound left on it . . .'

Sanja's fingers were tapping the plastic surface of the

TDK. I heard Minja's shrieks from inside the house, and Kira's faint voice soothing Minja. I followed with my gaze a small black spider that was spinning a web in the corner above the solar generator.

'Perhaps . . . perhaps there are more somewhere in the plastic grave?' I offered. 'Or maybe they weren't meant to last in the first place. Past-world technology was fragile.'

Sanja's expression changed, as if the outline of her face had become more focused. She lifted the square lid on the top panel of the machine and felt the round indentation under it with her fingers. Then she looked at my wooden storage box that was open on the worktop. Her eyes were fixed on the silver-coloured disc with a hole in the middle. The disc looked exactly the right size for the round indentation of the listening-device. Sanja looked at me and I saw my own thoughts on her face.

'May I?' she asked.

I nodded.

Sanja took the disc from the wooden box and fitted it into the indentation. It seemed made for the machine. The round knob in the middle of the indentation fit right into the hole in the middle of the disc. Sanja pressed the disc into it, and it clicked lightly into place. She closed the lid and pressed the arrow button. Through the plastic window I saw the disc starting to turn.

We waited.

There was no sound from the loudspeakers.

I saw Sanja's expression and felt disappointed myself. Then she reached out her hand to fiddle with the switches on the top panel. The first one she touched caused the glow-worm light to go off and the rotation of the disc to slow down, so she switched it back to the original position. Another one did nothing at all. When she moved the third switch, the loudspeakers gave such a loud crackle we both jumped. It was followed by a short stretch of silence, and then a male voice which said clearly in our language:

'This is the log of the Jansson expedition, day four. Southern Trøndelag, near the area previously known as the city of Trondheim.'

While the voice went on to record the day, month and year, Sanja cheered and I laughed. The voice continued:

'We started the day by measuring the microbe levels of the Dovrefjell waters. The results are not complete yet, but it seems that there is no discrepancy with the Jotunheimen results. If this turns out to be the case, our estimations about the spontaneous biological recovery and reconstruction process taking place in the area have been far more modest than the reality. Tomorrow we are going to plant purifying bacteria in the waters and then we'll continue towards Northern Trøndelag . . .'

The day outside grew into a thick, burning shell that surrounded the workshop, and horseflies climbed on the insect web walls, and we listened to the voice of the past-world. At times it would wither almost entirely, jump a little, or get stuck, until the sound found its flow again. Sanja didn't stop it, and didn't try to skip the boring bits. It had waited on the disc through generations. It was a part of a story that had nearly been lost in the plastic grave. We didn't speak, and I don't know what Sanja was thinking; but I thought of silence and years and water that ran ceaselessly, wearing everything away. I thought of the inexplicable chain of events that had brought this voice from a strange landscape and a lost world into this dry morning, into our ears that understood its words, yet comprehended little.

The voice spoke of exploration of waters, microbe

measurements, bacterial growth, landforms. There was an occasional lengthy break in the speech, and we began to discern separate sections. At the beginning of each one the voice announced a new date: the recording moved from day four to day five and so on. After day nine the voice stopped altogether. We waited for a continuation, but it didn't come. Minutes passed. We looked at each other.

'Too bad there wasn't more,' Sanja said. 'And too bad it wasn't more exciting.'

'I'm sure my mum would disagree,' I said. 'She's crazy about all sorts of scientific—'

The speakers made a loud noise. We stiffened, listening. A female voice spoke now.

'The others don't think I should do this,' it said. 'But they don't need to know.' The woman paused and cleared her throat. Then: 'Dear listener,' she continued. 'If you're military, you may rest assured that I did everything in my power in order to destroy these recordings instead of letting you get your hands on them. The fact that you're hearing this probably means I failed miserably.' The voice took a moment to think. 'But that won't happen until later. Right now I have a story to tell and you're not going to like it one bit. I know what you've done. What you're going to do. And if I have anything to say about it, the whole world will know what really happened, because—'

The talk was cut unexpectedly short. The disc continued to turn, but now the past-world voice was irrevocably gone. The recording was over.

Sanja and I stared at each other.

'What was that?' I asked.

Sanja tried to move the recording back and forward, she even tried the other side of the disc, but it was clear we had heard everything there was to hear.

'What year did the man mention at the beginning?' I asked.

Neither of us had paid attention to the year. Sanja started the disc from the beginning again. As we listened, I could see on her face that she had realised what I had. Without giving any more thought to it, we had imagined that the disc was from the past-world.

We had been wrong.

'It's from the Twilight Century,' I said.

'It can't be for real,' Sanja claimed, but she sounded unconvinced. 'It's just a story, like one of your books, or those suspense stories that one can buy to listen to on the message-pod, one chapter at a time.'

'Why would it have an hour of dull science stuff first, and the interesting bit only after that?'

Sanja shrugged.

'Maybe it's just badly written. Those pod-stories aren't always that great, either. My dad has a few.'

'I don't know.' I was trying to think feverishly where in the plastic grave I had found the disc.

Sanja took the disc from the machine with determination, placed it in the wooden box and snapped the lid closed.

'Anyway, it doesn't matter,' she said. 'We'll never know what that woman had to say. At least we got the machine to work.'

But I was thinking of unknown winters and lost tales, I was thinking of the familiar language and the strange words that were left smouldering in my mind. I thought of rain and sun falling on the plastic grave and slowly gnawing everything away. And of what might still remain.

I was almost certain I could remember where the disc had come from.

'We could look for more discs where we found that

one,' I suggested. I was getting excited about the idea. 'We could try to make the story whole. Even if it's just a story, wouldn't you still want to know how it ends?'

'Noria—'

'We could go for all day tomorrow, take some food with us and—'

'Noria,' Sanja interrupted me. 'You might not have anything better to do than serve tea and poke around the plastic grave,' she said. 'But I do.'

Somewhere inside the house Minja had started to cry.

The distance had grown between us unexpectedly. We had known each other since we were learning to walk on the village square, holding our mothers' hands as we took our first tentative steps. If someone had asked, I would have told them Sanja was closer to me than anyone else, save for my parents. And yet she sometimes withdrew into her shell, turned away from me, slipped out of my reach, like a reflection or an echo: a mere trace of what was only a moment ago, gone already, beyond words and touches. I didn't understand these moments, and I couldn't deny them.

She was far away from me now, far as hidden waters, far as strange winters.

'I have to go,' I said.

I shoved the wooden box into my bag. The feeling that we had found a secret passageway through time and space into an unknown world had faded away. The day had burned it to cinders.

I pulled the insect hood over my head and stepped out into the blazing heat.

On my way home the strap of the bag gnawed on my shoulder and I was weary. Sweat trickled down to my neck and my back, and my hair clung to my skin under the insect hood. The words recorded on the disc were bothering me. *The Jansson expedition.* It sounded like something out of my mother's old books. And the woman from across all this time – unexpected, hidden in the travel log – had considered her story so important that she had dictated it in secret and been ready to destroy the whole recording rather than letting the military have it.

I wanted to know what had meant so much to her.

I could see from far away that there were unfamiliar transport carriages outside our house. I wondered if we had received tea guests on short notice, and hoped this wasn't the case. My father hated visits for which he had no time to prepare well, and was cranky for days afterwards.

I turned the helicycle towards the woods from the road, and I tried to see between the tree trunks into the garden.

Breath curled into a knot between my throat and chest when I saw the blue military uniforms. There weren't just one or two, but many more.

A familiar helicarriage was parked outside the gate under the seagrass roof. When I came to the front yard, I saw approximately ten soldiers who were carrying complex-looking machinery to and fro. Some of the instruments reminded me of pictures I had seen in my mother's books. A makeshift fence had been raised around the teahouse, and in front of it a soldier with a sabre hanging from his belt kept watch. My parents stood on the veranda of our house, and a tall soldier wearing an official's uniform was talking to them, his back turned towards me. When he heard my footsteps, he turned and I recognised the face behind the insect hood.

'Good afternoon, Miss Kaitio. It is a pleasure to meet you again,' Commander Taro said and waited for me to bow.

CHAPTER SIX

They called it a routine investigation, but we knew there was nothing routine-like about it. Routine investigations were carried out by two soldiers and they lasted a few hours at most. Instead, a highly ranked official stayed on our grounds for nearly two weeks with six soldiers, two of whom took turns to guard the teahouse while four were exploring the house and its surroundings. They walked carefully planned, slow routes from one end of the garden to the other, back and forth, examining each centimetre. They carried flat display screens in their hands. The multicoloured patterns that took shape on them bore a slight resemblance to maps, with their ragged edges and varying, overlapping forms.

From my mother's books I had a vague idea of how the machines worked. They sent radio waves to the ground that the screen interpreted, with the patterns indicating the density and humidity of the soil. The soldiers also carried different drilling and measuring devices. One of them, a woman whose expression I rarely saw change, walked with two long metal wires crossed in her hands.

Occasionally, she would stop with her eyes closed, then stare at the wires for a long while, as if waiting for something. My parents told me that the teahouse was isolated and an intensive search was being executed there because the metal rod of the wire woman had on the first day twitched to point at the ground on the veranda.

My father stared sadly at the plank pile growing in front of the teahouse while the soldiers were taking the floor apart.

'It will never be the same again,' he muttered, his lips tense. 'Wood like that is hard to find nowadays, and the expertise for building a teahouse doesn't exist in any old village.'

In those days a silence wavered between my parents, dense with stirring, well-hidden fear and nameless, unspoken things. It was like a calm surface of water, extreme and unnatural: a single word dropped on it, a single shifting stone at the bottom would change it, create a circle and yet another circle, until the reflection was warped, unrecognisable with the force of the movement. We avoided talking about any but the most everyday things, because the presence of the soldiers grew invisible walls between us that we had no courage to shatter.

In the evenings I did not go to bed until I had privately checked that the soldiers hadn't taken their screen-devices towards the fell, and in the mornings my heart was thick and heavy in my throat when I woke up to the thought that they might have expanded their search outside the house and garden. I couldn't eat breakfast until I was certain this wasn't the case. In my dreams I saw the waters hidden in stone, and in the middle of the night I would wake to the strangling feeling in my chest that somehow, impossibly, the sound of the spring carried all the way from the fell to the house. I listened to the unmoving silence for a long time, until sleep sank me again.

At first I thought my mother was faking an interest in the equipment of the water seekers to keep up appearances and to cover her nervousness. As the days passed, I came to understand that behind her behaviour there was a real interest that she had a hard time concealing. She was aching to know more about the equipment, to try it for herself, to learn the mechanisms and applications. It had been over fifteen years since she had worked as a field researcher for the University of New Piterburg, and military technology was more developed than anything civilians could access. She walked with the soldiers, asking questions about their machinery, and I could see on her face how she was making mental notes on things so she could write them down in the quiet of her study. My father noticed this, too, and his manner became curt and distant towards her. Everything that was left unsaid during those days tightened around us like a web that might suffocate and crush us, if we didn't find a way out soon enough.

I wanted to talk to Sanja. I wished I hadn't left her workshop so abruptly. I had sent her three messages and asked her to come over, but she hadn't replied. I wasn't sure what to make of this, because she didn't tend to reply that often anyway. While my mother walked around studying the equipment of the soldiers, and my father stood by the teahouse, apparently hoping his presence would limit the damage caused by them, I carried books into my room and set up camp by them.

The recording on the silver-coloured disc was bothering me. I had always had a relatively clear idea of what the past-world had been like – or rather, of how little was known about the past-world. For all my winter daydreams and snow-longing, I had never questioned what I had been taught at school and what the books said. I had taken for granted that what was generally considered to be true really was the truth, and nothing beyond that mattered. But what if it wasn't so? What if the stories that remained were just darkened and distorted shards of a mirror – or worse: what if someone had deliberately shattered the mirror in order to change the reflection? *I know what you've done . . . And if I have anything to say about it, the whole world will know what really happened,* the voice on the disc had said.

After I had spread the books gathered from the house all over the floor, I eventually found two large world maps in them. I placed them next to each other for comparison. One showed the past-world, the world of cold winters and skyscraping cities. The other showed the present-world.

I stared at the outlines of the continents and oceans, changed, barely recognisable.

So much lost to salt and water.

I looked at the places nearest to me. The White Sea, east of my home village and Kuoloyarvi, had not reached as far inland, as close to us as it did now. The lakes and rivers in the Scandinavian Union had merged into wider waters, and the old coastlines were long gone.

That was not all.

Drowned islands, coastal plains, river deltas turned salt-bitten; and large cities, now silent ghosts of lives past in their shroud of sea, everywhere, everywhere.

On the old map North and South Poles were shown in white. I knew this stood for the ice that had sometimes been called eternal ice, until it became clear that it wasn't eternal after all. Near the end of the past-world era the globe had warmed and seas had risen faster than anyone could have anticipated. Tempests tore the continents and people fled their homes to where there was still space and dry land. During the final oil wars a large accident contaminated most of the fresh-water reserves of former Norway and Sweden, leaving the areas uninhabitable.

The following century was known as the Twilight Century, during which the world, or what remained of it, ran out of oil. With this a major part of the past-world technology was gradually lost. Staying alive became the most important thing. All that wasn't considered necessary for everyday survival faded away.

I thought about the words recorded on the disc. The male voice had spoken about Trondheim, Trøndelag and Jotunheimen. They belonged to the Lost Lands, as the contaminated areas of the Scandinavian Union were called. If the Jansson Expedition was real, what had they been doing in the Lost Lands during the Twilight Century? How had it even been possible or safe for them to go there? I nearly wanted to believe in Sanja's claim that the recording on the disc was just a story. It seemed true to me, but I knew that was what the best stories were like: you could believe in them, even if you knew they were imagination. Yet something about the disc didn't quite convince me. The story on it lacked the structure of a designed, made-up story. It had the shape of reality and truth.

I closed the books and piled them on my desk, but not until I had folded the corners of the map pages.

Six days after the arrival of the soldiers, Sanja appeared unexpectedly at our gate. She had walked all the way from the village, and she carried a pile of empty waterskins strapped on her back. They were the same ones I had used to take water to her as a payment for the repair job a few weeks earlier.

'Let's go inside,' I told her.

'My father said you have a local invasion going on here,' Sanja said as we got inside the house. 'Why on earth?'

She took off her insect hood. I helped her unload the waterskins off her back and hung them from a hat rack on the entrance wall.

'I guess they think we have a hidden well under the teahouse floor or something,' I replied. My voice sounded calmer than I would have expected.

'I should've known you're hiding some dark secret,' Sanja said and her expression dissolved into one of her lopsided grins. 'Don't they really have anything better to do? Maybe someone's pissed with your dad and dropped them a false lead just to create havoc.'

I smiled, but my face felt stiff. It seemed she had no intention of mentioning our quarrel, and I felt no need to do so, either. Some rifts will close on their own, I thought. There was no reason to force them open again.

'Are you in a hurry to go back?' I asked.

Sanja shook her head.

I made ice tea for us in the kitchen. Ice lumps crackled in the earthenware cups, as I poured the pale yellow, lukewarm liquid over them. We sat down at the table, and I got some dried figs out of the cupboard.

'I wish we had a freezer, too,' Sanja sighed and sipped her tea. 'I tried to fix one last year, but it only worked for a couple of weeks before breaking down for good. I'd have needed to go to the city for the spare parts and that would've been two months' food budget gone.'

'Do you find it weird how much past-world technology there still is in the plastic graves, the kind that is easy to fix?' I asked.

'What's so weird about that?'

'They always said at school that past-world technology was frail and can't be manufactured anymore, and that's what all books say, too.'

'And it was. Most of the stuff in plastic graves is rubbish.'

'What about books?'

'What about them?'

'Why weren't more past-world books preserved?' I knew the tea master's house had more books than any other in the village, and my parents had told me that they were rare even in cities. Few books were printed because of the price of paper, and past-world volumes were virtually impossible to come by, unless one had access to state libraries or military archives. At school we had only used pod-books.

'Most were in the big cities that drowned when the oceans changed their shorelines,' Sanja said.

'Yes, but have you ever seen a history book that was written before the Twilight Century?'

'What would be the point of a history book that didn't contain the Twilight Century and present-world era?'

'Still, they couldn't all be lost under water, could they? When the cities drowned, why weren't more past-world books rescued?'

'I don't know.' Sanja spread her hands. 'Maybe there was no time. People had to be rescued first. Maybe—'

A shout from outside interrupted her. I got up and walked to the window. I saw one of the soldiers – short, bespectacled – gesturing at two others, who came half-running to him. I didn't hear what he said, but after exchanging a couple of sentences all three headed towards the teahouse. I couldn't see the teahouse from the kitchen window, and after a moment they vanished from my view.

'What is it?' Sanja asked.

'I don't know.' I couldn't help wondering if the soldiers had found something. But there wasn't anything to be found in the house, teahouse or garden, was there?

It was as if cold water was poured over my heart. I understood, perhaps for the first time, how little my parents had told me. Was there a map indicating the location of the spring hidden in the teahouse that the soldiers had found? Was there something about the spring written in the current tea master's book, the thick and pale brown pages filled with my father's accurate handwriting of which he had only let me read parts while he was watching closely? Or perhaps in one of the other books, neatly locked in a glass case in the living room, in which late tea masters described ceremonies meticulously? I did not know, and my imagination wove swiftly a thousand stories, none of which ended well.

'You don't need to come if you don't want to,' I told Sanja. 'It's probably nothing.'

She followed anyway, when I placed my cup on the table, pulled the insect hood over my head and walked out. The lawn was full of holes and mounds of earth that we avoided, but I noticed that the rock garden and the tea plants next to it remained untouched save for boot prints crossing the sand. Amid the overturned ground my footsteps felt unsteady and the route unfamiliar.

As I walked around the corner of the teahouse, I saw my parents standing on the edge of a large hole opened in the grass. They stood side by side, and although they were not looking at or touching each other, at that moment they belonged seamlessly together, like stone pillars of some old building or the intertwined trunks of two trees I had seen in the Dead Forest years ago. Commander Taro was standing on the opposite side of the excavation, and the other soldiers had gathered around the hole. I stopped a few steps away from my parents. Sanja stepped to my side, and although I wasn't looking at or touching her, I knew she was close.

The hole was deep and steep-edged, and the slated sun of the late afternoon didn't reach to the bottom of it. Nevertheless, I could clearly see some kind of man-made, hard wall at the bottom, and even deeper, dark water glinted like a teardrop in the eye of the earth. I tried to read the expressions on my parents' faces, and for a second time within a short period I felt that they were strangers to me. I didn't know everything they knew, and I didn't know how much they had told me.

One of the soldiers drew water from the hole with a glass dish attached to a metal telescope rod. It was murky with mud, but Taro took the dish, lifted his insect hood, dipped his fingers in the water and licked his fingertips.

'It seems there is drinkable water on your grounds,' he said, gazing at my father. 'I assume you weren't aware of its existence?'

'If I had known, would I have kept the knowledge from you?' my father replied, not averting his eyes.

'You and your family can go now, Master Kaitio,' Taro said. 'Rest assured we will keep you informed on further developments.'

Slowly, my father turned to leave. He looked at my mother, and he looked at me, and his expression changed. He turned back to face Taro and then walked calmly to the commander along the edge of the excavation. A couple of soldiers tried to stop him, but Taro gestured at them to leave him alone. My father stopped in front of Taro. They stood there against the earth and the sky and the torn wreck of the teahouse, a tall official in a blue military uniform and a man whose hair was already brushed with grey in the simple linen garments of a tea master.

'You believe everything can be owned,' my father said, 'that your power reaches everywhere. Yet there are things that will never yield to man-made chains. I will dance on your grave one day, Taro. If my body is here no longer, my spirit will do it, free from the cage of my bones.'

Taro turned his head slightly, but did not take his eyes off my father.

'On second thought,' he said, 'now that we have searched the grounds, it's a good time to move on to the house. Liuhala, Kanto,' he directed his words to two of the soldiers. 'Escort Master Kaitio and his family back and begin the search. Make sure to be thorough.'

The two soldiers stepped towards my father. He made no attempt to move. I thought he was going to hit Taro, but eventually, after staring at him for a long time, my father turned and started towards the house without looking back again. The soldiers followed close behind him. My mother, who had been observing the scene in silence, took my arm and went after them, pulling me with her.

She walked slowly, and once we were outside the hearing range, she whispered to me, 'We have nothing to be afraid of, Noria. I've searched the grounds several times, and I know there's no spring here. It's just rain water in an old well filled with concrete.'

'Why didn't you tell them that?' I asked.

'It's better if they realise it themselves. It will humiliate them and chase them away. Someone might even apologise.'

'Not Taro, though,' I said and thought about the expression on the Commander's face, the unyielding quality behind it.

'No, not him,' my mother admitted.

When we entered the house, the soldiers had already begun to open cupboards and drawers, pulling things out and throwing them to the floor. I saw my father bent down at the kitchen door. He was holding his chest with one hand and his breathing was troubled.

'Are you all right?' my mother asked. My father didn't reply immediately. A moment later he straightened his back, banished the pain from his face and said, 'It's nothing. I just felt a little short of breath.'

I have tried to remember what my mother did, find a confirmation in her tone of voice or her gestures that she did not understand more than she said then. At other moments I have tried to overturn this notion, find something to give me certainty that she did understand and knew that my father had begun to turn away from life. I cannot find either, no sign to verify this one way or the other. There is a distance between us that I can never cross, the distance of time and change and irreversible endings, the past that never shifts its shape. Because I cannot bridge the ravine, I must walk along its edge and let it be a part of my life, one of those shadow-filled cracks that I cannot deny and into which I can never bring light.

My mother knew. My mother did not know.

I remembered Sanja, who had been sauntering a few steps behind us and stayed outside the door. I left my parents at the entrance to stare at the soldiers turning the rooms inside out and went to walk Sanja to the gate.

I stopped on the veranda. I didn't see Sanja right away, but then I spotted her. She was standing on the path to the teahouse. A blond-haired soldier I had often seen in Taro's company and therefore assumed to be his closest petty officer was talking to her. I couldn't hear their words and I didn't see Sanja's face clearly behind the insect hood, but her limbs were tense. The soldier told her something and Sanja moved uncomfortably. I walked to them. Sanja gave a start when she noticed me.

'I should go,' she said to me, or perhaps to the soldier.

'Say hello to your father,' the soldier said and started towards the teahouse.

'An old school pal of my dad's,' Sanja told me as we were walking towards the gate. 'He asked all sorts of weird stuff.'

Now that I think of Sanja, after all that has happened, this is one of the two images that emerge before my eyes uninvited, brighter than others that I have invited in vain: she is standing outside the gate, her black hair spilling to her forehead and cheeks, her body narrow and angular inside the rough linen fabric. The shadow of the insect hood is sharp on her face, and the tangled shapes of branches all around us are whisper-soft as they slowly carry her away from me.

I do not raise my hand.

I do not speak a word to forestall her.

I stand and watch the shadow-dance of the trees on her back, on her arms, I stand silent and still, and she walks away and doesn't look behind.

Two days later the soldiers finally took their equipment and left our grounds. The short, bespectacled soldier came to give us a scant-worded explanation: the water had been found to be rain water gathered in an old underground well that hadn't been used in decades. As the search continued, it became clear that there was no running water in the house or garden, other than the legal water pipe.

The last thing they did was to break the lock of the bookcase in the living room and pull out the three dozen or so leather-bound tea masters' books. When they began to carry them out of the house, my father protested.

'You won't find anything important in them,' he said. 'They're just personal family diaries. Besides, I could have given you the key, if you had asked,' he added bitterly.

The soldiers carrying the books didn't even stop to listen.

They left the garden full of holes, and their attempt at repairing the damage caused to the teahouse was nominal. My father marched to Taro.

'Are you really going to leave the teahouse in this state?' he asked. 'Do you realise how difficult it will be to find someone to restore it?'

Taro's eyes were black and hard and unmoving.

'Master Kaitio,' he said, 'as the representative of New Qian I have the duty to investigate all possibilities that might lead to discovery of fresh water. It is not my fault if they turn out to be misleading.'

And so they left, without apologies, without compensation.

I had imagined that once the soldiers were gone, things would go back to the way they were, but the strange silence we had assumed persisted, an unnaturally calm surface of water around us.

I waited for a stone to shift.

When it did, it was in a way I didn't see coming.

A couple of weeks after the investigation, I heard my parents talking to each other again in the kitchen.

'They will come back,' my mother said. 'They're not
going to give up.'

'They no longer have any reason,' my father replied.

My mother was silent for a long time and said eventually, 'I've made my decision.'

'We must talk to Noria,' my father said.

I had no time to get back to my room, so I pretended
I was on my way out. My father came from the kitchen.
I didn't need to turn to look. I recognised his footsteps,
and I knew he had stopped behind me.

'Noria,' he called softly. I stopped and looked at him.
In the twilight of the hallway a web of shadows was lying
on his face, a blue-grey dusk sifting through the windows.
'Your mother wants to talk to you.'

I walked after him to the kitchen, where my mother
was sitting at the table with an empty teacup in front of
her. It was as if the shadows followed us and entwined
around the large blaze lantern hanging above the table,
dimming its light. I saw them on my mother's face.

'Sit down, Noria,' she said.

I did. My father took a seat next to my mother. They
were a unified front again, like on the edge of the excavation, two stone pillars, two tree-trunks intertwined.

'Your father and I have talked,' my mother said. 'We
both want to give you a secure life, but we have different
opinions on how it should be.' She was silent and looked
at my father, who spoke in his turn.

'Noria, if you don't want to be a tea master, now is the
time to say it. I'm convinced Taro will leave us alone now
that he has searched the grounds. I doubt it will even cross
his mind to look for the spring in the fell, and if it did,
the spring is so well hidden that finding it is unlikely. We're
safe here. Unfortunately your mother believes differently.'

'Taro will see through what he's started,' my mother said. 'Life here cannot go back to the way it was. They got closer than you think already, Noria.'

'But they didn't go anywhere near the fell,' I said.

'There's something you don't know,' my mother replied. 'Tell her, Mikoa.'

'You know we use more water than most families,' my father began. 'And you know that some of it is quota water, but some comes from the spring. You must have noticed the difference.'

The water used in tea ceremonies always tasted fresh, as if had been just drawn from the spring. It was part of the art of tea. My father had taught me to always taste the water used for tea and to choose the freshest, cleanest, if there was a choice. Otherwise we used the water coming from the water pipes, which at the beginning of the month always tasted stale and slightly fishy, as was the case with purified sea water. Near the end of the month there was a clear improvement in the taste. Unlike in most homes, we did not save water, and we never ran out of it or needed to buy overpriced water from merchants.

'Do we use our water quota for the first few weeks of each month, and switch to the water of the spring when we run out?' I asked. 'But how do they come from the same pipe?'

'It would be too hard to carry all the water from the fell to the house,' my mother said. 'It would also be suspicious. One would need a helicarriage and large water containers and frequent visits. Someone would notice sooner or later the tea master returning from the fell several times a week with full barrels. We weren't the first ones to realise the impracticality of it. We don't know when the water pipe was built, but it was already there in Mikoa's father's time.

It's not been recorded in any of the tea masters' books. Whoever built it understood that it would be too dangerous to leave a written record of it. The pipe is skilfully constructed: it comes from deep inside the fell, is hidden in the earth and connects to the legal water quota pipe so far from the house that it can't be traced by searching the tea master's grounds. The only risk is that it needs to be opened and closed manually from the fell. We were lucky that it happened to be closed when the soldiers came.'

'The pipe is hidden as well as the spring,' my father remarked. 'Finding it is nearly impossible without knowing its location.'

'They're used to searching, and their machines are intricate.'

'They have no reason to come back.'

'They have no reason not to come!'

A silence fell between them. After a moment my father spoke, directing his words only to me.

'Your mother believes the tea master's house is no longer a safe place to live.' He glanced at her and waited. I saw her choose her words carefully.

'Noria, I've been offered a post as a researcher at the University of Xinjing. I've accepted.'

'Are we moving to Xinjing?' I asked. I didn't know for sure how far it was, but I knew the journey to the southern coast of New Qian was long. The trip across the continent must take weeks even on the fastest trains. My father and my mother glanced at each other.

'You're of age and therefore we can't make the decision for you,' my mother said. 'Do you wish to go to Xinjing with me, or do you want to stay here with your father? You don't need to decide right now, but I will need to leave before Moonfeast, so it's only a month away.'

I looked at my mother. I looked at my father. My throat felt thick. In the direction of the village, as close as the marked house, the soldiers were sharpening their weapons and didn't listen to pleas. At any time they might turn their attention towards us again, if they ever had turned it away at all. I had no way of knowing which one of my parents was right, and I couldn't both stay and go.

My choice wasn't clear to me, and I worried that the words I chose would set it in stone. Yet the silence was worse somehow.

I opened my mouth and told them what I would do.

CHAPTER SEVEN

Early in the morning of the eighth day of the eighth month we lifted my mother's trunk and seagrass bags onto the helicarriage my father had borrowed from Jukara in exchange for some fresh water. My parents climbed to the front seat and I sat down in the back under the half-open roof, and we started the drive towards Kuoloyarvi.

The scent of Jukara's helicarriage triggered a strange feeling of recurrence in me. I felt a lot younger, as if this was one of those rare, wonderful days when my parents took me to the city with them. I looked at the purple-blue stain on the coarse, worn fabric of the seat. I had dropped melted blueberry ice cream on it on one return trip home when I was eleven. My parents had been upset with me, and I had scrubbed the seat until it was clear that it would never be quite clean again.

For a moment I felt like a multi-layered Qianese box or a hollow wooden past-world doll fitted with many smaller dolls, one inside the other. A younger version of myself, or perhaps several, nested under my skin, swinging her feet that didn't reach to the floor from the seat, not imagining the day when her parents would not be safely within arm's reach – or if she did, she closed it quickly out of her mind.

The journey to Kuoloyarvi lasted nearly three hours. As we approached the sea, the landscape changed slowly. Once the village and the Alvinvaara fell were behind us, we passed the forests of the watering areas, their jagged, dark-green edge cutting the sky far on our left. This had always been my favourite stretch of the road on the way to the city. As a child I had dreamed of steering the carriage into the woods and driving among the tall trees, their cool shadow around me a welcome shelter from the scorching sun. But I learned early I could never do such a thing: the forests were guarded and closed from civilians, just like food plantations and the few remaining lakes.

Later, when the glinting, wavy skyline of Kuoloyarvi with its vault-shaped buildings and solar panels began to loom ahead, I saw the water desalination plants on the horizon, at the edge of the sea. They were stark and solid and huge, like a row of ancient, blind stone giants. Their security was notorious. Even the roads that led to them were watched, and I had heard stories of travellers being arrested just for walking too close to one of them.

It was mid-morning when we arrived at the border of the city. I saw from far away that there were more soldiers than usual. Normally the gates were only guarded for the sake of appearances, and not all travellers were stopped. This time, however, there was a long queue of helicarriages slowly crawling into the city, and beside it two slightly faster-moving lines for those who travelled on foot. We took our place at the end of the helicarriage queue. When we reached the gate, a guard in a blue uniform stopped us.

'What is your business in the city?' he asked.

'I'm on my way to Xinjing,' my mother said. 'My family is seeing me to the train station.'

'All the way to Xinjing? Are you on state business?'

'Yes, I've accepted a job at the University of Xinjing.'

'May I see your train tickets, your passpod and the letter that proves your connection to the university?'

My mother found in her bag the secondhand message-pod that had been assigned to her by the university. She placed her finger on the display in order to activate the passpod feature. The screen lit up and my mother's ID information emerged, including her ticket reservation. She handed the message-pod to the guard, who examined it. She also produced the paper letter sent from Xinjing. The guard seemed almost impressed at the sight of real paper, but didn't say anything. He nodded to my father and me. 'And you, do you have any proof of your identity?'

'I'm afraid not,' my father said. 'One used not to need a passpod in order to enter the city. Is there a particular reason for this?'

'We have our orders,' the guard said and did not elaborate. 'May I have your fingerprints, please.'

He handed his multi-pod to us and we pressed our fingers to the display. Our names and some code numbers emerged, and my father gave the pod back. I saw the guard scribble a couple of sentences on the screen with his pod-pen.

'You and your family can go, Master Kaitio,' he said after taking a careful and lengthy look at my mother's passpod and letter. It sounded more like an order than a permission. 'You and your daughter must notify the guards when leaving the city,' he remarked to my father.

My father nodded, his mouth a tight line in his face, and steered the helicarriage through the gate.

*   *   *

I had only been to the train station a few times before. Kuoloyarvi was not a big city, and most of the traffic coming to the Scandinavian Union arrived by ships further south, to the ports of the Ladoga Bay in the Baltic Sea. There were only four tracks. The long train stood at the platform with its doors open. The name 'Brilliant Eel' was painted on the side of the locomotive with decorative characters. There were solitary travellers, couples and families lifting trunks on board and saying goodbyes. We helped my mother carry her luggage inside the railcar compartment. There was still time before the train would leave, but she said, 'Don't stay and wait. I'll send you a message when I get to New Piterburg.'

The train journey would continue from New Piterburg to Ural and from there across New Qian to Xinjing. I thought of all the things I wouldn't see because I wasn't going with her, things I had only heard about: algae cultivation areas in the coastal seas and factories turning it to fuel, rubber tree plantations and blazefly farms, sea-ships and the large, lavishly decorated tearooms of the cities. And somewhere, under the waves, arching like an ever-clouded sky, the ghost cities of the past-world, sharp-edged and mute as memories.

My mother kissed me goodbye.

'I'll write to you,' she said. 'And the New Year is only a few months away. I'll come for a visit then.'

I didn't know what to say, so I held her for a long time.

When she finally released me, I walked out to wait and through the window I saw her talking to my father. Their lips were moving and their expressions were changing, but the thick glass muffled the words, making them inaudible. They embraced, and I couldn't understand why they wanted to tear their lives apart.

I turned away.

A grey-faced man walked inside the station building with a large seagrass bag on his shoulder.

A group of soldiers walked near the entrance, their boots heavy on the stones, their hands resting on the hilts of their long sabres.

A little girl in a blue summer dress was skipping rope and humming a shapeless sing-song. Her mother was eating roasted sunflower seeds and kept glancing at her watch.

Eventually my father descended from the train.

'Shall we go?' he asked.

I looked at my mother, who was sitting behind the window, colourless, faint as a faded picture in an old book in the middle of the bright day. She looked at me while we walked away, looked even when I was no longer looking back, I am certain of it. If she wished to change her mind and step off the train and return to the tea master's house with us, she did not act upon it.

Before starting the journey towards home, we went shopping at the Qianese market. As soon as we got there, I knew our destination was a stand where a tall, dark-skinned, slightly crooked woman sold items. Her name was Iselda, and I remembered her from my childhood. My father asked her to present us with her best-quality teas. Iselda placed three small knots of fabric on the sales table and opened them. I expected my father to examine them one by one, but instead he nodded to me. I had never before been allowed to choose the type of tea without his directions.

I took each knot of fabric in turn in my hand. The leaves of the first tea were green-black and oblong, and it smelled slightly sweet. The second tea was a brighter green in colour, its leaves tied up in large buds that would open into flowers once hot water was poured on them.

Its scent was fresh and light – I could imagine that combined with the water of the fell spring it would produce an extraordinary aroma. The greenness of the third tea was silver-brushed and its leaves were twisted into the shape of drops. What determined it, however, was the scent. The scent of the third tea *flowed*. That is the only way I could describe it. It was the scent of freshly picked tea, but it was also the scent of humid earth and of wind sweeping shrubs, and it wavered like light wavers on water, or shadow: one moment it was strong in my nostrils, the next it fled nearly out of reach only to return again.

'This one,' I said and handed the tea to my father.

'How much?' he asked the tradeswoman.

Iselda mentioned the price of one *liang*, as was customary when trading tea. When I heard it, I was sure my father would refuse. Yet his expression didn't even stir. He told Iselda a lower price. I prepared myself for a bargaining that would take its time, but Iselda only looked at him for a moment and then nodded.

'We are taking half a *liang*,' my father said. 'That should be enough for the graduation ceremony.'

He dug an empty fabric pouch from his bag, and Iselda measured the tea into it. We also bought a couple of *liang* of another, cheaper tea for everyday use, and some spices and groceries that couldn't be found in the village.

On the way home I tried not to look at the empty front seat of the helicarriage. I looked back towards the city, at the dusty plain and the narrow thread of the sea on the horizon, radiant in the late-afternoon sun like the scale coat of a giant dragon disappearing slowly from sight.

After my mother was gone, my father occupied himself entirely with the preparations of Moonfeast. He had hired a few men from the village to help restore the teahouse and the garden, Sanja's father Jan among them. I'd noticed Jan spending a lot of time looking at the expensive wood and the few fine furnishings my father had ordered from the cities; Jan was a skilled builder, but he rarely had good materials to work with. While my father was busy supervising the repairs, cleaning the house and collecting the harvest were left to me. The berry bushes and cherry trees had suffered somewhat from the turmoil caused by the water searching, and the soldiers had overturned part of the root vegetable patch. Nevertheless, not all had been lost, and I was kept busy cooking gooseberry jam and drying cherries and plums for the winter, tapping seeds from sunflowers and amaranth into sacks, picking almonds and pulling carrots from the soil. On top of these things I had to order feastcakes from the baker, check the water-skins, get my tea master's outfit from the village tailor and go through the ceremony with my father once a day.

He seemed to have decided he wouldn't speak of my mother's departure. On the fifth day after she left I was cleaning the house vigorously. My father saw me carrying a water bucket, a scrubbing-brush and some wet cloths towards my mother's study. When I placed them on the floor and pushed the door open, he said, 'Don't.'

I looked at him, and then I looked away, because I didn't want to see his face.

'Leave it the way it is,' he said.

'If you say so,' I replied, but I thought: it cannot remain that way. Not if you want it, and not if I want it. Dust will gather around the legs of the shelves and spiders will weave their webs in the corners, and mute book pages will grow yellow between the covers. The glass of the windows slips downwards like slow rain, even if we don't see it, and the landscape outside is different every day: the light falls from another angle, the wind tugs at the trees slower or faster, the greenness of the leaves draws away and one ant more or less walks on the trunk. Even if we don't see it right away, it is all happening; and if we look away long enough, we will no longer recognise the room and the landscape, when we eventually look at them again. This house is different since she left, and we both know it.

My mother sent messages from along her journey. They had a light, in-awe-of-the-big-world tone to them.

I've never seen such a huge port in my life, she wrote from New Piterburg. *It has grown so much in the past fifteen years. And you should see the people who travel on these trains! Yesterday I sat at dinner with a family of five who had come all the way from the Pyrenees by boat and were on their way to Ural. I swear the only thing preventing their noisy kids throwing the train off the tracks was the presence of soldiers. I'm thinking of you. Hugs, L.*

Not as much as we are thinking of you, I replied to her in my mind. You have in your reach the whole world unmarred by our footprints; they cannot wear away quietly under your eyes. All we have is this house and its lack of you, and we protect the imprint you left behind, so it would stay here a little longer, so you would still recognise it as your own, when you come back. If you do.

I got up early on the morning of Moonfeast day. The tea master's outfit was hanging from the curtain pole in front of the slightly open window, swaying in the draft. It wasn't yet time to wear it. My father had told me the day before we would take a walk to the fell after breakfast. I guessed we were going to fetch water from the spring for my graduation ceremony, but I knew there was something else, too. Otherwise he wouldn't have asked me to go with him. I dressed in simple everyday clothes and sturdy trekking shoes, and had the rest of the millet porridge he had left on the table for me. I filled a small waterskin, hung it on my shoulder and shoved a couple of sunflower-seed cakes into my pocket. I picked the insect hood up from the clothes rack at the entrance on my way out.

I found my father raking the rock garden. The builders and gardeners he had hired had done a surprisingly good job. There were only small traces of the grass having been disturbed, and the rock garden was exactly as it used to be, save for the unmoving ripples of sand that had been brushed away.

The teahouse had taken the heaviest damage. Part of its floor had needed to be replaced with a different type of wood, and the contrast between the old and new boards was distinctive. Yet now the hut was whole and usable again. I'd reminded my father that imperfection and change belonged to the art of tea, and they must be given the same value as perfection and permanence. He'd looked at me and I'd seen the surprise in him.

'You'll be a better tea master than I know how to be anymore,' he'd said.

He stepped off the rock garden and raked his own footsteps away. The sand rested in the middle of coarse stones like a deserted seafloor.

'Let's go,' he said. 'We have a long day ahead of us.'

We walked to the fell along the same route as the first time, when he had taken me to the spring. On the side of the fell, just before reaching the boulder garden, we turned in a different direction. A little later my father stopped and pointed further down the slope. It was split by a long, ditch-like furrow, smooth-worn with stones and sand gathered at the bottom. Its rocky walls were smeared with lichen.

'Do you know what that is?' he asked.

I knew, of course. I had seen many enough before.

'The channel of a dried stream,' I said. 'There's been no water in it in decades, because so much lichen has grown on top of the rocks.'

'You read the landscape well,' my father said. 'But there's more you must learn. I should perhaps have told you about the secret essence of the tea master's work much earlier. But it's customary that the wisdom isn't passed from master to apprentice until the day the apprentice becomes the new master. When we reach the spring, you'll find out what I'm talking about.'

We turned back and my father asked me to show if I could find the way to the cave mouth shaped like a cat's head without his help. The route was familiar to me from my childhood, so I found it easily. Again, on my father's prompting, I sought the hidden lever at the back of the cave, opened the hatch on the ceiling and climbed ahead of him into the tunnel going to the spring. My father followed and handed me one of the two blaze lanterns, their light glowing in the dark. As we walked towards the roar of the spring, I saw humidity concentrated on the walls of the tunnel.

We reached the cave, where water sprang from the dark wall in bright threads into the pond before vanishing again inside the fell. I stopped at the edge of the pond. My father walked to the other side and lowered his blaze lantern close to the water. I saw on the stones the pale stain I vaguely remembered having noticed on my first visit. About half a meter above the throbbing surface of the water, a stout metal wedge covered in a worn layer of white paint was driven into the rock. It shone faintly in the half-light.

'This is the side of the tea master's work that remains invisible to everyone else,' my father said. 'Since ancient times, tea masters have been watchers of water. It is said that in the past-world each tea master had a spring they took care of on their grounds. The springs had different qualities: one produced water with healing powers, the water of another granted a longer life, the third spring gave you peace of mind. There were also differences in the taste of the water. People would come from far away to enjoy tea that was made with the water of a well-respected spring. It was the duty of the tea master to see that the spring remained clean and wasn't overused.' My father's face was like sun-brittled paper on which the shadows of the cave and the light of the lantern fought for space. 'As you know, in the present-world nearly all springs have dried up, and the rest have been claimed by the military. It's possible there are secret springs such as this elsewhere, but I don't know of them. It's possible that this is the last one.'

The weight of his words and everything buried in them lay between us. He brought his lantern right to the surface of the spring and pointed at the water. Under the surface, near the bottom of the pond, I saw another white-painted wedge, nearly blurred invisible by the water.

'Do you see that mark?' my father asked.

I nodded.

'If the surface of the water sinks lower than that, it means too much water has been drawn. The spring will need to rest and gather its strength. It's the tea master's task to see that it happens.'

'How long?' I asked.

'Several months,' my father said. 'The longer, the better. The spring hasn't been pushed too far in my time, but it happened twice in my father's time. Both times he let it rest for nearly a year before it recovered completely.'

'What about the other mark?' I pointed at the wedge in the rock above the water surface.

'It's equally important at the very least, and requires constant monitoring,' my father said. 'If the water rises that high, more of it must be directed into the water pipe than usual, and fast, because it's in danger of rising from underground into the dry channel we saw outside. This hasn't happened in my time, either, but if we didn't use water from the spring every month, it might.'

'How quickly?'

'I don't know exactly, but I believe it would take about two months.'

I understood now why he came to the fell so frequently.

'You need to learn to control the water levels and to use the pipe, Noria. I'll not pass the task to you entirely yet, because from this day on we'll be sharing the tea master's responsibility in this village. But one day it will be placed in your hands, and therefore I'm teaching it to you now.'

My father took a few steps towards the cave wall. When he lifted his lantern, I saw a lever that had been turned to point to the left. He gestured for me to come closer.

'This controls the flow of the water into the pipe we use in the house. It is currently closed, because we still have some of this month's water quota left, and the water in the spring isn't unusually high. Now is a good time to open the pipe, because we'll need natural water for your graduation ceremony, and the month is in half. You do it.'

I took the lever and turned it to point to the right. The water in the pond stirred like a restless animal, and although I didn't see much difference in its swirls, it seemed to me that alongside the roar there appeared another, slightly different one.

'Water from the fell will now be flowing into the house pipe until this end is closed again. I usually close it after about two weeks, wait for two to three weeks and then open it again. The most important thing is to come here every week to check the water level and control the consumption of water accordingly. Next week it'll be your turn.'

My father filled the two waterskins he had brought directly from the spring, and we each strapped a skin on our backs.

'What would happen, if the spring dried and wouldn't go back to normal? If it stopped giving water altogether?' I asked when we had made it out of the cave and were walking towards the house.

'We'd live by the water quota, like everyone else,' my father replied. 'It would be enough for us. The garden would suffer somewhat, but we'd be fine.'

He was quiet for a moment. The sun had crawled to the sky, already languid with autumn, but still hot. I rolled my sleeves down so the insects would have less to bite. My father was looking into the horizon and I saw that he wanted to tell me something.

'Past-world tea masters knew stories that have mostly been forgotten,' he said quietly. 'But one is recorded in every tea master's book we kept in our house. The story tells that water has a consciousness, that it carries in its memory everything that's ever happened in this world, from the time before humans until this moment, which draws itself in its memory even as it passes. Water understands the movements of the world, it knows when it is sought and where it is needed. Sometimes a spring or a well dries for no reason, without explanation. It's as if the water escapes of its own will, withdrawing into the cover of the earth to look for another channel. Tea masters believe there are times when water doesn't wish to be found because it knows it will be chained in ways that are against its nature. Therefore the drying of a spring may have its own purpose that must not be fought. Not everything in the world belongs to people. Tea and water do not belong to tea masters, but tea masters belong to tea and water. We are the watchers of water, but first and foremost we are its servants.'

We walked on in silence. Pebbles crunched under my feet. The scent of burning fires rose from the direction of the village.

'You look happy,' my father noted, when we reached the house. 'That's good. Today it's time for you to be happy.' He smiled at me. 'It looks like the baker's errand boy has left the feastcakes at the gate while we were away. Would you get them and bring them to the kitchen, please?'

I nodded and walked towards the gate, where three boxes of cakes were piled upon each other. When I turned to look, I saw my father had stopped and bent down. There was something rigid and painful about his posture, but the day was bright, and my mind was elsewhere, and I smelled the freshly-baked cakes in the wind. I did not look twice in his direction.

CHAPTER EIGHT

Memory has a shape of its own, and it's not always the shape of life. When I think back now, I look in that day for omens and signs of what was to come, and sometimes I believe I see them. It's a strange and hollow comfort, one that never carries me for long. Past-world seers used to read tea leaves to tell the future. But they are only tea leaves, dark residue of things gone by, and they spell no pattern except their own. Yet memory slips and slides and shatters, and its patterns are not to be trusted.

I remember standing in my room, my hair still dripping wet from the bath I'd had, water trickling down my chest and between my shoulder blades in narrow rivulets. My graduation outfit, which I would be wearing in tea ceremonies until its seams came apart, lay on the bed, empty like a skin not yet worn or perhaps already shed, waiting to be filled with meaning and movement, or else buried. The sharpest edge of this memory is the radiance of the day on the other side of the window: a blazing core of fire brimming with light, more brilliant than any day before or after, as if the sky was bursting to full flame before being glazed over by nightfall, before my world changed. I know this is not possible. I have seen radiant days before and after, and the brilliance I remember has an unnatural, blinding blade to it. But that day of my life has taken the shape of memory, and that is the only shape in which I can conjure it now. Its true, unchanged form is no longer within my reach.

I remember putting the tea master's outfit on. It felt new and stiff around me.

I remember pulling my hair back with a large needle. It was heavy with moisture caught between the long strands.

I don't remember walking to the teahouse, but I must have. There was nowhere else I could have gone.

Something was bothering my father. I had known it as soon as he crawled into the teahouse through the visitors' entrance and looked around him. I suspected I had made some mistake I couldn't recognise, but the ceremony had already begun and could no longer be interrupted. Master Niiramo, who had been invited from Kuusamo, had taken his place on a cushion by the back wall and removed his insect hood. I had no choice but to wait for my father to sit down next to him and carry on.

Niiramo had been invited for reasons of protocol. There were always two older tea masters present at the graduation ceremony, the teacher of the graduating apprentice and another master, an outsider. Niiramo performed tea ceremonies in Kuusamo and was on good terms with the local military regime. My father didn't think much of him, but it was difficult to get tea masters to leave cities during Moonfeast, which was traditionally a popular time for ceremonies, and Niiramo had been easy enough to persuade with some help from Bolin.

Slanted light fell through the skylight above the hearth, casting a sharp shadow across my father's face. I breathed in the smell of smoke and wood and water. I saw the seam where my knees touched the floor: next to an old, darkened, smooth-worn pine board there was a fresh, paler one, yet unscratched and unbattered by time. I was aware of my father's and Niiramo's gazes on me. They were not here as my guests, but as my judges. Niiramo had seemed surprised when he had first seen me, and was now staring at me with an expression I could only decipher as mild disapproval.

My movements felt cast in stone when I began to prepare the First Tea.

I looked at the teaware I had chosen for the occasion: simple, worn earthenware cups and plates with cracks in the glazing and no decorations whatsoever. They were among the oldest in the tea master's house, another remnant of the past-world; possibly used by our ancestors in their faraway home, long before sea began claiming islands and coasts. Their muted colour of leaves turning into earth gave me comfort, caught me in a web of something far older and stronger than myself. I was standing on a path that reached across centuries unchanged, yet always attuned to shifts in the texture of life, steady as breathing or heartbeat.

Echoes of tea masters that had come before rippled through me as I counted the bubbles at the bottom of the cauldron and poured water into the pots and cups. I thought of their imprint on the memory of the world: the flow of their movements I mirrored with my own, their words I quoted as I spoke, the water that had run through earth and air when they walked on stones and grass-stalks, the same water that pushed sands to the seashore and brushed across the sky still. Their wave coiled across time and memory, spreading like rings on the surface of a pond, eternally repeating the same pattern. This curious feeling carried and confined me at once.

I kneeled before Master Niiramo with my tray. As he reached out a hand to pick up a cup, a strong scent of perfumed balm mixed with sweat oozed from him. His skin was well kept. His suit was simple, but I recognised the fabric as expensive and the buttons as valuable metal work I hadn't seen often. He clearly had extra meat on his bones. I bowed my head and offered the next cup to my father.

My eyes swept across the empty corner where my mother would have been sitting if she were here. She had sent a voice message earlier wishing me luck and saying her train would be passing the Aral Bay soon. I tried to imagine the landscape she was crossing, and for a moment it was as if I could feel the dusty smell of the cushioned seats in the train compartment, hear the voices and footsteps of children running down the narrow corridor and feel the constant movement of the floor under me. But when I tried to see outside, the colour of the plain was unclear and the forms of the horizon blurred into a strange sky. The landscape remained unexplored, and the empty space in the room took my mother's shape, persistent as a shadow.

The graduation ceremony was longer than the standard one. In addition to tea and sweets, it also included a light meal, and it could last several hours. There was little conversation. I settled into a strange, unhurried rhythm into which the drowned must settle when the sea takes the weight off their limbs.

I imagined the room filled with a soft wrap of water that slowed down all movements and muffled all sounds, washed me clean inside and out, made everything fade and crumble.

My father's face made of water-soaked wood, Niiramo's shape of stone dissolving into sand. My own body an undulating stalk of seaweed in the waves moving back and forth. All this already out of my reach, something I couldn't stop and forestall even if I tried.

I let them drift away.

Slowly, like the moon gathers and turns the tides, my muscles relaxed, the tightness withdrew from my face and my breathing flowed more freely. The tenseness was still there, but it was at a distance now, no longer armour on my skin, locking me down.

The room simmered with the heat radiating from the hearth and the steam rising from the cauldron. The air was completely still. My hairline was moist and I felt the fabric of the graduation outfit sticking to my armpits and thighs. Sweat glistened in beads on Niiramo's brow. My father's face was flushed. I had left the small window on the entrance wall open before the beginning of the ceremony, but the fresh air outside seemed to have packed itself into a block against the opening, not knowing how to stream in. I got up from my cushion and opened the slightly larger window on the opposite wall. Even though the day was calm, draught blew in immediately and the air began to flow through the room again.

Niiramo placed his cup down and looked at me.

'Miss Kaitio, are you sure that both windows need to be open?'

From the corner of my eye I saw my father stirring restlessly.

'It is much more pleasant in the room with some fresh air, don't you think?' I replied.

'Noria, Master Niiramo expressed his wish that the window should be closed,' my father remarked. The shadow crossing his face had shifted slightly. It fell over his bare neck now.

Niiramo stared at me, and I wasn't sure if I should interpret his expression as a smile.

'Miss Kaitio can do as she sees best,' he said.

I left the window open, bowed to Niiramo and took my place next to the hearth again. Niiramo said nothing more, but I was now certain of the smile: the kind that a rich merchant smiles when he catches a messenger boy stealing goods. The dark mood didn't pass from my father's face during the meal, and it seemed to me he was stealing secret glances at Master Niiramo.

I waited until they had finished eating and collected the plates. I took them into the water room, removed a linen cloth from the top of a bowl of sweets and brought the sweets into the main room. I served yet another round of tea with them.

There was no more water in the cauldron.

I knew it was time for the evaluation.

'Noria Kaitio,' Niiramo said and bowed. 'Take your place, please.'

I bowed in response, walked into the water room and pulled the sliding door closed after myself.

The room had no windows. It was used for storing water, trays, ladles, cauldrons and teapots. If I reached my hand in any direction, it would meet the wall, or some of the tea utensils. Hair-narrow strands of light framed the sliding door and the tea master's entrance on the opposite wall. Inside a blaze lantern hanging from the ceiling, blazeflies were flittering languidly against the confines of their glass prison. Shadows hovered on the walls, opening and closing like floating nets, curling closer and withdrawing again. I heard Niiramo and my father talking in low voices.

I thought of my mother again, her journey that could have been mine: another life in which I had buried my tea master's outfit instead of accepting it as my second skin. Bright as a reflection in a clear mirror, I saw myself, walking and learning the scent and twists of the unfamiliar streets between the buildings of a strange city like one learns a new language. And beyond that, a landscape of my own, for me to discover and make my home.

I heard some shuffling from the tearoom, then footsteps on the veranda outside, and then a soft noise as the sliding door of the visitors' entrance was pushed closed. I could guess either Niiramo or my father – or both of them – had gone to get something from the veranda.

The city and the landscape shrivelled away. There was only darkness at the bottom of the mirror, and no other life but this.

A soft ring of a bell sounded from the tearoom. It was time for me to enter again. I swept the hair from my face and opened the sliding door. I had been right: at least one of them had gone to the veranda. Niiramo was holding a scroll, and my father had a thick, leather-bound book in his hands.

'Noria Kaitio,' Niiramo said.

I bowed.

'As the evaluating tea master, I must point out the mistakes you made while performing the ceremony.' He was quiet. I waited. The softening veil of water had withdrawn from the room, there was only a dry and stony desert, a sphere of burnt air I could barely breathe. 'It is clear you know the etiquette of the ceremony well,' Niiramo continued. 'But it is equally clear that you deliberately change it according to your own will where change is not advisable.' He looked at my father and smiled his rich merchant's smile.

'I presume you know the rule by which only one of the teahouse windows must ever be open during the ceremony?'

'Yes, Master Niiramo, I am familiar with the rule.'

'Would you care to remind us why it exists?'

I quoted exactly as I had been taught.

'So the guests could take pleasure in the scent of the tea and the humidity of air created by the water. Draught in the teahouse drives the aroma and the humidity away.'

'I would be curious to hear why you took the liberty of breaking this rule.'

I bowed again, although I felt annoyed at having to answer such a stupid question.

'For practical reasons, Master. The heat in the teahouse was suffocating. As the host, I thought of the comfort of my guests.'

Niiramo scrutinised me. I didn't avert my gaze.

'Whatever your reason, it was still an exception to the form and as such, a mistake,' he said.

I forced myself to remain quiet. Niiramo continued, 'Another mistake, on which I'm sure your father agrees with me, was your choice of teaware.'

I thought of the teacups and plates, their surfaces cracked by change and time, their steady forms under my hands, connecting me to the past-world.

'Why do you consider it a mistake?' I asked.

Niiramo's smile twitched and deepened in his fleshy, smooth face. I thought of a narrow, long maggot digging into a rotten piece of fruit.

'You must realise that a tea master preparing for such an occasion should choose the most valuable teaware available. It demonstrates respect towards the guests and understanding of the privileged nature of the tea master's profession. I happen to know,' at this point he gave my father a look, 'that your father enjoys Major Bolin's favour, and I can see from your house and garden that you have some wealth. I'm convinced you own better teaware, and you could surely have had a whole new tea set made for the occasion. That would have been wisest.'

'But Master Niiramo—' Niiramo's eyebrows rose higher on his sweaty forehead when I spoke without permission. My father looked horrified. I cut myself short and bowed in order to request permission to speak, as was part of the hierarchy between master and apprentice. Niiramo nodded.

'Master Niiramo, the ceremony is not about showing one's wealth, but embracing change and accepting the fleeting quality of the world around us. It was my intention to honour this.'

Niiramo's smile didn't disappear. A sweat drop trickled down his cheek towards the skilfully crafted collar.

'Are *you* telling *me*, *girl*, what the tea ceremony is about?'

Anger gathered in my throat like burning dust.

'You should know without being told,' I said before I could stop myself.

'Noria,' my father said.

Niiramo began to laugh a slowly accumulating, low laughter. The sweat droplet fell from his quaking cheek to the collar of his jacket and the fabric absorbed it.

'You amuse me, Miss Kaitio,' he said. 'You have a lot to learn, about the ceremony and the world. I'll let time and experience take care of it. In thirty years you'll find yourself evaluating another young tea master's graduation performance, and when he tells you that the ceremony is not about showing one's wealth, you too will laugh.'

Never. Not in this life, not in ten thousand others.

Master Niiramo's laughter faded slowly. He looked at me.

'Then, of course, there is the unfortunate fact of your gender,' he said. 'Your father would have done wisely to mention it to me beforehand. I'd like to know why you believe that a woman can practise the profession of a tea master successfully.'

I understood now why Niiramo had looked so surprised when he had first seen me. Had Major Bolin purposefully neglected to mention that I wasn't a man when talking Niiramo into this? I looked at my father, but he couldn't help me. This was a battle I had to fight on my own.

'Master Niiramo, might I ask you in turn why you believe a woman is not fit to be a tea master?' I enquired.

'It is written in the old scriptures,' Niiramo replied. 'Li Song writes, "A woman shall not walk the path of tea masters, lest she be ready to abandon her life as a woman."'

I didn't think the citation precluded women's right to be tea masters in any way, but instead of arguing about wordings I said, 'I believe it is possible to change the surface of things while retaining their core intact, just as it is possible to retain the surface appearances while carving the core hollow.'

Niiramo was quiet. I wondered if I had gone too far. The room was silent. Outside the wind chime sounded once, twice, three times.

Eventually he spoke.

'I want you to understand this. If you were a candidate

101

in one of the cities, I would demand you to retake the test. Yet I know the same standard can't be expected in these backwater areas and, of course, not from a female apprentice. You have learned your craft solely from your father, and have never had a chance to make yourself familiar with the customs and knowledge of other tea masters. I see no obstacle to granting you the title of a tea master as of today's ceremony, even if it wouldn't have fulfilled the criteria under other circumstances or judged by a less benevolent master. However, I would advise you to be more alert about etiquette in the future, particularly if you receive guests from the cities or the military.'

I wanted to say something, but I saw my father's expression, now closer to despair than annoyance, and I remained silent.

'Are you ready?' Master Niiramo asked.

I bowed.

'Noria Kaitio,' Niiramo read from the scroll. 'Today, on the fifteenth day of the eighth month, Year of Koi Fish in New Qian time, you have been granted the title of a practising tea master,' he continued. Niiramo handed the scroll to me. Under the text were his and my father's signatures. Master Niiramo moved to the side and my father stepped in front of me. I accepted the leather-covered book he gave to me and read the oath I had learned by heart:

'I am a watcher of water. I am a servant of tea. I am a nurturer of change. I shall not chain what grows. I shall not cling to what must crumble. The way of tea is my way.'

I bowed low, and my father lowered his head. When I looked up, I saw his eyes moisten. He opened his mouth to speak, but sound caught in his throat.

'I nearly forgot,' Niiramo disrupted the silence. 'Commander

Taro sent his congratulations. He was right: your water has an extraordinarily good aroma.'

'I should have warned you about the teaware beforehand,' my father said to me in the kitchen, when we were wrapping two cups used in the ceremony in fabric for Master Niiramo as a gift, as was customary. 'I knew he would be picky about it. I don't approve of the way he spoke to you, but we never need to see him again.' I had a feeling he was going to scold me because of my behaviour, but thought better of it.

'Are you coming to Moonfeast?' I asked him.

My father shook his head.

'I've seen it all enough times. Sleep is more alluring to me now than the feast.'

Before leaving the house I took the scroll and the blank tea master's book into my room and placed them on the bed. I glanced at myself in the mirror. My face was still red from the ceremony, and the tunic of my master's outfit had dark, moist stains in the armpits. I changed into clean clothes and spread the outfit on the bed next to the book.

As I turned to put the book on my desk, I saw a thin white parcel that shone pale as moon on the dark wooden surface, and I recognised my mother's handwriting in the letters spelling my name across it. My father must have brought it into my room before the ceremony.

The envelope was big: not a stiff mail pouch woven of seagrass, but made of real paper. Inside I discovered a large, thin shawl of fine wool. I knew my mother couldn't have found it in our village, and possibly not even in the Scandinavian Union. Anything but the coarsest wool was difficult to come by. She must have ordered the shawl from faraway cities. I looked for a note, and my hand

caught a small white slip of paper inside the envelope. I
pulled the paper out and read:

*To Noria, the new tea master, from your proud mother.
Be happy today!*

I brought the shawl close to my face. I expected it to
smell of her hair soap and scented oil, but it only carried
a faint smell of wool and paper. There was no trace of her.

I wrapped it around myself anyway.

I arranged the master's outfit on a hanger and hung it
from the curtain pole. Just then I happened to glance out
of the window and saw Niiramo standing outside on the
grass, waiting for his helicarriage to arrive. His face was
weary and his eyes closed, and he brought a handkerchief
to his brow in order to dab the sweat dry. His shoulders
were slumped, as if extreme, previously hidden exhaustion
had taken hold of him.

I shoved a small waterskin into my bag and flung the
bag over my shoulder. Then I picked up a blaze lantern
and a box of feastcakes from my desk and left.

When I reached her family's house, Sanja was already
waiting for me, sitting outside in an armchair that had
seen better days. Minja was nodding sleepily in her arms,
sucking on a piece of cloth filled with seeds. Sanja sprang
up when she saw me and Minja woke up.

'How did it go?' she enquired.

'You have a permanent invitation to my tea ceremonies,'
I said.

'Congratulations!' she exclaimed and grinned. 'I'll skip
it, though, I've never been to one of those things and I
wouldn't know what to do.' Sanja embraced me, dangling
Minja with one arm. She was caught between us and began
to protest loudly. 'Wait, I'll be back in a minute.'

Sanja vanished into the house, and after a moment she returned, holding a basket covered with cloth. She had left Minja inside, probably with her mother.

'This is for you,' she said.

I took the basket and lifted the cloth. Under it there was a box Sanja had clearly made herself. Not for the first time, I admired her skill with things I could never have done. I knew how to cite texts and perform movements and bow my head before guests, but she knew how to take things apart with her hands and put them together again in a different way, reshaping them until something new and astonishing emerged. She had fashioned a rectangular, multi-coloured box out of pieces of scrap metal and plastic and wood, an uneven, glistening surface where vine-like patterns climbed across the sides and the lid, entwined and spiralled out of sight again.

'Do you like it?' she asked, and her face was a little less pale than usual. It was strange to see her so uncharacteristically shy. 'It's for tea.'

'It's gorgeous,' I said. 'Thank you!' I hugged her, pushed the box into my bag and handed the basket back. 'Shall we?'

Sanja nodded. We started walking towards the central square of the village. A few stars shone glass-clear above, and the full moon glinted pale and sharp-edged as it cut its way higher through the thickening blue of the evening.

'Look!' Sanja said and pointed at the sky.

Initially I didn't know what I was looking at, but then I saw it. Apart from the metallic moonlight, a flicker of fishfires brushed the dark outlines of the fells. It wavered slowly like a stretch of cloth in near-still water.

'It's only just beginning,' Sanja said.

The sounds and scents of Moonfeast floated around us

as we walked through the village. The backyards of the houses we passed were decorated with coloured blaze lanterns, and the rattle of occasional fireworks threw sparkles above the roofs. The smell of fried fish, vegetables and feastcakes wafted in the air. People were carrying harvest-meals and drinks to tables, and from some yards we heard music and buzzing voices.

From far away I saw the Moonfeast parade weaving its way around the village square. The Ocean-Dragon fashioned from junk plastic, plaited reed and waste wood glistened silver-white, swimming in the rhythm of the drums and chanting, as dancers carried it through the air. A group of children dressed up as fish and other sea-creatures followed the dragon's movements, a shoal flashing their junk-plastic scales against the falling darkness. I played with the thought that the fishfires we had seen were actually lit by them, like in stories where the reflection of fish swimming with the Ocean-Dragons cast them to the sky. In the middle of the square a large full moon of painted wood was propped up on a high stand over the whole scene. When we came closer, I saw the eyes of the dragon glow with yellowish light. It took me a moment to realise that there must be a blaze lantern inside the head. In the haze the pale, narrow figure of the dragon was like a passing ghost, floating mute and other-worldly above all sound and movement.

I was beginning to enjoy myself. I felt Moonfeast drawing me in. Sanja was dragging me through the crowd towards a food stand. We bought roasted almonds and dried seaweed snacks. I saw Sanja twisting and changing her weight from one foot to the other while I paid for the food. I could guess where she wanted to go next.

'Let's try that one,' she said to me and pointed at another

stand near the entrance to an alley leading away from the square. As we made our way through the crowd, we passed a group of villagers talking in hasty, serious voices. One of them was listening to a message-pod.

'It must be a fabrication,' I heard someone say. 'There hasn't been anything in the news.'

'You know how the news is,' another one said, 'and I wouldn't put it past the Unionists. My brother-in-law says he knows some of them, and—'

'My cousin saw it, that's what he says,' said the man holding the message-pod. 'He was right there, and he says it's complete chaos.'

It was a conversation that I would remember later, but back then I had other things in my mind.

Sanja was right: the stand had a small picture of a blue nymph painted in the corner of the canvas awning. Everyone knew what it stood for, and while it wasn't strictly illegal, most self-respecting merchants refused to sell it.

'We'd like four blue-lotus cakes, please,' Sanja told the merchant, an elderly woman with large brown birthmarks on her face.

'Aren't you a bit young for that?' the woman said, but Sanja gave her the money and she said nothing more, only dropped the cakes into the fabric pouch Sanja handed to her.

I looked into the sky. The fishfires had grown; they were spreading their thin veil across the night.

'To the Beak,' Sanja said. 'It has the best view.'

The Beak was a sharp cliff jutting out of the side of the fell near the plastic grave. A narrow staircase climbed there from the edge of the village. It would be the best place to see the fishfires, unless we wanted to walk back to the tea master's house and from there to the fell.

When we arrived at the Beak, we saw we weren't the only ones to have thought of the place. A couple of dozen people were sitting there in small groups or isolated couples. We knew some of them from the village school and stopped to say hello, but Sanja whispered, 'Let's climb further up, there must be a less crowded place there!'

After a while we found a smooth landing of rock where we could see the sky clearly. Sanja spread her worn shawl on the ground. We placed our blaze lanterns on it and arranged a picnic meal of almonds and cakes around them. The fishfires above us reached all the way across the sky, wavering, calming down and rising again in high folds like the sea.

We didn't talk much, yet the silence woven between us was not separating or empty, but a connecting silence where I felt at peace. Sanja was fumbling a cord of woven coloured seagrass on her wrist. I recognised the decorative ribbon sewn on the sleeve ends of her shirt and the long hem of her skirt. I had seen it somewhere before. An image of her mother sewing a ribbon to the edge of a tablecloth before Sanja's Matriculation celebrations surfaced before my eyes. It had looked a little worn already back then. The ribbon had probably been attached to the sleeves and the skirt-hem to cover their tattered appearance.

I gnawed on my blue-lotus cake and waited for the drifting feeling of languor.

'When the Ocean-Dragons roam, it means the world is changing,' I said.

Sanja chewed on her roasted almonds and drank water from her skin.

'It's just a story, Noria,' she said. 'Fishfires are colliding particles caused by the closeness of the North Pole. An electromagnetic reaction, no more exciting than a light bulb or a glow-worm. There are no dragons living in the sea, no shoals of fish following them or the flashing of scales in the dark sky.' She picked up a blue-lotus cake and tasted it. 'These were better last year,' she remarked.

'I know what fishfires are,' I said. 'And I still see the dragons. Don't you?'

Sanja looked at the sky for a long time, and I looked at her. Under the dim-green glow of the fishfires her face was different than in any other light, like a bone-smooth seashell veiled with algae. Her hands were two starfish in the abyss of the night. I could imagine them drifting away, being pulled into craggy mazes where daylight didn't reach, where translucent, blind creatures didn't make a sound or dream of another world.

'Yes,' she said after a long silence. 'I see them.'

Sanja placed her hand on my arm. I felt its warmth through the thin fabric of my tunic, each line of her fingers as if they were drawn on my skin with sunlight. Blazeflies glowed quietly in the lanterns, Ocean-Dragons roamed and the world turned slowly, unnoticeably, unstopping.

In the still of the dawn I walked home with my new shawl wrapped tightly around me. The road from the village to the tea master's house didn't seem long, or the shadows of the trees tall. After passing through the gate I clinked the windchime hanging from the pine lightly with my fingernails. I could still taste the previous day's meal and the night in my mouth, and I wanted to chew on mint leaves. I turned towards the rock garden instead of walking directly into the house.

I remember that grass stalks brushed my ankles, the cool humidity of the morning hour sticking to my skin.

Memory slips and slides and is not to be trusted, but I remember.

I stopped in my tracks when I saw it.

A dark and narrow figure stood at the edge of the rock garden, by the tea plants, and waited.

My flesh and bones were stony and tight around my heart, and I couldn't bring myself to take another step.

The figure turned around and walked away, until it had disappeared behind the tea plants. The branches moved for a moment where it had brushed them in passing, and then they were silent and still.

With heavy limbs I ran into the house.

There was no light or movement in the blaze lantern hanging from the entrance ceiling, and it took a while before my eyes got used to the half-light.

My father was lying on the floor, his face twisted with pain and his breathing laboured. There was a broken waterskin next to him. The water had spread into a puddle on the floor and wet my father's clothes.

'What happened?' I asked him and tried to help him up. With great difficulty, he got to his feet, but he couldn't stand straight.

'Nothing,' he said. 'I'm just a little tired.'

'I'm going to call the doctor,' I said.

I walked him into my parents' bedroom and put him under the covers. After a moment he grew restless.

'I need to get some water from the kitchen,' he said. 'My mouth is dry.'

'I'll get you water,' I told him, but he insisted on getting up and walking to the kitchen and pouring himself a cup of water.

It was the last time I saw my father get out of bed without help.

PART TWO

The Silent Space

'Not one grain of sand stirs without a shift in the shape of the universe:
   change one thing, and you will change everything.'

Wei Wulong, 'The Path of Tea'
7th century of Old Qian time

CHAPTER NINE

We are children of water, and water is death's close companion. The two cannot be separated from us, for we are made of the versatility of water and the closeness of death. They go together always, in the world and in us, and the time will come when our water runs dry.

This is how it happens:

Earth settles where water was, takes its place on human skin or on a green leaf sprouting from sand, and spreads like dust. The leaf, the skin, the fur of an animal slowly takes the shape and colour of earth, until it's impossible to tell where one ends and the other begins.

Dry and dead things become earth.

Earth becomes dry and dead things.

Most of the soil we walk on once grew and breathed, and once it had the shape of the living, long ago. One day someone who doesn't remember us will walk on our skin and flesh and bones, on the dust that remains of us.

The only thing that separates us from dust is water, and water cannot be held in one place. It will slip through our fingers and through our pores and through our bodies, and the more shrivelled we become, the more anxious it is to leave us.

When the water runs dry, we are of earth alone.

I chose the place at the edge of the rock garden, under the tea plants. The sky was covered in clouds, and the thin grey light weighed on the winter-worn grass like sea on underwater landscape. It bent my bones and tilted the ground towards me. I thought of the silence of the earth, but air and water flowed under my skin still, and I had to make use of the brief daylight hours while they lasted.

I took off my coat, placed it next to the shovel and picked up the hoe.

I was careful not to damage the roots of the tea plants. I hoed and shovelled until my muscles ached and my mouth was dry. When the first blazeflies began to glow in the gooseberry bushes, the hole at my feet was large enough.

I washed myself in the bathroom with cold water and picked up the message my mother had left on the message-pod. Her voice was swollen with sorrow.

'I've had no news from the visa office,' she said. 'All railway connections between Xinjing and Ural are still suspended, and no one's allowed to travel further than the nearby villages. Noria, the only thing I can do is try to arrange a ticket and visa for you to come here once the connections resume. I only hope I can find a safe way to send them to you. I'd give anything to be there with you.' There was a pause. I heard her breathing. 'Please send me a message to let me know how you are,' she added in a broken voice.

The pod beeped and went quiet.

I listened to the message again and then twice more. I

knew I should choose her name from the list and talk to her, but my mouth was so full of silence there was no room for words. Eventually I pressed the green button. *Recording*, the screen announced.

'I'm okay,' I said and tried to make it sound true. 'I'll write to you tomorrow.'

I sent the recording and placed the message-pod back on the wall rack.

I went to bed and stared at the darkness until I could see the outlines of the furniture in the faint light of night turning to dawn.

When I eventually got up and went to the veranda, I couldn't tell if the weather was unusually cold or if I was just feeling shivery because I hadn't slept. I came back to my room and put on the thickest coat, trousers and shawl I could find, and pulled two pairs of socks on my feet before slipping on the sandals. On the way out my eyes fell on my father's insect hood that rested folded flat and wrapped in protective fabric on the shelf at the entrance next to my own. I picked it up, took it to my mother's study and closed the door.

The guests began to arrive around ten o'clock in the morning. The first were plasticsmith Jukara with his wife Ninia and sister Tamara, and Major Bolin with his heli-carriage driver. Soon after them four tea masters who had been acquaintances of my father greeted me at the gate, followed by some cousins and second cousins of his from the nearby villages. I had had to compile the guest list partly by guesswork, because my mother's family was from near New Piterburg, and she had no siblings or cousins this far north. My father had barely kept in touch with any family members of his. I couldn't remember meeting most of his relatives more than once or twice as a child, when we had attended someone's wedding or name-giving, where my father had been asked to perform a tea ceremony. These people were strange to me; we had no memories or words in common. I was alone among them.

The three lament-women of the village approached through the trees. They looked exactly the same as I remembered they always had. As a child I had been afraid of them. They wore loose, dark garments and their heads were covered with scarves, and expressions on their wrinkled faces changed like tides. Some people claimed they saw things that others couldn't see. They spoke little, and followed death wherever it went, and when they lamented, stones seemed to ache around them.

I couldn't remember inviting them, but I did not turn them away. Someone must weep on a day like this, I thought, and I had nothing but numb silence in me.

Sanja and her father Jan were the last to arrive. Sanja hugged me, and I was certain she could feel me shaking against her.

'Mum had to stay at home. Minja's not well,' she whispered quickly before withdrawing from me and continuing with Jan to the garden where the other guests were already standing around the grave and the coffin. I closed the gate and followed in their footsteps.

The bamboo coffin rested on a stone bench where the men from the burial office had placed it the day before, and at the end of the bench stood the water urn. The coffin still looked too small to me. It was barely larger than the hearth in the teahouse floor, and I thought, not for the first time, of how fleeting death was, how impossible to grasp and see and understand. My father was not here, not in the coffin or in the urn. They held mere matter his spirit had been bound to, and he no longer belonged to it more than light belongs to a faded flower that it once made grow.

I had asked Bolin to take care of the speech formalities. He welcomed the guests and spoke about my father briefly. Then he opened the leather-covered book he was holding, and read out a passage. I was aware of him speaking, but the words drifted away, their husks strange and hollow.

He closed the book, placed it carefully on the ground and nodded to Jukara. Together they lifted the coffin from the bench, carried it to the grave and slowly lowered it into the hole. As the closest family member I was the first to leave my greeting. This early in the year there were no flowers yet, and most trees had shed their leaves months ago, so I had picked an evergreen tea plant branch. I dropped it on the coffin, and in the shallow grave its dark brown and green dissolved into the bamboo. Only the smallest, brittlest buds shone as scattered stars against the dark background.

Most guests left a pebble or a mussel shell found in the long-dried riverbed as their last greeting. Their rapping was rain-soft on the bamboo lid. Bolin sprinkled silver-grey knots of tea leaves on the coffin.

When everyone had left their greetings, it was time for the water urn.

The lament-women began to sing.

It started as a quiet song that grew gradually, beautiful and ugly at once, like weeping forged into a waxing and waning melody that shrouded everything within its reach. Their language was old and strange. Its words sounded like a spell or curse, but I knew it was one of the past-world languages, now nearly lost, only remaining in the songs they and few others knew.

The lament spun a slow web around me, divided into countless threads that floated far away as glowing paths, through the fabric of things remembered and lost and forgotten. I lifted the water urn from the stone bench and walked to the edge of the grave where the tea plants stood. The song of the lament-women rose and fell, it grew leaves and branches and roots on my skin and under it, and my own outlines faded, because what I carried within couldn't be contained in them: I was a forest that reached upwards and crumbled down again, I was the sky and the sea and the breath of the living and the sleep of the dead. Strange words carried me; a lost language directed my footsteps.

I bowed down to pour the water on the roots of the tea plants.

When the urn was empty, I carried it back to the stone bench. The song waned like wind.

The ceremony is over when there is no more water.

The guests began to move towards the house. I stood on the pale grass among bare trees for a long time, looking at the tea plants, and they did not grow slower or faster. Only when Sanja stopped next to me and placed her arm around my shoulders, did I feel my own outlines again and was no longer floating shattered in space.

'They're waiting for you,' Sanja said.

'I think he'd want me to stay a little longer,' I said.

'The dead don't need pleasing, Noria,' she said.

If anyone else had said it, or if she had said it in a different way, I would have walked into the fell there and then and left the guests in the house and not returned until they were all gone. But Sanja's hand was solid on my shoulder, and I had never heard her voice so soft.

She turned to look me in the eye and swept a strand

of hair from my face that I hadn't noticed. I followed her into the house.

It was too dark in the living room, because I had entirely forgotten to think about light. The spring equinox was still over half a month away, and the day behind the windows was not bright. Relatives I may never have met before held short speeches. Ninia and Tamara took care of bringing food to the table. I had promised them two weeks' water supply in exchange, and since all water pipes in the village had been closed, no one refused such offers. The lament-women ate and drank more than anyone else, but I didn't blame them. Sanja sat next to me all the time.

I looked around, trying to remember where I knew everyone from. There was one guest I couldn't place: a blond-haired man sitting in the corner wasn't talking to anyone and didn't seem to know anybody. I was fairly certain he wasn't family, and nearly as certain that he wasn't from the village. Yet there was something familiar about him.

'Do you know him?' I asked Sanja.

Sanja glanced at the man.

'Never seen him in my life,' she said.

He was in civilian clothing, but something about his gestures and the way he was watching the people in the room made me wonder if he was a soldier. Around the same time as weekly water patrols were made compulsory for everyone and the punishments for water crimes became harsher, soldiers had begun to appear in all large gatherings, either openly in their uniforms or disguised as civilians. I hadn't believed these stories at first, but I had once mentioned them to my father who was too ill to go to the village any more, and he had said, 'They're watching closely now. They don't want to risk organised resistance after the events of Moonfeast. They're gripping us tight and will squeeze until no one has the courage to stand against them. It has begun, but it will not end any time soon.'

An unexpected shudder ran through me and anger weighed in my throat like hot stones, and then tears were pouring down my face. I let them. After a while they dried up, but I could still feel them charring and stinging behind my eyes. They would burn their way through again.

The guests trickled out little by little. When nearly everyone had left, Bolin came to me.

'Could I speak to you for a while, Noria?' he said. I noted that he used my first name instead of calling me Miss Kaitio as usual. He had known my father for a long time and helped with the funeral arrangements more than necessary. I thought he wanted to talk about his next tea visit.

'I'll see you the day after tomorrow,' I told Sanja. 'Thanks for coming.' She squeezed my hand.

'Send me a message or come and see us any time,' she said. Jan nodded his goodbyes to me, and they left.

'Could you bring the chest from the helicarriage?' Bolin told his driver, who gave a small bow and walked outside, boots clanking on the floor planks. We were alone in the dusky living room, where only a couple of dim lamps separated light from shadow. Bolin had been coming to my father's tea ceremonies since I was six or seven years old, and he had always treated me well and with respect even before I had any skill with the ceremony. He had been my father's friend, as much as my father had any, and I trusted him well enough not to be afraid. I offered him a cup of tea, but he shook his head.

'Noria,' he began.

I waited. He seemed to be looking for the right words. A lone blazefly was whizzing softly against the window, and I wondered if I had left a lantern unclosed somewhere. I would need to sweep up dead blazeflies from the corners later.

Eventually Bolin spoke again.

'There are people who believe there is water on your grounds,' he said. 'I don't know if it's true, but—'

'It's not true.'

'I'm not here to fish for information,' Bolin said, and his face was grave. 'I don't know if your father ever mentioned this, but we grew up together, and once upon a time I would have trusted him with my life. He didn't understand why I chose an army career, but we salvaged what we could of our friendship. Therefore I know he would have wanted me to warn you.' He went quiet for a moment. 'The power is no longer in my hands. In name, perhaps, but every day, every hour it's slipping to someone else, and soon there won't be anything I can do for you. The power that used to be mine is Taro's now. You must be as careful as you can, Noria.'

I wondered then how much exactly Bolin had been doing for my parents and me. I remembered my father saying that we had his protection. I began to understand I didn't know what it really meant. Protection – from whom? The image of the blond-haired, unfamiliar funeral guest crossed my mind, the memories of the soldiers investigating the garden.

There were always foods in our kitchen that many other villagers only had at Moonfeast or Midwinter celebrations, and almost no one else had a freezer. Did he have something to do with them – and had some of the books in the house come through his hands? Had he been keeping water patrols

121

away so my father could continue to practise in peace? How much of this was his doing – and most importantly, how would things change if his protection was removed?

'I will be careful,' I said.

Heavy footsteps crossed the veranda, and there was a knock on the door.

'That will be my driver,' Bolin said. 'I brought something for you. Come in!' he shouted.

There was a clank, as something heavy was placed on the floor. I heard the door being eased open, wood scratching against wood, and a moment later the driver walked in. His face was very red, and he was carrying a large wooden chest, which he put down in front of me.

'Open it,' Bolin said.

I lifted the lid. Inside were dozens of old, leather-bound books.

'I've no doubt that Taro found nothing of interest in them, or I wouldn't have been able to get them back,' he continued. 'They'd have been destroyed if I hadn't pulled the few strings that I still can. Think of it as my final favour to your father. I know how important these books were to him.'

Tears blurred my eyes again as I ran my fingers along the spines of the tea masters' books. I recognised one as my father's. He had not acquired a new one after the soldiers had taken it. Little else remained of him now.

'Thank you,' I said. 'Thank you.'

Bolin's face had a weary expression I could only inter-pret as sadness. The lamps glowed softly, and nothing looked different, but everything had changed.

'I will still be attending the tea ceremonies, and I know you will be able to keep up the quality of your father's work,' Bolin said. He hesitated and then patted me clum-sily on the shoulder.

'I'd like to know one thing,' I said. 'Why did you bring Taro here last summer?'

I knew the accusation was clear behind my words. His answer surprised me.

'I had no say in the matter. There is no power that lasts, Noria. Even mountains will eventually be worn down by wind and rain.'

He looked old and vulnerable, and I didn't know what else to say to him. I saw him hesitate, just like I had a moment earlier.

'There's also something I would like to ask before I go,' he said. 'I understand you may not want to talk about it, but I'd like to know. How did Mikoa die?'

I was quiet. The day grew darker, the year turned slowly towards spring, water flowed in its stone-shell of the fell, and I was as cold as if my bones had turned into ice.

'I don't want to talk about it,' I eventually said.

Bolin bowed low and left.

This is how it happens:

On the night of Moonfeast my father collapses to the floor, and he lies silent and still, while water and darkness creep into his clothes and hair and onto his skin.

Meanwhile, three unionists pour oil all over their clothes and hair and skin. Then they climb the stairs of the head-quarters of the local military regime in Kuusamo and start the fire.

The next day an old couple from our village is taken away by men in blue uniforms, and by the evening everyone knows their son and two other people burned themselves as a protest against the Qianese occupation.

The weeping-song of the lament-women sweeps through the village for three days.

First there are more water guards each passing month. Then, just before the Midwinter celebrations, the water pipes are shut down altogether, and the only way to get water is to queue for rations on the central square.

The pod-news talks about tamed terrorism in the Scandinavian Union, about minor unrest in distant areas, fast-flaring and equally swiftly calmed riots in cities, as if the war is scattered, incidental, insignificant. Yet at the same time there is less and less food in the markets; pass-pods and visas are more difficult to get, and notifications about volunteers killed in battles are on the rise.

When the moon grows dark and new to mark the beginning of the year, my mother can't come home because the railway connections are suspended.

I watch all this through my father's illness, and while I see what is happening, it is like faint, shapeless mist at the edges of my life. My father is the centre holding it all: the pain chaining him that I can't alleviate; his faltering life diminishing before my eyes that I can't hold in the confines of the world. I let everything else pass by, even though I know I must face it later.

He lies in my parents' bed, too wide for him alone, and his skin is sun-brittle paper, thinner every day. I can see the angles and arches of his bones through it.

Bolin tries to arrange medicines for him, but it is getting difficult even for military officers to find them. The doctor who comes shakes his head, sticks needles into his limbs, leaves and comes again, doesn't know what is wrong with my father.

I think my mother's absence gnaws on him, all change gnaws on him, and he just no longer has the strength to live.

Eventually he stops eating.

Eventually he stops drinking.

He knows, like in a dream you know that the other person in the room is familiar, even if you don't know their face.

He orders me to prepare the last ritual.

He is my guest only once in his lifetime, and a tea master does not reveal any feelings in front of guests.

After he has finished the tea, he waits in the teahouse until death presses a hand on his heart and the water in his blood runs dry.

When Bolin hears what has happened, he arranges for a doctor from the military hospital to come and store the organs, because there is a shortage. When it is done, he sends a helicarriage for the body.

In the burial office I choose a bamboo coffin, which looks too small, and a silver-coloured urn, into which my father's water will be gathered. The burial director tells me all will be ready in two days. I step back into the helicarriage and go to the baker's shop to order the funeral cakes.

My mother is not here and she should be. There is no train she can board and no letter she knows will reach me, and every day I wake up hoping she is still breathing, even if I can't feel it.

My father is not here and he should be. He is lying in a chamber of metal and stone, where the water that flowed in him is turning into ice and leaving him. After two days he will be nothing more than dust in a bamboo coffin and water in a silver-coloured urn.

I am here, and all words are mute ashes in my mouth, and no water will quench my thirst.

CHAPTER TEN

The queue dragged on at an agonisingly slow pace. The sun stung my eyes and my bare face was covered in the fine grit that the strong late-winter wind was whipping around. I regretted that I hadn't unwrapped my insect hood in the morning. There weren't many horseflies yet, but the sand clouds were no better. I kept glancing at the water-rationing point, which was still so very far away. I had other plans for the day and couldn't wait to get out of the queue, but I knew I had to show my face at the village square at least twice a week in order not to appear suspicious.

I had walked to the fell first thing in the morning to check the surface level of the spring, and I had spent yesterday washing laundry and pruning gooseberry bushes in the still-bare garden and sowing vegetable seeds in burned-clay earthenware pots. Trying to keep the house as it had been while my father was still alive and my mother still lived at home felt like trying to catch wind between my palms. Dust gathered in thick, grey threads on the webs that spiders spun in the corners while I wasn't looking. Long-legged, soft-winged insects that were the colour of dead leaves came seeking a faint glint of light inside the house and lost themselves in the maze of walls and closed spaces. Their dried bodies would crunch under my feet in unlit rooms, and I would find their lightweight debris slowly accumulating in places I had no time or energy to sweep often: twig-fragile legs, scale-glittery wings torn off hollow bodies, black-eyed heads with broken antennae twisted towards silence forever. The change was stronger and faster than me. The house was different, and my life was different, and I had to submit to it, even as my blood screamed against it.

The moon had only grown full once after I had dug the grave. The grass covering it was bruised and black earth showed through the stalks. Even though I saw it every day, my father's death remained unfathomable and strange to me. I couldn't place it in these rooms where his life had belonged. His imprint was so strong that it was like he still walked here, not knowing how to leave, stepping out of sight just as I turned around, leaving the teahouse right before I slid the door open. It was a gentle and sad presence, not a frightening one. I spoke his name sometimes, knowing he wouldn't reply even if he heard me, wouldn't place his hand on my shoulder. We inhabited different worlds now, and the dark river between us had only ever been crossed in one direction.

The queue moved forward and Sanja yanked the cart in which her family's empty containers and my waterskins lay. Sand rattled in the wheels as they turned. There were still at least a dozen people ahead of us.

'Fancy seeing you here,' a voice said behind me, and a short-fingered hand with chipped nails touched my shoulder. I turned around and saw Jukara's wife Ninia, who had joined the queue. She was one of the few people in sight already wearing an insect hood. Behind its transparent mesh her round face looked colourless and the skin sagged on her bones. She had painted her lips a brighter red than usual. I wondered where she had managed to get lip-colour and what its price had been.

'Hello, Ninia,' I said.

'Of course, you only need water for yourself these days,' she continued, and her sun-bleached eyebrows drew into a woeful expression. She patted my arm. I felt something burning behind my eyes. 'Have you heard from your mother?'

'The pod-connections are weak,' I replied, and my voice did not sound entirely solid in my ears. I had sent my mother several messages every week, but I had only received one back after the funeral. There was nothing but bad news coming from Xinjing, if any, and my mother's silence frightened me more than I wanted to admit. 'How are you?'

'The little ones are suffering,' Ninia said. I knew she was referring to her grandchildren. 'Stretching the water rations for the whole family is hard work. Still, we're lucky, because Jukara has regular repair jobs at the camp, and the officials often pay extra, if you know what I mean.' She seemed to realise that she might have said too much. 'It's tough, it's tough,' she continued. 'But you probably have it worse, poor thing, with both parents gone and only the tea ceremonies to support yourself.'

Sanja must have seen my reaction, because she interrupted.

'Excuse me, there's something on your face. Under the left eye. No, on the other side,' she said when Ninia lifted her hood and brushed her cheek.

'Is it gone?' she asked.

Sanja inspected her closely and creased her brow.

'I think I made a mistake. It seems like a wrinkle. Or maybe a shadow made by your new insect hood,' she told Ninia, whose nostrils flared.

'That's right, decent hood fabric is hard to find these days,' she said and pursed her lips.

I turned to look the other way, so she wouldn't see the smile that twitched on my face despite the knot of grief in my chest. I knew Ninia's insect hood wasn't new. I had seen the lipstick stain permanently stuck to its hem which she usually attempted to cover with a scarf.

'How's your family, Sanja?' Ninia opened the conversation again, although her tone had turned several degrees cooler.

Sanja's expression darkened. Minja had been unwell for weeks, and Sanja was worried about her. The water given out at the village square had so far been clean, but there were rumours circulating about people in the cities and other villages who had fallen ill after drinking their water rations. Sanja had told me her parents whispered that the military was making people sick on purpose by distributing contaminated water. I didn't want to believe it, but I still preferred to use my rations on washing or watering the garden rather than drink them.

'Not too bad,' she said. 'Dad has a lot of work, he's been hired to convert those old outskirts buildings into living quarters for the new water guards.'

'And your mother and sister?' Ninia queried.

'They're as well as you are,' Sanja said.

Ninia went quiet for a moment.

'Give them my regards,' she said then, and her face showed clearly that the conversation was over for now.

'What a cockroach,' Sanja muttered under her breath.

Eventually our turn came. I pulled out my message-pod and placed my finger on the screen. My identification code and name popped up. I handed the pod to one of the soldiers rationing the water. She connected it to her multi-pod and filled my waterskins. I watched her insert the information that my water quota for the week had been used up. *Citizen: Noria Kaitio. Next ration: three days left*, the screen read. The soldier handed the message-pod back to me. I switched it off and put it in my pocket.

I lifted the full skins into Sanja's cart while she waited for her containers to be filled and her ration information to be entered into her family's message-pod. The containers seemed terribly small to me. I used the same amount of water every day just by myself: washing and cleaning the dishes alone took half of it.

When the containers were full and Sanja had received her message-pod back, she placed lids on them and we began to pull the cart together out of the square. We walked past some stalls where people had put secondhand kitchenware, furniture and other items on display. An elderly woman was trying to swap a pair of shoes for a bag of flour. The day was surprisingly chilly, given the time of the year, and I felt cold despite the effort of hauling the cart on the uneven stones. A thick wall of hazy-dark clouds rested on the horizon of the bright skies like a wide, soaked stretch of grey wool fabric.

'I hope it rains tonight,' Sanja said. 'I put the barrels and the gathering-pool outside already.'

I, too, longed for rain, a soothing, purifying torrent that would wash me and the landscape, would tint the world different and new even for a brief moment. I didn't think the clouds promised anything more than a drizzle, but I didn't say this.

There were blue-clad water guards and people returning home with their water rations on the streets, but otherwise it was quiet. In the months following Moonfeast, the villagers had begun talking in hushed voices while the number of soldiers increased and more barracks were built for them in the outskirts. As the water shortage worsened, a stagnant stench of people and life seemed to crawl into the houses, spreading its sticky fingers all over the streets and yards like lichen grows over rocks in a dried riverbed. Every time I walked into the village, it stuck to my nose, unpleasant, before I grew unaware of it.

The stench seemed to intensify when we approached the medical centre we had to pass on the way. The old brick building had a waiting room too small to contain more than a dozen people at a time, and at least ten women were waiting outside with their children. Two babies were screaming at the top of their lungs, while a few slightly older children seemed too weary to move or even speak. A young woman who couldn't be much older than me was trying to get a baby with cracked lips and swollen eyelids to drink from a bottle. A black-haired, pale-skinned girl who was maybe three years old had soiled herself and the mother was desperately trying to calm her down. When she saw us, she took a plastic mug that was hanging from her belt by a piece of string and said, 'Could you spare a cup of water for us? My child is thirsty and sick, and we've been waiting for hours.'

Sanja looked at me. This was new. The village had seen water shortages before, but no one had ever needed to beg for water. The little girl's cheeks were hollow and eyes big.

'Let's stop,' I told Sanja.

The woman was holding up her mug. I took my water-skin and poured some water in it. She clenched my arm with her free hand and squeezed.

'Thank you, miss! You're a good person. Thank you, thank you, may fresh waters flow your way!' She continued her flood of thanks and I was beginning to feel embarrassed. Just as I had closed the waterskin and placed it back in the cart, another woman approached me. Two small children were holding on to her hands.

'You wouldn't have a drop for us, too, would you?' she asked.

Sanja threw me a pointed glance.

'We need to go, Noria,' she said.

She was right. I saw everyone waiting outside the medical centre looking at me hopefully, pondering their chances and best ways of asking for water. If I stayed, I would have nothing left in my skins.

'I'm sorry,' I told the woman. 'I'm really, really sorry, but I can't. This is all I have for myself.'

She looked at me, her face settling to disbelief and then something nastier.

'You're the tea master's daughter, aren't you?' she said.

'Come on, Noria,' Sanja said.

'I should've known. Tea masters have always thought they're too good for this village,' the woman continued.

Blood rushed to my face and I turned away, pulling the cart across the cracked surface of the street. I heard the crowd behind muttering and thought I made out my own name, but I wanted to hear nothing more.

'Just ignore them,' Sanja said. 'It's not your fault that you can't help everyone.'

My face felt hot and my throat was thick. I didn't know

what to say. I wanted to get out of here. I tried to think of what was ahead, what had been the real reason for my coming to the village today. Even through the blend of humiliation and confusion, I felt a faint flash of excitement.

We turned from the street corner to take a circuitous route. I had time to see a low, grey-plastered house with a blue circle that had appeared on its door four weeks earlier, and the gaping dark windows with no movement or sound flickering behind them. Our feet chose a different direction on their own. These days walking in the village was not straightforward, but new paths born of wordless pacts had slowly come to replace the old ones as the mark of water crime had claimed space along the streets. There were now a dozen houses carrying the blue circle. The grey-plastered one was the latest among them. Their mute spectres stood along the edges of the roads, surrounded by a ring of silence that no one would cross unless it was unavoidable. The residents of the neighbouring houses continued their lives as if there was a swirling, all-swallowing emptiness in the place of the criminal house that would sweep them off the face of the earth if they as much as glanced in its direction.

There were whispers in the village that the people who lived in the water crime houses had been seen once or twice, picking something up from their doorstep or standing quietly outside, never leaving their own front yard, usually early in the morning or late in the night. These tales were received the same way as any ghost stories: with a mixture of fear and curiosity that faded into disbelief in daylight.

The truth was that no one still knew for certain what happened to the residents of the marked houses. It was easier not to ask.

Silence is not needed to chain tame things.

A cold gale tugged at the roof-corners and lashed us occasionally through the gaps between the houses. In one backyard a bone-thin man I recognised as a teacher at the village school was rubbing his scalp with light brown powder, a mixture of clay and bitter tree-bark flour, which was sold in market stalls as dry shampoo. I was used to soapwort, which grew behind the teahouse in thick tufts, and I liked the way it foamed between my fingers when mixed with bathwater. For the first time it occurred to me that someone might wonder why I never bought dry shampoos or soap flakes. I didn't know how many changes I would have to make to make my life appear the same as any other villager's.

As we approached Sanja's house, I couldn't wait any longer.

'I'm going scavenging,' I said. 'Do you want to come?'

Sanja sighed.

'I can't. There's too much to do at home.' She glanced at my waterskins. 'Do you want to leave those at my place and get them later?' she asked. 'You'll never be able to haul them all the way to the plastic grave and back.'

'You can keep them,' I said.

Sanja looked at me as if I had just offered her a flight on the back of an Ocean-Dragon.

'Don't be stupid!' she said. 'You're not going to get more water until next week. Of course I can't take them.'

'I don't need them,' I said. 'I've got water at home for the rest of the week. Please, keep them.'

Sanja looked like she was going to insist, but let out a deep breath instead and said, 'This once, but don't you dare try this again.'

*   *   *

134

The pungent smell of the plastic grave floated towards me. I passed a place where people were trying to fill waterskins and buckets from the shallow, murky-watered brook that ran near the edge of the grave. My parents had always warned me to never drink from it. They said the water was contaminated by the toxins of the grave and would make me sick. Villagers had tended to avoid it in the past, but lately whenever I came here I saw someone trying to draw from it. I had once told an elderly woman the water was not good for drinking.

'What would you have me drink, then?' she had said. 'Air, or sand, perhaps?'

That was the last time I had spoken to anyone at the brook.

I nearly stopped when I recognised a red-lipped face behind the insect hood among the handful of water-seekers. Ninia was crouched at the edge of the brook, filling a transparent skin with yellow-brown water. There really was something cockroach-like about her stubby figure, brown clothes and laboured movements, but just as this image took shape in my mind, I also felt a stab of shame. *What is she doing but trying to survive as best she can? What is any one of us doing but that?* I guessed Jukara's employers weren't paying quite as well as she had suggested. She turned her face away from me, and I couldn't tell if she had not seen me or if she chose to pretend she hadn't.

I walked past without stopping.

In the ever-changing, eye-betraying terrain of the plastic grave it was hard to discern landmarks, but I knew my way. Near the centre of the grave concrete elements twice as tall as me stuck out of the rubbish mountain. I stopped next to them and looked towards the edge of the grave, until I spotted an ancient, rusted-through carcass of a large past-world vehicle. The places where the wheels had been were still visible, as was the dead dashboard, but the seats and all still-usable metal parts were long gone. No one seemed to ever move this piece of dead weight, because it would have required the strength of at least five people, and there didn't seem to be much to find in this corner of the grave. I walked to the skeleton of the vehicle.

Out of habit I pushed my hand through a hole in the dashboard and felt around until I reached the smooth surface of a plastic box approximately the size of a saucer. I didn't need to take it out: it was enough to know that it was there. It was one of the time capsules Sanja and I had hidden in our favourite places when we were younger. They contained things like pebbles, dried flowers, home-made seagrass wristbands and treasures found in the plastic grave. We had always painted the date on the inside of the lid of each capsule, then dipped our fingers in paint and pressed our fingerprints next to it. On the outside we had marked the date when we were allowed to open the capsule, usually at least ten years in the future. This was the last one we had made, and for many years we had always checked that is was still in place every time we visited the grave.

I pulled my hand out, wiped it on my trousers and started walking towards the edge of the grave from the wrecked vehicle. After twenty steps I came to a shallow hole I had left a few days earlier. No one else seemed to have been there in the meantime.

I took thick gloves from my bag, pulled them on and began to move things.

I hadn't talked about this to anyone, but the silver-coloured disc had brought me here. After my father's death the quiet house seemed to wrap me in heavy sleep, as if the earth was pulling my blood towards its promise of unbroken rest. The silence wasn't just the silence of the empty spaces my parents had left behind, the lack of their breathing and words and footsteps inside those walls. It was also the silence of everything they had left untold and unsaid, everything that it was now up to me to learn and find out without them. I was only beginning to understand how little I knew: of the spring and other tea masters, of the strange laws and threatened balances of secret alliances and bribery we had lived by, of this whole dark grown-up world stretching like a lightless desert in all directions around me and blurring into the horizon. I was angry with them for leaving me alone without the knowledge I needed. *Why didn't you tell me?* But they were not here, there was only earth and wind, and they had no words.

I didn't quite understand yet why the story of the silver-coloured disc was so important to me, because I didn't know how to pull together the threads that made it so. One of them was my fear that one day I would find the surface of the spring too low, or blue-clad soldiers in the cave with their sabres pulled, and another was a budding notion, or perhaps a near-vain hope, that there had to be more than this to life, that outside the village, somewhere under the sky, there must be a reason to believe that the world wasn't dry and scorched and dying beyond all repair. Yet the threads had begun to intertwine in my mind, and not knowing yet how to put the thought to words, I felt an urge to do what I could to restore the story of the disc and find the missing pieces. I looked for them in the books in my mother's study, and I looked for them among the rubble of the past abandoned in the grave. I was aware of the hopelessness of the task, but it served to take my mind off the irreversible silence of the empty house, and there was something calming about it: a promise of change, a buried chance that might still see the light of day.

The wide and shallow hole I had dug within the weeks after my father's death had a lot of broken past-technology. It had taken days to find the right place, but I was now fairly convinced that this was where I had first found the silver-coloured disc a few years ago. I had recognised some of the machines lying in the area, remembering that Sanja had rejected several of them because they were too broken to ever be made whole again. All the essential parts were missing, too, so they were no longer useful for her experiments. As far as I recalled, the disc had been close to the surface, but the plastic grave had changed several times since, and if there were any other discs, they could lie a lot deeper – or far from where the first one had been. Still, I didn't know where else to start looking.

The shadow of the concrete elements turned and grew taller. The first stiff horseflies of the spring pushed their new and heavy bodies into the air around me, then landed on mushy garbage piles again to rest. I would need my hood soon. My limbs ached and my clothes were sticky against my skin. I kept finding nothing but the usual junk: pieces of kitchenware and tattered shoes with broken heels, unrecognisable fragments, endless plastic bags. I moved to the side a crushed past-machine with some wires sticking out from under the cracked shell – it was one of the things that Sanja had deemed useless, and therefore I had no idea what its original purpose had been – and stared at the plastic-bag tangle before me. I decided to go home after dragging it out of the grip of the grave, even though I didn't believe I would find anything interesting under it.

The bags were tied into a long chain that was painfully tightly stuck. Their brittle plastic ripped in my hands as I tried to get a proper hold of the rustling clot. Eventually I felt something give way, and the knot slid smoothly out of the grave. I gathered it into a large ball and threw it to the side.

In the hole I had just made I could see nothing except more plastic bags.

I closed my eyes. My neck muscles felt strained and a headache was creeping up the back of my skull. It seemed to pull my scalp into unpleasant knots, like a too-tight ponytail or plait.

It was time to go home after yet another fruitless search.

I opened my eyes. The broken past-machine I had moved out of the way earlier lay next to me. It wasn't big. Its hard plastic shell was broken in several places, as if it had been smashed on purpose, and on one side there was a round glass lens that resembled the bottom of a small blaze lantern. The glass was badly cracked. Part of it had fallen out.

I must have seen the same wreck of a machine dozens of times on my treasure-hunts. I must have held it in my hand and moved it dozens of times. If I had looked at it closely years ago, when Sanja chose to leave it behind and I brought the disc back home with me, I wouldn't have noticed anything worth remembering.

Now sunlight caught on a matte metal plate, no bigger than half of my little finger, engraved and embedded on one side of the machine.

I stared at the engraving, and the world seemed to stop around me.

I read the text again and again.

M. Jansson.

The machine nearly fell apart in my hands when I wrapped it in a rag, pushed it into my bag and climbed up from the hole. Plastic crackled, stirred and murmured under my feet as I walked across the grave as fast as I could manage.

Even if the past-world story recorded on the silver-coloured disc existed in the plastic grave, my chances of finding it had seemed non-existent. Now, for the first time, I dared to think that there might be a real possibility, no matter how minuscule, that I would be able to find a continuation to the story of the disc. The thought grew in my mind like a green and tender branch bursting towards sunlight.

When I got home, I walked straight into my mother's study and took the machine from my bag. I unwrapped the rag around it and placed it on the only corner of the desk which wasn't covered in books and handwritten notes. I rolled the blind down, because the sun had turned its light to this side of the house while I was away. A grey-blue shadow fell into the room.

I sat down on the chair and stared at the piles of books. I stared at the paper on which I had written in as much detail as I could everything I remembered of the recording on the silver-coloured disc. I stared at the past-world machine. It was as mute as a dead insect. The strands of late afternoon burned sharp and defined between the slats of the blind.

The Jansson expedition. The Twilight Century. The Lost Lands. M. Jansson.

I knew I didn't have all the pieces, and that I might never have them. I also knew there was a place where I hadn't looked yet.

140

The house was silent and still, the teahouse empty and quiet, and no one walked outside. If my father's spirit wandered in the rooms or among the trees, it was peaceful, and guarded the landscape it had lived in. The light of the message-pod did not blink. Ants drew their thread-thin paths on the stone slabs of the garden and in the corners of the house, the wood of the walls grew wearier, dust fell on the shelves unnoticed, and there was no one to tell me what to do or ask me what I was doing.

It was dusky in the living room. The lid of the chest lifted easily when I propped it open against the wall, and a faint scent of old paper and ageing ink drifted into the air.

The spines didn't have dates, years or tea masters' names on them, so I had to look for the right book for a while by leafing through the first pages of the leather-covered volumes. Eventually I found the one that had the years I was looking for written on the front page in unfamiliar hand.

I turned the page and began to read.

CHAPTER ELEVEN

I drained the last drops from the teacup and placed it on the floor next to a pile of books. My neck ached. Weightless speckles of dead dust drifted in the shaft of sunlight filtering through the window. I moved the books that I had already searched and the notes I had brought from my mother's study, then settled on my back in the empty space created on the living room floor and closed my eyes. A crease in my shirt caught under my weight pressed against my muscles. My thoughts swirled in a tight tangle, and every time I grasped one thread, attempting to follow it, the rest clenched into a more persistent knot.

I had spent the past two days reading the tea masters' books, and so far I had leafed through seven of them from the Twilight Century. In the latter half of the century four tea masters had lived in the house. The first of them, Leo Kaitio, hadn't cared much about writing. He had only filled one leather-bound book during his lifetime. The entries were brief and their content dry. 'Rain this morning. The tea visit of Second Lieutenant Salo and his wife went as expected. Must remember to have shoes repaired.'

'January even warmer than last year. A crack in the earthenware teapot.' I had needed to check in my mother's old
books to make sure I remembered correctly what January
was: it had been the name of the first month of the year
in the old solar calendar. Despite this complication, I had
skimmed Leo's notes quickly. Near the end of the book
the handwriting changed, and it took me a while to understand the reason. To be certain, I had opened the next
book in order, with the name Miro Kaitio scribbled on
the first page. He was presumably Leo's son. A quick
glance at Miro's handwriting confirmed my suspicions: the
writing on the pages Leo had left blank in his book was
likely to be Miro's.

Miro had not inherited his father's curtness, but had
clearly spent a large chunk of his free time writing. He
had filled six books with tiny handwriting and also scribbled notes on small pieces of loose paper folded between
the pages. Some of his entries were undated. The section
on the final pages of Leo's book was one of those. There
must have already been a shortage of writing supplies at
the time. Miro had probably adopted his father's book
for perusal in some moment of despair when he had run
out of paper.

Miro's entries were completely different from Leo's. He
wrote about his thoughts and dreams, about his feelings
during the tea ceremonies and outside them. He would
write lists of things that made him smile (a cat curling in
one's lap, the first bite of a crisp apple, sun-warmed grass
under one's bare feet) and things that made him irritable
(a chafing shoe, spectacles so old one can no longer see
with them, running out of ink when one most needs it).

I opened my eyes and got up to my feet. I rose too
quickly: the room darkened and I had to lean against the

wall until I stopped feeling dizzy. I went to the kitchen and poured myself another cup of tea, which had grown lukewarm. I came back, sat down on a cushion and picked up the final one of Miro's books, which I had only read halfway through. The pages felt fragile and dry against my fingers, as if they might fall apart, scattering the thin black words across the floor for wind to carry away. This link to the past was brittle and threadbare, like a bridge too weather-worn to cross safely. Yet the words themselves were strong. They drew me in so that I lost track of time and had to remind myself of what I was looking for. I was enchanted by the way this tea master who had lived long before my time described his days, his full moon nights spent awake, grains of sand scattered across the teahouse floor by visitors' shoes, snow that melted immediately into glistening-dark earth and that some winters didn't fall at all. These stories and fragments of a life long faded reaching to me from the yellowed, delicate pages were so luminous, so detailed and colourful that I couldn't take my eyes off them. The bones of this man and the water in his blood had returned to earth and sky long ago, but his words and stories were alive and breathing. It was as if I myself lived and breathed more truly and inevitably while I was reading them.

Shadows changed outside, and I listened to the rustling of paper under my hands.

I didn't close the book until there was barely enough light to see the words. Bridges fell apart and past was once again barely more than a web of indiscernible words behind an opaque screen, and the silence of the house enclosed me. Another day was gone, and I had not found what I was looking for.

Before going to sleep I went out to rake the rock garden.

The faint lines in the sand grew nearly invisible in the late evening. As I was finishing, I happened to glance at the road going to the village, and I thought I could make out two human shapes watching the house at the edge of the woods.

I froze, and my heart was beating in my chest.

The rake slipped from my hands. I squatted to pick it up from the sand, and when I straightened my back, the edge of the woods was empty and still.

The following morning I went to look for traces, but the hardened ground and the thick-scattered rug of pine needles didn't reveal anything. In the dusk, the shadows of trees may look like figures that are watching relentlessly.

A couple of days later I got an unexpected message from my mother. I walked into the house with two skinfuls of water I had queued for in the village and saw the message-pod light flashing. I almost dropped the skins to the floor and rushed to switch the pod on. The display lit up and I read my mother's round, rolling handwriting.

Dear Noria, she wrote, *I'm sorry I haven't been able to write more often. I miss you and hope you will be able to join me here soon. I'm doing everything in my power to make this possible. Meanwhile, could you please send me something of yours? Nothing large, but something you use often, such as a spoon from the teahouse or one of the pens you use to write in your tea master's book. I would just like to have a keepsake to feel closer to you while we can't be together. Don't bother to clean or polish it; I want it just as it is. My pod is running out of power and I cannot charge it until tomorrow in daylight, so I must keep this brief. Love, Lian.*

I sank down to the floor. My relief was enormous. My

mother was alive. I hadn't heard anything from her in over a month. I picked up the pod-pen and wrote, *Are you ok? I miss you.* I sent the note immediately, but there was no reply.

Then I read the message again, because something about it was bothering me.

The more times I read it, the stranger I found my mother's request. I knew she loved me, but she had never much cared for material things. When she had moved to Xinjing, she had left most of her books behind without second thought, and she tended to recycle anything that could be recycled without attaching any sentimental value to it. I had watched her give all my toys away, convert my baby clothes into furniture covers or carpet rags and calmly dispose of a stone collection I had compiled on the windowsill of her study. As far as I knew, she hadn't kept a single childhood drawing of mine, and the shawl I had received for my graduation was the only piece of clothing she had ever given to me that did not have a purely functional value.

It was unexpected that she would suddenly want something of mine as a keepsake. I was also concerned that she hadn't told me at all how things were. It was possible that she hadn't received all my messages. It was also possible I hadn't received hers. The connections were poor because of the war, and the messaging services were probably being monitored. I had tried to keep my messages as neutral and harmless as I could, and I didn't see why they would have been censored, but it was impossible to know all the workings of the military.

Although I didn't understand my mother's request, I placed the message-pod back on the wall rack, went to the kitchen and picked up from the worktop an unwashed spoon I had used that morning. There was a brown stain marking the metal where a few drops of tea had dried on it. I wrapped it in a piece of cloth, searched in a bottom drawer for a seagrass pouch used for sending mail and dropped the spoon inside. I fetched my tea master's book from my room, tore out a page and scribbled a few lines on it: *Dear mother, this is your keepsake until we meet again – Love, N.* I folded the paper and pushed it into the pouch, then closed the mouth and fastened it with a piece of string. I could send it from the village the next day. I only hoped it would find its way to Xinjing.

Days grew longer and warmer rapidly over the next two weeks as the spring reached towards summer. Water flowed across darkness, dissipated from sun-baked stones and ran away. When I wasn't thinking of the books or the expedition or my parents, I was thinking of Sanja. I wanted to talk to her, tell her how I had been searching for my way out of the silence since my father's death, but I never seemed to find the right moment. She had been weary and quiet lately, and I thought there were things she was not telling me. She almost never had time to go scavenging. When I asked why, she would avoid answering.

I was still wading through Miro's entries. I was trying to put his tales in some kind of order, although I knew it would inevitably be imaginary. The task was made more difficult by the fact that during Miro's time there had been two other tea masters in the house. Miro had assumed the title when his father died, but he hadn't had any children of his own, so his apprentice had been his cousin Niko Kaitio. However, Niko had died young, a mere few months after his graduation, so his son Tomio had inherited the apprenticeship and the title. Niko and Tomio didn't have Miro's literary tendencies, and Miro had unhesitatingly hijacked the blank pages in their books for his own writings.

The book I was currently leafing through had been written well before Miro's time. I had earlier marked the final section, which was filled with Miro's writing, but this was the first time I had come back to read it. The entry was dated the final year of the Twilight Century, which I knew by Tomio's journal to also be the year of Miro's death.

I know the time of my last ceremony is almost at hand, and I wish to record this story before my heart stops. I haven't written it down before, because I didn't consider it safe to do so. But now four decades have passed since these events took place, and I don't believe that knowledge of them can any longer harm anyone. A time may come when it is all well that someone other than water remembers and knows, for too many stories are lost, and too few of those that remain are true.

I quickly counted forty years back from the date. It was consistent with the year mentioned on the silver-coloured disc. I crossed my legs on the cushion, placed the book on my lap and read on.

I had only been working as a tea master for a few years, and my father had died the year before, when one evening after dark there was a knock on my door. As I opened it, I found two men and a woman standing on the veranda. They told me their names and said they would be willing to do some work in the garden and house in exchange for food and water. This was nothing out of the ordinary at the time. Many people had lost their homes and possessions in the wars, and for many the only way to find water and shelter was to travel from village to village in search

of work. Yet these people didn't look like ordinary vaga-
bonds. Their clothes seemed fairly new and they had the
restless air of people on the run. One of the men was
wounded. A stained rag was tied around his arm, and the
surrounding skin was badly bruised. Under the edge of
the cloth showed a tattoo: a narrow-bodied Ocean-Dragon
that carried a snowflake in its claws. The way they said
their names – one too quickly, another stammering – made
me suspect the names were made up. But they were clearly
exhausted, as if they had been travelling for days without
sufficient rest, and they carried nothing but a small bag
made of one of those old weatherproof materials. I decided
they didn't look too dangerous and accommodated them
in the teahouse for the night. I didn't keep anything of
value in the teahouse, so I wasn't worried about being
robbed, and I've always been a light sleeper, so I knew I
would hear if they tried to sneak up into the house in the
middle of the night. There was a sturdy lock on the door
that couldn't be opened without quite a noise. I gave them
some bread and tea, blankets and pillows and a lantern,
and showed them the way across the garden. I then came
back to prepare a soothing ointment for the wound, but
when I returned with it to the teahouse, I found them all
fast asleep. I left the jar outside the door.

The next morning while they were still sleeping the
baker's errand boy came to bring me bread and had some
new gossip to share. He told me that soldiers had been
making rounds in the village the night before, knocking
on doors and looking for three war criminals. When my
guests woke up, I invited them in for breakfast and watched
them closely. They were hard to read. Their manner was
good and fairly formal, as if they were highly educated.
This supported the possibility that they might have been

brought up enjoying some privileges of the military. At the same time, some of the remarks they made struck me as strange, even inappropriate for someone from a military background. I found that I could not place them. I needed to know more.

As we were having another cup of tea, I mentioned to them what I had heard earlier in the morning. They fell silent and their faces turned to stone, and I knew it was them the soldiers were after. I asked them to give me a reason why I shouldn't report their location.

The men began to object to this, but the woman silenced them with a single movement of her hand. When her sleeve end moved, I noticed that she had a dragon tattoo on her wrist, similar to the one I'd seen on the wounded man's arm.

She told me they were returning from the Lost Lands, where they had been investigating the drinkability of the water and the recovery of the areas from the catastrophe. This surprised me, because I had thought it was illegal to go to the Lost Lands. When I said this aloud, the woman admitted that their expedition was illegal and secret. I saw in her companions' expressions that they would rather have kept all this to themselves, but the woman took a sip of tea, straightened her back and continued to talk.

The army of New Qian had somehow learned about their expedition and begun to trace them. Their leader had been killed on a water-fetching trip near Kolari, and they had been on the run ever since. A few days earlier one of their companions had gone missing and taken some of the backups of their recordings and the video camera they had used to shoot material. The rest of the backups were with them, and they didn't want the army to get their hands on those. They didn't know if their friend was dead or

150

alive. Their intention was to hide near the village for a few days in the hope that the soldiers would head elsewhere.

The three of them were looking at me. The shorter, brown-haired man was holding a hand to his wound, which seemed to cause him constant pain. Sweat glistened on his face. The tall man's expression didn't give anything away.

The woman asked for me not to report them.

I asked them why they had come to the tea master's house, and why they believed I would help them.

'My father was a tea master,' the woman said then. He had been killed in the water wars when she was very young, but she remembered his stories about tea masters who understood water.

I asked if there really was pure, fresh water in the Lost Lands.

The woman looked at the two men. I saw the taller one take a deep breath and eventually give a silent nod.

'There is,' she said. 'And we want it to belong to everyone, not just the military.'

I thought about her story. I couldn't see why she would lie to me about something like that. Their fate was in my hands. The rewards for catching war criminals were decent, and if I wanted to report them, all I had to do was call the village police right now. There were three of them and only one of me, that was true; but I was in good health, and they were weak. I would be out of the door and out of their reach before they knew it. They seemed to understand this, too.

I told them I would help them.

If their relief was not genuine, it was the best pretence I had ever seen.

I took them to the only place I trusted to be secure. It was important that even they themselves didn't know the way there, so I had to take them one by one, blindfolded and along a circuitous path. This was the condition of my offer of refuge, and after short negotiations, they complied without a complaint. I knew there was a possibility they might be able to combine their knowledge and guesswork about the location into a certainty and track the route again later, but it was a risk I had to take. When they were all safely in the hiding place, I made another trip to the house to fetch food and clean clothes.

They stayed for two weeks. I went to see them every two days, and every time I told them the latest news from the village. They didn't tell me much about themselves, but I learned some things: they were all academics, and they seemed to belong to some larger underground organisation striving to end the water restrictions. After a fortnight they wished to leave, because the place was beginning to get cramped for them, and they were worried (or so they claimed) about putting me in danger by staying too long. As far as I knew, the soldiers had taken their search to other nearby villages, so I believed it was as safe as it was going to be for them to leave. I drew a map for them showing a route out of the village that was the least likely to be guarded and gave them food and water. They wanted to make it to Kuoloyarvi first and then continue to New Piterburg. One by one I walked them from the hiding place to the slope of the fell, where I had left the food parcels. It was just before dawn and early spring, and the sky was already brightening into morning.

They thanked me for my kindness and said they had no way of repaying me. I replied that some things didn't need repayment.

The woman smiled. Her eyes were dark in the morning dusk.

'You do realise none of us will probably see the time when water runs free again?' she said.

'I do, but that's not enough of a reason to give up hope that it might happen one day.'

'To some it would be,' she said.

They left, and I watched their narrow figures, until they vanished into the folds of the fell.

I don't know what happened to them. I never heard of them again. I don't know their real names, or if they saved the knowledge they carried with them. Perhaps the knowledge saved them. I'll never know if they told me the truth or if I did the right thing. But this is my last story, and after I have recorded it on these pages, my water may run dry freely.

I closed the tea master's book and stared at the paper-littered floor. The pieces were moving in my mind, trying to form an understandable image. Could these travellers hunted by soldiers who had visited the tea master's house have belonged to the Jansson expedition? The likelihood seemed extremely small. On the other hand, it might have explained how the silver-coloured disc had ended up in this very village. If they had been afraid of getting caught and wanted to prevent the military from laying hands on their information about the Lost Lands, they could have thrown their recordings into the grave.

I was even more curious about whether Miro had really hidden them in the fell – perhaps even in the spring itself. It would have been unheard of. Everything about my father's words and behaviour had made it clear that only tea masters and their apprentices, once they had learned enough, could go to the spring, and perhaps occasionally family members – I was certain my mother had been there. However, Miro would have violated all traditions and unwritten laws by hiding strangers he had no reason to trust in the cave. But what other place could he have meant? He hadn't mentioned taking water to them, only food. It struck me as odd that he hadn't described the hiding place at all. It was uncharacteristic of his detailed writing style, so it seemed like a deliberate choice.

The message-pod beeped at the entrance. I hoped it would be my mother. I hadn't heard from her since she had asked for the spoon a few weeks ago. My leg muscles were prickling after the long sitting as I walked stiffly to read the message. It was from Sanja.

Could you sell a few skinfuls by instalments? Hurry!! Today if you can, she wrote. A cold weight fell into my stomach. Sanja had never asked for water. I thought of Minja immediately. There was still daylight left for several hours, and I would make it back from the village before the curfew.

I'm on my way, I replied. I left the books spread around the living room floor, filled three large waterskins, carried them to the helicycle cart and started the slow ride towards the village.

CHAPTER TWELVE

The front door was locked. I knocked on it, but there was no sound from inside. I knocked again. Nothing but silence. I took off my coat and cast it on top of the waterskins to cover them from sight. I walked around the house to Sanja's workshop. I tried the door, but it was latched on the inside. I peered through the mesh walls: there was a half-assembled past-machine on the worktop next to a half-eaten seedcake, and the blades of a small solar fan were cutting the heat of the day. Sanja was nowhere to be seen.

I thought of the past-world stories I'd heard about ghost ships whose crew seemed to have evaporated without explanation: of a pen dropped on the table mid-sentence, of steaming laundry in the copper and still-warm tea in its cup when rescue arrived.

'Sanja?' There was no answer. 'Sanja!' I cried out again. 'Kira? Jan?'

There was no sound from Sanja or her parents. Even Minja's voice didn't echo in the house. I turned to go back to the front door, but then I heard a clank from behind me. When I looked in the direction of the sound, I saw

Sanja scrambling up from the workshop floor. Her face was flushed.

'Is everything alright?'

Sanja turned to me and wiped sweat from her brow with the back of her hand.

'You were quick.' She switched off the desk fan, opened the door and stepped out of the workshop.

'I didn't see you,' I said. 'I didn't think there was anyone here.'

'Oh, I was just rummaging under the table,' she said, but avoided my gaze. I was certain there was no place in the room that I could have missed by mistake.

'Is everything alright?' I repeated. Sanja's shoulders fell.

'No,' she said. I saw tears twitching behind her face. 'Minja . . .' Her voice was coarse and cracked. 'She's not alright. Mum took her to the doctor – again – but it was no use last time, either.' She swallowed and raised her eyes. 'The medicines need to be dissolved in water.'

I took a step towards her, then another, and she didn't move away. I hadn't seen her cry since she stumbled in the fell when she was ten and sprained her ankle. She gave one sob against my shoulder and then she was quiet. We stood there for a long time, in the scorching sun-sting of the late afternoon. Eventually Sanja withdrew from me and sniffed.

'Sorry,' she said.

'Don't be silly,' I said and poked her arm. 'I brought water.'

I was relieved that she could still try a smile.

'I'll do repair jobs until the end of the world, if you won't accept another payment,' she said. I opened my mouth to argue, but she interrupted, 'It's only fair. It's not like you have a well in your garden.'

I didn't look at her then; I wasn't sure what she would see on my face.

'I left the skins in the front yard,' I said. 'Let's go, before someone snatches them.'

We collected the skins from the cart and carried them to the door. When Sanja opened it, a thick stench that made me think of dirty hair and sour milk pushed through the gap. There were empty mugs and greasy plates with food remains stuck to them on the living room table and under it. I noticed children's clothes soaking in murky water at the bottom of a washing tub in the corner. Some of them had large dark stains. Piles of dust floated along the floor in the draft when we passed them.

Sanja looked at me and then she looked around, as if realising for the first time in days how the house looked.

'It's a dreadful mess,' she said. 'Minja can't hold any food, and we haven't even been able to wash all her diapers.'

I saw she was embarrassed, because she had asked me in to witness the traces of the illness.

'You can do it now,' I said and tried to smile.

We carried the waterskins into the kitchen. I helped Sanja pour a little clean water in a baby bottle. She rinsed the bottle, filled it again and took from a cupboard a fabric pouch, from which she dosed two spoonfuls of white powder in the water. She shook the bottle a little so the powder would dissolve. Its pale mist floated in the cloudy liquid.

We heard footsteps from the veranda. Sanja went to the door with the baby bottle. Kira stepped inside, holding Minja in her arms. I hadn't seen Minja in a few weeks and my stomach turned. She was thin and fragile, and her usually bright eyes were just two shadows in her bone-sharp face. Kira was pale and her posture was sunken.

'They can't admit more patients,' she said. 'The nearest hospital that has space is in Kuusamo.'

'What do they expect us to do?' Sanja asked.

'They said to give the medical solution to Minja and wait for the fever to go down.'

'But that's what we've been doing for the past two weeks! Did you tell them we haven't got enough water?'

'Sanja,' Kira said. 'The medical centre is full of patients who are even worse off than Minja.' Her voice was weary and crushed. 'They have two doctors and three nurses, and a few volunteers from the village. They owe three months' worth of water debt to the black market. They don't even know if they can continue to run the clinic next month.'

The air between us grew heavy. Sanja and I realised at the same time what Kira must have understood earlier: the doctors had no choice but to send Minja home to die.

Sanja handed the baby bottle with the medical solution to Kira.

'Is it clean enough?' Kira asked.

'Yes,' I said. Both Kira and Sanja looked at me sharply, and a realisation passed across Kira's face.

'You do know we can't pay, don't you?' Kira asked. The words were addressed to Sanja as well as to me.

'You don't need to,' I replied.

Kira sat down in a worn armchair, took the baby bottle and offered it to Minja. Minja barely had the strength to open her mouth, but after a long coaxing Kira got her to lick a few drops of liquid from the bottle. She carried Minja to the bedroom.

'Sanja, would you come here a bit,' she called.

'I'll wait here,' I said to Sanja, who nodded. Kira lowered her voice behind the door, but I could hear her words nevertheless. I believe she wanted me to hear.

'You shouldn't have asked her for water,' she said.

'What else can we do?' Sanja asked defiantly. 'I can't finish the water pipe. It's nearly impossible to find the missing parts now, and the prices are sky-high.'

Kira sighed.

'I know, Sanja. And finding water shouldn't be your responsibility. If Minja was healthier, I might be able to make rounds doing sewing in the nearby villages with her, or try to find work at the army boots factory in Kuusamo. I just wouldn't want to owe a debt of gratitude to anyone.'

I had heard enough. I walked out to the veranda and pushed the door closed carefully. I sat down on the step and looked around me: at the limp sunflower sprouts nodding in the sand, at the sunshade woven of seagrass sheltering a couple of dust-pale, straggly chairs, taut in their wooden frames. The surrounding yards and houses looked the same – drab, tired reflections of each other, exhausted under the weight of the afternoon.

I didn't know how long it had been when Sanja got out of the house and closed the door quietly behind her.

'They're both asleep,' she said. 'It's been a rare sight in this house lately.'

I kept my voice low, but the words left my mouth sharper than I had expected.

'Are you out of your mind?'

Sanja's head twitched towards me. My chest tightened when I saw the recent weeks on her face, but I continued.

'Do you realise how dangerous it is for you to be building an illegal water pipe? If the water patrol finds it—' I thought of the empty workshop, the clank, her sudden appearance. 'It's under your workshop, isn't it? Your construction site.'

Sanja's features were hazy with exhaustion, but annoyance, or perhaps despair, focused them for a moment.

'The water rations are not enough for us, and we can't afford to buy more,' she said. 'Dad has managed to make an arrangement and get part of his salary in water, but sometimes it looks and smells like dirty underwear has been soaked in it.'

I frowned.

'Couldn't you complain to someone?' I asked.

Sanja snorted.

'Who? The same officials that give it to us illegally?'

I saw what she meant.

'Stop,' I said. She stared at me in disbelief. 'Don't go anywhere near the water pipe again.'

'You've clearly never had to choose,' she said, 'if you'd rather be thrown into jail for a water crime, or let your family die of thirst.'

I fell speechless for a moment, because she had rarely said anything this harsh to me. The hardness of her words seemed to have taken her by surprise, too. She took my hand and squeezed it.

'I'm sorry, Noria,' she said, 'I didn't mean . . .'

'How much do you need?'

'Noria—'

'How much?'

She looked directly at me. Her eyes were dark and bright.

'Much more than you can afford. Two skinfuls a day,' she said.

'I'll bring it to you.'

She shook her head.

'You need your own water. You can't.'

'Yes, I can,' I said.

It seemed to me that she was going to ask something. I was grateful when she didn't. I didn't need to lie.

Something had changed between Sanja and me, something for which I had no words back then and perhaps have none even now. She hadn't spoken to me about the water pipe or Minja's illness. I hadn't spoken to her about the spring.

Secrets carve us like water carves stone. On the surface nothing will shift, but things we cannot tell anyone chafe and consume us, and slowly our life settles around them, moulds itself into their shape.

Secrets gnaw at the bonds between people. Sometimes we believe they can also build them: if we let another person into the silent space a secret has made within us, we are no longer alone there.

I began to bring water to Sanja regularly. She accepted it without a word. Mist was dispelled from Minja's eyes, her gaze was able to grasp things going on around her again. Words returned to her tongue. Her limbs were still thin as faded, winter-bare twigs, but her life was no longer in danger. Kira's behaviour towards me was a mixture of gratitude and awkward, curt avoidance. Jan never mentioned the water at all when I saw him, which was rarely enough, but he asked me a few times if there was need in the tea master's house or garden for repair or construction jobs that he could do. I always said no.

Meanwhile, I had reached a dead end in my search for more information about the Jansson expedition. Inspired by Miro's last diary entry, I had leafed through all the rest of the tea masters' books, but only found occasional, short notes, none of which told me anything I didn't already know. The plastic grave guarded its secrets, if it had any.

My visits produced no results save for a wound I got from a sharp piece of metal and a handful of components I put in my pocket for Sanja. Silence raised its wall against me everywhere. The light on the message-pod remained dark. Soft grass pushed mute stalks from the soil of the garden, and my father's dust rested soundlessly in the shroud of the earth.

Then, one late spring morning, the silence was broken.

The day was like any other day leading to summer. The overcast sky arched in the colour of polished metal, and the tender flames of light-green leaves flickered on the branches of the sparse trees and bushes. The streets were quiet. I passed a house in front of which an aged couple was sitting under a seagrass sunshade. I saw tears streaming down the woman's wrinkled cheeks. The man had put his arm around her shoulders. I turned my gaze away.

When I reached Sanja's house with my waterskins, she was waiting for me at the door.

'Have you heard?' she asked. I saw her expression and my heart clenched.

'What happened? Is everything alright?'

'Yes. I mean, no.' She paused and agitation crossed her face. 'The grey-plastered house with the blue circle on the door. Near the medical centre?'

I remembered the blank windows and drawn curtains, the empty path across the front yard, the neighbours who averted their gaze on the street.

'The residents had not been taken away, as everyone thought,' Sanja said. 'They were held inside for nearly two months under house arrest, guarded night and day. They couldn't go anywhere, but the soldiers were bringing just enough water and food for them to stay alive. This morning

162

they were forced out and . . .' She tried to fit the word in her mouth. 'They were executed.'

'Are you sure?' The bright blue circle surfaced before my eyes, glaring as a bruise against the chipped paint of the house, the colour of the sky reflected in water, the colour of military uniforms. I found it hard to believe, despite everything that had happened after last Moonfeast.

'My father saw it,' Sanja said. 'He was on his way to the central square. He saw the soldiers drag the people out of the house and cut their throats in the middle of the front yard. Everyone passing on the street saw it.'

I tried not to imagine the scene, but my mind leapt ahead of me: the glistening metal pressing into the fragile skin and reflecting the colour of the earth, the movement of a blue-clad arm, the pool of blood spreading on the pale sand of the yard and the sunlight shattering in it.

'Is this what it's going to be from now on?' Sanja asked in a tight, strangled voice. 'Anyone can be executed in their own front yard or captured inside their own home any time?'

'It will end,' I said. 'It must.'

'And if it doesn't?' Sanja stared at me and I couldn't remember ever seeing such bare despair on her face. 'People won't stop needing water. They'll have to risk their lives building illegal water pipes. I—'

I realized what she was trying to tell me.

'You haven't continued building your water pipe, have you?' I asked. She turned her face towards the ground, and her dark hair fell to cover it.

'We can't depend on your water forever, Noria,' she said. 'You'll need it yourself.'

I thought of the past tea masters, their choices and their duties. I thought of Miro, who had done what he believed

163

to be right, against all tradition. I thought of my parents, who were not here, and of Sanja, who was.

'Come,' I said. 'I want to show you something.'

We walked into the fell as we had walked many times as children, playing wise and fearless explorers in a strange and wild landscape. Grave clouds were building a darkening wall on the horizon, gradually enclosing the sky. My feet knew the paths and did not slip on the stones. Behind the landscape there loomed another, bound in memory: its paths were wider and the fell-tops tall as distant mountains, boulders larger and harder to climb, dry riverbeds deep wounds in the sides of the rock. Compared to this image emerging from across the years, everything looked meagre and tame now; and yet I felt as if I was walking step by step further into a steep, dark, drowning landscape, even more overwhelming than the fell had been in my child-eyes. I could almost hear the stones of the path shaking behind me, its outlines crumbling into the sand. If I turned to look, I would only see desert and far in the horizon the sharp, dark-green tips of the forest, but the house and the village would be gone, all roads buried, and we'd have no choice but to continue towards the blind spot we were approaching.

Sanja didn't ask where we were going, but followed me in silence.

When we reached the mouth of the cave, she said, 'I remember this one! The headquarters of the Central And Crucially Important Explorers' Society of New Qian.'

'Follow me,' I told her. I crawled to the back of the cave and sought in the folds of the rock the lever which my fingers found easily by now. The stone felt dry, coarse and cool. The hatch in the ceiling of the cave opened. The restless light of the blaze lanterns was reflected in Sanja's eyes in the dusk, as if her thoughts were glowing and flittering.

'What is this place?' she asked.

'The place that doesn't exist,' I said.

The familiar coolness of the fell poured slowly over us, as we walked deeper into its heart. I heard Sanja's footsteps behind me, and the strange enchantment that had begun outside didn't let go. The faint echo of the spring bounced off the walls in whispers, and I couldn't get rid of the feeling that if I turned around, Sanja would disappear into the folds of the cavern, become a shadow among underground shadows. Our movements haunted the walls, thin as cobwebs. I didn't stop until we reached the cave in which the water rushed from the rock into its pond.

I heard Sanja gasp behind me. She stepped next to me and grasped my arm. I felt the shaking of her hand and the narrow moon-slivers of her fingernails on my skin.

'This,' she said. 'All this water. Is it yours?'

'Yes,' I said. The grip of her fingers tightened. 'No,' I corrected.

Sanja turned towards me, and a start ran through me. She was furious.

'How could you?' she spat out. 'How could you hide this? The people in that house—' Her voice was shaking. 'Minja. She could have . . .'

Shame flooded my face. I couldn't look her in the eye.

'How could you?' she repeated.

Fear coiled into a heavy knot inside me. I didn't know what I had expected – gratitude? Relief? Perhaps excitement, because I had given Sanja a part in my secret? I had known I'd be putting myself in danger by bringing another person to the spring, but I had never thought the danger might come from her direction. Now I was no longer certain.

'You must promise you won't tell anyone,' I said more hastily than I had intended. 'I can only help you if the spring remains a secret.'

'You don't have the right,' she said. I still couldn't bring myself to look at her.

'Sanja,' I said, and I could barely hear my own voice. 'What do you think will happen if anyone finds out about this?' She was still holding on to my arm. I raised my gaze.

Shadows thickened on her face and her body was tense. Then something moved behind her eyes. Her shoulders relaxed, her expression softened, and her voice was quiet again.

'It's still not right,' she said.

'I know,' I replied.

It was cool in the cave, as always, and the humidity crept into my bones, but Sanja's face was flushed from walking. Her tolerance of cold had always been better than mine.

'What are you doing?' I asked. She had begun to take off her clothes. She dropped her cardigan on the stones, pulled the shirt over her head and undid her shoelaces.

'Do you know how long it's been since I last bathed in clean water?' she asked. She shrugged off her remaining clothes and stepped carefully to the edge of the pond. She found a place where the rock was worn even and sloped into the water. I saw her shudder, when she pushed her feet into the spring, but she edged herself into the water without stopping, until it was up to her waist. She waded deeper and squatted.

The water enveloped her like a smooth stone thrown into it. She surfaced, shivering, black hair against her skull, and in the wavering lantern-light she was so pale and narrow that she seemed almost translucent: a water spirit caught on the edges of reality.

'Is it cold?' I asked.

'Come and try for yourself,' she said.

Secrets carve us like water carves stone.

If we let another person into the silent space a secret has made within us, we are no longer alone there.

I took off my clothes and stepped into the spring. I hardened myself against the piercing chill of the water, letting it settle on my skin, even as it cut into my limbs and pinched along my back. The pebbles at the bottom of the cave were polished round and slippery, and I couldn't see through the water where I was stepping in the semi-darkness. My foot slid, and Sanja reached out her hand to support me.

I took it. I closed my eyes.

Time trickled on somewhere far outside the cave, wind swept over rocks and light changed slowly, and we were silent and still.

On the surface nothing will shift, but slowly our life settles around the things we cannot tell anyone, moulds itself into their shape.

Eventually Sanja let go of me and stepped back. She took one step, then another. Her eyebrows knitted into a confused crease. She lowered her gaze, trying to see into the spring through the water in the twilight. She swept the bottom with her foot. I stepped closer and felt something smooth and even under the sole of my foot, like a plate made of some hard, shiny material.

'Noria,' Sanja said. 'What's this?'

The box was of polished wood, and there was a thin layer of dark, slippery algae on the surface. It was as thick as maybe two or three tea master's books placed on top of each other, but more oblong. Two wide leather belts were tightened around it, holding it closed. There was no lock on the box. We turned it in the light of the blaze lanterns. I began to unbuckle one of the belts.

'Are you sure it's safe to open this?' Sanja asked.

'No,' I admitted. 'But don't you want to know what's inside?'

Sanja nodded and began unbuckling the other belt.

Inside the box there was another, metal one, tightly sealed, but that one wasn't locked, either. Water had seeped through the outer layer, but there was no humidity inside the metal box. It held a thick, plastic wrapping through which we could see a knot of fabric. I peeled the plastic away and unfolded the cloth, which turned out to be a faded-brown shirt. We stared at the contents of the knot, speechless.

In the folds of the fabric rested six smooth, shiny, silver-coloured discs.

That night it rained, rained until the dust of the earth foamed mud-dark, and narrow brooks ran across stones and yards and withered tree-trunks. People opened their mouths and drank directly from the sky and thanked nameless powers. Water rattled into buckets and tubs and onto roofs, and its sounds enclosed the landscape within their soft fingers, stroking the soil and grass and tree roots.

I sat with Sanja on the veranda of the tea master's house, watching the languid glow of the blaze lanterns on the walls and floorboards. I felt the warmth of her skin next to me.

Seven silver-coloured discs glistened on the wooden table.

Night came quietly, and nothing needed to be otherwise.

CHAPTER THIRTEEN

'Could you play that last bit again?' I asked.

Sanja pressed the button with two arrowheads pointing to the left on the past-tech machine. My wrist was aching from writing. I shook my hand while reversed words chirruped in the loudspeakers. Sanja took her finger from the button, and a voice said, '—until we have confirmed all results. It is nevertheless clear that at least Saltfjellet-Svartisen, Reivo and most of the land between Malmberget and Kolari belong to the areas where the water resources are partly potable already, and according to our estimates, will be entirely so in less than fifty years.'

'Stop there,' I said. Sanja paused the disc, and I wrote the last sentence down in my notebook.

We had arranged everything in a neat circle on the workshop floor: the past-machine, the discs, the books I had brought from my mother's study. I reached for the heavy volume which included a map of the Lost Lands from the past-world era and traced the place names with my finger. Reivo was the first one to catch my eye. I drew a circle around it, and when I leaned back, the muscles in my neck and back tightened to painful knots.

'I think I need a break,' I said. We'd been sitting for hours.

Sanja shrugged.

'You're the one who wanted to write everything down. I'll go get some tea.'

While she stood up, I continued to look for the places mentioned on the recording and marking them on the map.

'I still don't understand what you're going to do with the info, though,' she remarked on her way out.

'Neither do I,' I said, but that wasn't entirely true.

The silver-coloured discs were laid in a row on top of the fabric they had been wrapped in. Numbers from one to seven were painted on them. We had been able to determine their order by the dates mentioned at the beginning of each. So far we had listened to four of the discs in full, and I had written the contents of each one down so I could try to organise them into a coherent story. However, there was a problem: occasionally the words were hard to discern, time had worn the sound threadbare in places and some sections were so badly scratched that the machine skipped them every time. On top of this long parts were missing, days and whole weeks between the log entries. I suspected there had originally been ten discs, perhaps more.

I was now certain that all the discs had come from the same place. There were two distinct male voices on them, and one was clearly the same we had heard on the first disc. I was also convinced that the mysterious group of explorers Miro had kept safe in the Twilight Century was what had remained of the Jansson expedition, and that he had hidden them in the cave in the fell. I couldn't think of another explanation for how the discs would have ended up in the spring. I still hoped to be able to trace the route of the explorers, but listening with the notebook and map was agonisingly slow, and I knew already the story could never become complete and whole. There was too much time between our reality and the Jansson expedition, too many details blurred by years and images swept into the dust of the world that no longer was. We could only summon an indistinct shape whose features and outlines the distance dimmed down.

Yet despite the passage of time and decay there was something in all of this that made me burn and flicker, as if my skin was suddenly too strained and the confines of my life too close, whichever way I turned. The Jansson expedition had really existed. They had lived and breathed, they had packed their fast past-vehicle full of food and water and scientific instruments, and somehow they had carried it all and themselves across the guarded border to the Lost Lands. They had climbed stony paths that no one else had walked in decades, and looked from the slopes of the fjords down to the drowned, water-weary villages. They had dipped their fingers in the brooks running from the cliffs and in the dark, ice-still lakes, and when their equipment had shown the water to be drinkable, every step on their way had acquired a purpose.

In my dreams I was with them, in this strange landscape, where the voice of water was ever-present. Yet I couldn't see their faces or talk to them. They were in the background, out of reach, almost as if I was nothing but a bodiless spirit myself, held by a dark stream, unable to cross to the land of the living. Sanja was always next to me, and everything around us was lucid: the white fell-tips, the crisp air, the clear water mirroring the sky, bright and incomprehensible as another world, flaring with light.

The distance from dreams to words is long, and so is the way from words to deeds. Yet the more I listened, the shorter it grew.

The door slammed. Sanja walked into the workshop and placed a lukewarm cup of tea in my hand. A drop she had spilled travelled down the side of the cup and over my fingers.

'I don't think I can do more today,' I told her. 'Will you walk me home?'

This meant, of course, 'Are you coming to get water?' But we never said this aloud. It wasn't planned. Talking about water had not turned awkward only between the two of us, but everywhere in the village. It was too easy to make the mistake of sounding like one was either boasting of one's own water situation or begging for water from others.

'I can't today,' Sanja replied. 'Mum's got work for this week in the army kitchen, I need to stay home with Minja. I'll come tomorrow.'

'Can't do tomorrow. I have tea visitors coming.'

Sanja looked disappointed, but I knew it would be impossible for me to make time for her. The vice mayor of Kuoloyarvi was a demanding customer, and tea visits always filled the day from the crack of dawn until late evening. I couldn't afford to lose more guests. Many of my father's regulars had stopped coming after his death despite their condolences and assurances that of course they would keep visiting now that I was the tea master in the house. In my father's time new clients had usually found their way to his ceremonies via Major Bolin's recommendation, but Bolin seemed to have been right when he

172

had told me his time as our benefactor was over. I hadn't heard a word from him since my father's funeral.

'Can you come the day after?' I asked, and Sanja nodded. I pulled the insect hood over my head, took my notebook and my bag and stepped through the mesh door into the dust-dry afternoon.

As I passed through the gate of Sanja's house, I saw a soldier approaching from the outskirts of the village. I averted my gaze. Everyone in the village had learned to do so. However, when we passed each other on the road, he greeted me. I looked at him in surprise. It took me a while to recognise him: he was the same blond-haired soldier I had seen talking to Sanja last summer, when Taro had come with his people to search for water on our grounds.

I turned to the road winding out of the village. I saw from the corner of my eye that the soldier had stopped at Sanja's gate.

The tea ceremony wasn't the first one I had performed alone after my father's death. I had learned to seek comfort in his invisible presence: memories of him were so solidly connected to the teahouse that it felt as if he was still seated there, watching my movements, ready to guide me without strictness. Yet this time my mind reflected him as a dark and serious figure, as if he knew. I replied obediently to the vice mayor's questions about the picture hanging on the wall, I offered the tea sweets prepared according to particular instructions and I brewed the tea until it was strong, just as he wished. Still, the whole time I couldn't descend to the peace that focus demanded.

A broken promise is not light to bear. It's hard to please the dead, and sometimes harder not to do so.

The tea visit left me feeling drained. When I eventually

locked the teahouse door late at night and walked into
the house in the light of the blaze lantern, my limbs felt
heavy and fragile as glass, and I was too weary to prepare
supper. In the thin night-light of the early summer I fell
into my bed and slept.

Knocking at the door woke me up.

'Noria?' I heard Sanja's voice from the veranda. 'Are
you home?'

'Just a minute,' I called and scrambled to my feet.

I looked out of the window. The sun was shining brightly
into the garden. I slipped my feet into my sandals and
walked a little shakily to open the front door. Sanja was
standing on the veranda, holding four empty waterskins
bound together in her hand.

'I sent you a message earlier,' she said. 'I thought maybe
you forgot to reply, but I came as we agreed.'

I had completely forgotten that she was coming. I
glanced at the message-pod on the wall. Indeed, the red
light was flashing. I swept hair back from my face.

'I didn't hear anything,' I said. 'What time is it?'

'Not that late,' Sanja said. 'Nine at most. I'm a bit early
anyway.'

I opened the door wider and stepped aside. Sanja came
in with her waterskins and removed her insect hood. I
only noticed now that she was holding a mail pouch woven
of seagrass, which she handed to me.

'I ran into the mailman in the village. When he heard
I was on my way here, he gave this for me to carry. Said
it would spare him the walk.'

I took the mail pouch. Because I was certain it was
from my mother, I opened it right away. Inside was a
message-pod, slightly battered, but still in relatively good
condition, and no letter of any kind.

174

'Strange,' I said, and Sanja's expression revealed that she agreed. 'Are you sure it is for me?'

'That's what the mailman said.'

I tried to switch the message-pod on, but the screen remained dark.

'The battery must be empty,' Sanja said.

I felt like a rustling, hollow shell, and realised I had not eaten since yesterday morning.

'Would you like tea?'

Sanja nodded and followed me to the kitchen. I placed the message-pod on the windowsill, where it was in direct sunlight. It wouldn't take long to charge. When the water was hot and the tea was steaming in the cups on the table, I put my finger on the message-pod screen. The display flashed. Sanja had been right. The screen switched on and the recogniser was reading my fingerprint. There was nothing unusual about this: all message-pods had been coded to recognise the user's account or family account by the fingerprint, and in theory every registered citizen could use their account on any message-pod available. Yet the name that appeared on the display was not mine. *Aino Vanamo*, the message-pod announced. The birth year was the same as mine, but the date was not. The place of birth was recorded as Xinjing.

'What is it?' Sanja asked and got up from her seat to look at the message-pod. Her eyebrows rose when she saw the screen.

'You try,' I prompted. Sanja placed her finger on the screen. *Sanja Valama*, the display told me. I put my finger on the display again, and the identification for Aino Vanamo reappeared.

'Brilliant,' Sanja gasped. 'A fake passpod!' I knew her expression: it meant she was already wondering about how the message-pod had been hacked, and if she could do the same. 'It's been programmed to connect the fake identity to your ID data record,' she continued. 'But in anyone else's hands it's a completely ordinary message-pod.'

A red light and number 1 were flashing in the corner of the display to show that there was one message. I tapped the light with my fingertip.

If this finds you, began the message, *it's important you do as I tell you. It is not safe for you to stay where you are. Contact Bolin. He will help you to get a train ticket. Once you know when you are coming, send me the information using this message-pod. Don't use the other one, but leave it behind when you leave home. I hope to see you soon.*

There was no signature, but I knew the handwriting: it belonged to my mother.

Sanja and I were quiet for a long while. Eventually she asked, 'Are you going?'

'I don't know,' I replied. I understood now why my mother had asked me to send some object. She had needed my fingerprint for the fake passpod, but couldn't ask for it directly out of fear that our mail was being monitored. She must have had to bribe someone in order to make sure that I received it. I had sent the spoon over a month ago, so the passpod had probably been on its way for several weeks.

I should have been excited about my mother's offer. If she was asking me to come, it meant that Xinjing was relatively safe despite the war. My life would be easier without the constant hiding and guarding of the spring, without seeing the narrowing faces in the village, without the fear of seeing which house would be the next to bear a blue circle on its door. I wouldn't need to carry water from the fell or take it to Sanja, nor clean the house and tend to the garden and make the tea sweets alone. We could do things together again, as we had before her departure and my father's death. The same weariness that had wrapped me the night before and was still clinging to my bones crashed into me so gravely that I suddenly wanted to lie down on the kitchen floor and just let things happen around me. I wished for someone else to take responsibility for my life, for everything that had only recently become part of my everyday routine. Xinjing shone distant, veiled in soft mist, easy and welcoming as a dream.

Yet the same thing I wanted to escape demanded that I stay. Who would look after the spring, if I left? Who would Sanja go to, when she needed water for her family? Would the punishment not be placed on her if I left the spring in her care, the military found out about it somehow and I was elsewhere, at the other end of the continent? I could not put her in such danger.

Behind all this loomed a possibility that had only begun to materialise into a clear path from scattered shards: the water that was not here, but in the Lost Lands. I could follow my mother's wishes and travel to Xinjing, or my father's and stay here to guard the spring. Or I could do as I wanted, and choose an unfamiliar path that was not dictated by either one of them.

That day all possibilities looked equal, but even then one of them had already begun to reach beyond the others, to bend me towards itself.

We drank tea and ate amaranth bread, which we dipped in sunflower oil. I saw Sanja trying not to devour the food.

'I've always wondered if it would be possible to crack

the ID protection somehow,' she said. 'I have an idea about it. I might be able to do the same.'

I knew she would have loved to take the fake passpod to her workshop to study it, but didn't want to ask directly and I was not ready to offer it to her. I would need the pod if I decided to travel to Xinjing, and I was worried she might remove the fake information by mistake.

When we had finished our tea and bread, Sanja took her waterskins to the kitchen tap and filled them. I would need to go to the spring next week to close the spare water pipe leading to the house. We carried the skins together into her cart. We had begun to keep a large seagrass trunk in the cart in which we would lay the waterskins flat. On top of the skins we placed the fake bottom Sanja had built, and when it was in place, we loaded the trunk with old clothes and empty, broken waterskins. If the water guards stopped Sanja to check the trunk – which happened occasionally – they would only find repair and sewing jobs, which I had commissioned with Sanja and her mother.

I watched as the wheels of Sanja's cart left tracks in the dirt of the road when she walked away. A threadbare shirt sleeve flickered from under the closed lid of the trunk like a white, wind-torn flame.

Sanja had begun to come with me whenever I walked to the spring to check the surface level of the water. The weather was turning hot, and many times the fell was the only place where it was cool. Those days we went to the cave only to escape the heat of the day. Previously I had walked to the spring, glanced at the surface of the water and turned back. Now our shared trips to the fell became frequent. We would sit by the dry riverbed, eating food we had brought or watching clouds passing in the sky. Sometimes I would read a book while she was drawing in a notepad I had given her. The core of these visits, however, was always the spring, and although we never spoke of it, I believe she felt the way I did: that the threat of the spring drying and being lost to us did not seem real, and when we walked into the cave and to the edge of the water, it was every time like entering another world. The boundless luxury of water belonged to us alone, and I didn't want it to be otherwise.

Time is not to be trusted. A few weeks can seem like the beginning of forever, and it's easy to be blinded when you believe nothing needs to change.

That day we had spent perhaps an hour, perhaps two at the spring; we had no reason to keep track of time. The sun was hot and the insects fierce, and the shadows of the cave rested soothingly against our skins burnt by the early summer. My garden was waiting to be weeded at home, and Sanja had a table full of repair jobs in her workshop, but we were loitering. Sanja was in a good mood and was designing an installation of loose stones in the faint light of the blaze lanterns we had brought.

'What are those?' I asked. She had fashioned an angular pile of stones and placed a circle of small stone figures with painted, angry faces around it.

'That's a house,' Sanja said and pointed at the stone construct at the centre of the circle. 'Those are water guards.' She pointed at the stone figures surrounding the house. 'And those two are us.'

A little further away outside the stone circle there were two more figures. She had moulded a piece of plastic to represent a bucket wedged between them. Both were smiling widely.

'Don't the guards notice?' I asked.

'They're looking the wrong way,' Sanja said. 'I need a piece of your hair,' she announced and began measuring it from a strand that had run loose from my ponytail.

'What for?' I asked and pushed her hand away.

'So I can finish you,' she said.

'No, I'd rather be bald,' I laughed, but she chased me around the cave, and eventually I let her cut a piece of the ends of my hair with her penknife. She placed the hair on top of one stone figure and a small, flat pebble to keep it in place. Then she cut a piece of her own hair and secured it the same way to the head of the other figure sneaking out of the sight of the guards.

'The resemblance is unmistakable,' she said.

We were still in high spirits when we started our walk back along the tunnel. We were certainly not quiet, and our footfalls and laughter echoed, multiplied by the walls. When we reached the hatch, Sanja turned the lever on the wall without warning, and a cold shower gushed from the water pipe on the ceiling to my neck. I screamed and slapped her face with my wet ponytail.

'Come on, when we get out you'll just be happy your clothes are cool and wet,' she said with an innocent face.

'Then I'm sure it's not something you'd want to miss,' I said and pulled her under the spraying water. She spluttered, wriggled herself free from my hold and closed the pipe from the lever. I was still wringing water from my tunic, trousers and hair, when she opened the hatch from the other lever and slipped through it into the cave.

'I'll be there in a second,' I called out to Sanja. She was quiet, and I didn't see her on the other side. I thought I heard a faint crashing noise. 'Sanja?'

I filled the small skin I had brought with me and lowered it into the cave. Then I slid through the hole carrying two blaze lanterns and my soaked insect hood. When I raised my eyes, my voice fled.

Sanja was standing near the mouth of the cave with her back turned towards me, holding one blaze lantern. The other one was lying in shards on the rock floor next to her insect hood. At the cave entrance stood a man's figure, outlines sabre-sharp against the jagged light of the day. In the pale-grown glow of the lanterns I discerned his features.

'This is something we don't see every day in this village,' Jukara said. 'Two young women appearing from the folds of the fell dripping wet.'

Sanja turned her face towards me then, and in my mind I have tried to read her expression thousands of times, to understand its every detail. The memory slips and slides and shatters, but of two things I was sure then, and am still now: Sanja was as surprised as I was, and yet under her surprise another feeling was surfacing.

She looked guilty.

We didn't have any kind of cover story to offer to Jukara, of course. The mistake seemed ridiculously childish and careless afterwards, but it had been made, and neither of us knew how to correct it. We had been so certain of the security of the hidden cave that we had never stopped to think how we would explain our presence in the fell, if someone found us there. I guess we could have said we were just having a picnic, if the situation had been different. But Jukara had seen the hatch, and the gushing water, and our dripping clothes. We had no way of convincing him that there was no water nearby.

He didn't ask, or threaten, or blackmail. He didn't need

to. It was obvious that if I didn't offer water to him and his family, the cave would be teeming with soldiers the next time I went there – if there would be a next time.

'It's my fault,' Sanja said later that evening, when Jukara had left the tea master's house with five full waterskins. 'I'm so sorry. I didn't know this would happen.'

'What are you talking about?' I asked.

'I had to go to see Jukara last week,' she said. 'I ran out of patching plastic, and I didn't know of anyone else in the village who might have some to sell. He charged a high price and behaved oddly. Asked stuff about you.' She looked at me.

'What did he say?' I asked, now wary.

'Complained that you never take repair jobs to him anymore, even though your father was his best customer.'

It was true. Even before my father's illness I had usually taken repair jobs to Sanja in secret, and after his death I hadn't had anything repaired by Jukara.

'He also said things about your father,' Sanja continued. 'He said he'd always wondered how your father had so many waterskins to repair, even though he wasn't supposed to have more water than anyone else in the village. He . . .' A flush rose to Sanja's cheeks and she went quiet.

I waited.

She continued, 'He asked me if I thought your family had a secret well or some other water source.' Sanja raised her hands to cover her eyes. 'Noria, I didn't mean to give anything away! I was just so surprised I dropped the box of plastic patches he had sold me, and they scattered all over his workshop floor. I didn't say anything, and neither did he. But he must have suspected something before, and when he saw me startled, he must have decided to follow us into the fell . . .' Sanja's voice faded.

I didn't know what to say to her, so I said, 'It wasn't your fault. If he suspected something, I'm sure he would have followed us anyway.'

Later, when Sanja had left, I unfolded my maps and opened the notebook in which I had written the contents of the discs. I looked for roads that had been in use in the Twilight Century, and others that might still be good enough for travelling. I began to connect place names I had heard on the discs, and draw a route towards them from my home village.

CHAPTER FOURTEEN

Once the silent space around a secret is shattered, it cannot be made whole again. The cracks will grow longer and wider, reaching far and branching out like an underground network of roots, until it's impossible to say where it started and if it will come to an end.

I still don't know for certain how the word spread in the village. I don't believe Jukara meant for it to happen. Access to the spring was too great a privilege and gave him too much power. He wouldn't have given it up voluntarily. I understand this now, because somewhere beyond words and light, in a place I could not see myself, I had felt the same: the spring was my privilege, a compensation for a duty that would have otherwise gone unrewarded. I had not yet realised that one cannot expect rewards for all actions.

Perhaps Jukara told Ninia. He must have, because he couldn't have come up with endless stories about officials who had suddenly turned more open-handed and explanations for his visits to the tea master's house, not with a wife like Ninia. And telling her was the equivalent of summoning a village meeting and announcing the news there. Whispers welled and grew into chatter, until even those who had not been present heard it.

In the end it doesn't matter how the rest of them found out about the spring. It did not change the outcome. When a woman with greasy hair and unwashed clothes appeared at the gate with three sharp-boned children and asked in a frail voice if I could sell her some water on credit, I could not turn her away. After her came others, a wide-eyed young boy who said his parents were too ill to work, an old man who kept muttering about his son who had disappeared in the war, and more women – young women with babies, old women with dry wombs and a strained walk and weary eyes, middle-aged women asking for water for their parents or spouses or children.

I coiled a leather strap around Mai Harmaja's arm to keep the waterskin in place.

'Is it too tight?' I asked.

'No, you can tighten it up a bit more,' Mai said. I pulled the strap tighter. 'Feels steadier now,' she decided. The waterskin was already fastened to her upper arm by the pit, and it seemed to me that her skin was turning purple around the leather band. Mai rolled her sleeves down and wrapped a thin sun-shawl over her shoulders, and nothing showed that there were five skins under her loose garments: two tied to her thighs, two to her upper arms and one to her waist. Water sloshed slightly, when her feet fell over the creaking boards of the veranda. Mai was one of the volunteers at the village medical centre, and my third water guest of the day.

'Someone's coming!' Mai's son Vesa called from near the gate. His footsteps sent small dust clouds flying, stains in the brightness of the day, as he came running towards the house. He was nine years old and feeling important, because we had given him the task of watching the road leading from the village to the tea master's house and letting us know immediately if he saw someone on it. 'They have a helicarriage.'

'Go into the teahouse,' I told Mai. 'Wait for me there.' She nodded. 'You too, Vesa.' Mai started walking towards the teahouse along the stone slabs of the path, and Vesa rushed after his mother in a galloping half-run.

I had to act fast. I ran into my room and changed into my ceremony outfit, which I always kept clean and ironed. On my way out I glanced at the veranda to make sure I had not left full waterskins there before turning towards the gate. I stopped on the small hillock next to the windchime hanging from a pine tree and looked out to the road. In the approaching helicarriage I saw a driver and two men in blue uniforms, whose features I could not discern. I knew I had arranged a tea visit for Thursday, but it was only Wednesday. Could I have mixed the days up? I tried to keep the teahouse clean, so I could carry out a tea ceremony with short notice if needed, but I hated visits for which I had no time to prepare. And now I had to get Mai and Vesa out of the teahouse with their waterskins without making the situation look strange.

Fortunately, the water pipe running to the house from the fell was closed. I only dared to keep it open one day a week, because if a water patrol had inspected the grounds, I wouldn't have been able to explain why the water pipes were still working in the tea master's house, unlike elsewhere in the village. Therefore I would store as much water as I could when I kept the pipe open, and usually filled the villagers' skins from those reserves. Now I was grateful for my caution.

The helicarriage flitted between the trees as it made its way through and stopped under the seagrass roof by the gate. When the guests stepped down from the back seat, I saw their faces and started. One of them was a stranger to me, but the other one was the same blond-haired soldier I had seen outside the gate of Sanja's house only a few weeks earlier.

'Welcome to the tea master's house,' I said and bowed. 'May I inquire the reason for your unexpected visit?'

The blond-haired soldier bowed back to me.

'I don't believe we have been introduced,' he said. 'I am Lieutenant Muromäki and I work under Commander Taro. This here is Captain Liuhala.' His companion nodded towards me. 'I come here by Major Bolin's recommendation. I believe you are expecting us to a tea ceremony today.'

My lungs tightened and my breathing caught in my throat. The ceremony had been arranged in writing, as was customary, and as I had not been familiar with Muromäki's name, I hadn't made the connection with the face I now saw before me. I hoped my voice sounded steady as I replied, 'I was expecting you tomorrow, Lieutenant Muromäki. The letter I received mentioned tomorrow's date, and I confirmed the date in my reply to you.'

Muromäki tilted his head. He looked like a narrow-faced dog catching the scent of a prey animal in the wind.

'That is strange, Miss Kaitio,' he said. 'I am certain I dictated this date to the scribe. Tomorrow is not at all possible.'

'I have tea guests at the moment,' I said. 'But they were ready to leave. If you can wait for half an hour, I will have time to tidy the teahouse for you. I'm afraid the sweets are not quite fresh. I had intended to make some more tomorrow morning before your arrival.'

'If you do have tea guests, why are you not in the teahouse?' Muromäki asked.

'I forgot to bring the sweets from the house before the start of the ceremony.'

'We'll return to the matter in half an hour, then,' Muromäki said. I bowed to him again, and he and his companion returned to the helicarriage in the shade.

I went to the kitchen and found half a bowl of old tea sweets in one of the cupboards. I checked quickly that they were not mouldy and tasted one: it was dry, but not rancid. They would have to do. I carried the bowl to the teahouse. I nearly entered through the visitors' sliding door, and at the last moment I remembered to use the master's entrance behind the building. Mai and Vesa looked at me questioningly when I stepped into the room.

'You must be careful,' I told them. 'There are two soldiers at the gate. They believe you are here as my tea guests. I will walk you to the gate. When you take your leave, thank me for the ceremony, call me Master Kaitio and bow low. Are you sure you can carry all these waterskins safely?' I asked Mai. Her face had fallen and she had begun chewing at the nail of her little finger.

Mai made a couple of movements, as if to test her muscles against the weight of water.

'Yes,' she said.

'Are you ready?'

Mai looked at Vesa. He nodded, his head moving up and down again and again. After that, she nodded too. I pointed at the visitors' entrance.

'When you are outside, wait for me.'

*　*　*

188

It felt to me as if Mai's waterskins were splashing loudly on each step towards the gate as we walked up the garden path. I saw Vesa's movements from the corner of my eye, and I was afraid he would start skipping or do something else unsuitable for a tea visitor.

When we eventually reached the gate, I bowed to Mai. She bowed back stiffly, and Vesa followed suit.

'Thank you, Master Kaitio. It was a pleasure visiting you.'

'Thank you, Mrs Harmaja. May clear waters flow your way.'

Muromäki had stepped down from the helicarriage to stretch his legs. When Mai and Vesa walked to the grit road between the trees, he spoke to Vesa.

'You're a little young to participate in a tea ceremony.'

I caught a glimpse of Mai's alarm, but she collected herself surprisingly quickly. The presence of water patrols and soldiers watching the village had taught us all to cover our tracks; our muscles and faces and tongues still recalled the normal shape of life and were quick to resume it when needed. Mai placed a heavy hand on Vesa's shoulder and said, 'Just trying to teach the boy some manners. He wants to be an official when he grows up.'

Muromäki smiled, and I thought of a hungry dog again.

'Is that so? Good luck with the career, lad,' he said and mussed up Vesa's dark hair with his hand.

Mai nodded to Muromäki and steered Vesa on.

'Goodbye, madam!' Muromäki called after them. They walked slowly, and Mai's steps were not light. Vesa kept glancing back over his shoulder, his eyes wide, but Mai turned his head firmly towards the road ahead of them. The movement of her hand was stiff.

'I will chime the bell, when everything is ready,' I told

Muromäki. I turned around and rushed to the teahouse, and at every step I wondered if he had noticed something out of the ordinary.

The cups tinkled against each other as I placed the tray on the teahouse floor, but Muromäki showed no sign of having noticed the trembling of my hands. I concealed my nervousness behind the form of the ceremony as best I could: I let the familiar movements flow on their own, and at the same time I attempted to furtively read traces of suspicion or victory in him. I found none. Muromäki was unexpectedly familiar with the etiquette and didn't ask unusual questions. He spoke with Liuhala in a low voice and nothing suggested that this was anything more than a brief respite from work for them.

The soft roaring of the near-boiling water in the cauldron soothed me. I reminded myself of the idea built within the heart of the tea ceremony: before tea, everyone is equal, even if their lives never cross outside the walls of the teahouse. I slowly began to believe that he had come here only for the ceremony and was not carrying out Taro's commands, and that his coming on the wrong day had really been a misunderstanding. Muromäki did not mention Taro again, and did not talk about anything but the quality of the tea, the teaware and the unusually cold last winter. I found myself thinking: could there be a world in which people don't need to choose sides, where everyone can sit together drinking tea without some holding power and others living in fear? It was a world of which tea masters had always dreamed, which they had built, which they had guarded – but had it ever been real, could it ever be?

In that world, which perhaps was not this one, Muromäki bowed and took the tea I offered, and I didn't need to label him a friend or foe in my mind.

In this world, I bowed to him at the end of the ceremony and walked out through the tea master's entrance. The illusion of a space where power didn't exist crumbled in the dusk of the teahouse. I walked Muromäki and Liuhala to the gate and didn't know if I had just served a friend or foe.

Those weeks surrounding the summer solstice, when water flowed in secret from the fell to the tea master's house, and villagers found myriad ways of transporting it to their homes – under their clothes, inside hidden compartments in carts, under scrap wood and furniture and garments I pretended to be selling or sending for repairs, and so on – I spent every moment I could spare behind the closed door of my room, examining maps and notes. I looked into place names, I looked into roads, estimating their usability, measuring distances, researching the terrain and guessing at the time it would take to travel by helicarriage from one place to the next. I spent a week calculating the hours and days it would take to journey to the Lost Lands and back, I estimated the amount of food and water the helicarriage could accommodate, and how much slower the weight carried would make the travelling. I captured a handful of blazeflies inside a lantern and began dropping fruit pieces for them in order to see how long they would live and produce light, if I didn't let them go.

Eventually, on a cloudy day when Midsummer was already half a month behind, I told Sanja about my plan.

We were sitting on cushions on the floor of her workshop. I had an open notebook in my lap. A large fly trapped inside buzzed up and down the mesh wall, moving from the floor to the ceiling and back again. Sanja was fitting a silver-coloured disc with the number seven painted on it into the past-machine. The other six were piled in the box where we kept them. This was the only one we had not finished listening to.

'Sanja,' I began. 'Have you wondered what it's like in the Lost Lands now?'

'Why would I?' she asked and pressed the lid of the indentation on the machine closed. I shrugged, but didn't reply. She raised her gaze and stared at me. Her eyes narrowed. 'You can't be serious,' she said.

'Why not?' I think I only understood then how serious I was. I dug up a map from my bag that I had packed earlier to bring with me.

'Noria,' Sanja said. 'You've got nothing but a few fragments of the past. Even if the expedition was real, we don't have the whole account of their journey. If there was clean water in the Lost Lands in the Twilight Century, there's no guarantee whatsoever that there is some now. And how would you ever get there?'

'By the roads.' I spread open the map on which I had drawn the possible route. 'Rovaniemi is on the border of the Lost Lands. I think I'll be able to get a helicarriage, which will be easy to drive all the way there. I've researched these maps, and these old books, and the notes, and current news, too. I'm fairly certain that there are several unguarded roads crossing the border north of Rovaniemi. Past-world roads were wide and well-constructed, they were made for fast vehicles. Many of them must still be usable, because there are people living in those areas, just outside the Lost Lands. The Jansson expedition used the past-roads, we can follow the same route they—'

'Wait a minute,' Sanja interrupted. 'What do you mean, "we"?'

I realised I had spoken without thinking. I blushed.

'I thought maybe you'd like to go with me,' I muttered, embarrassed.

Sanja stared at me, and I realised I had never imagined I'd be going alone. In all my daydreams she had been there with me, reading the map, navigating by the stars, climbing the mountains and exploring the caves with me. I hadn't really considered the possibility that she might not want to go, or what I would do if my only chance would be to go alone.

'Noria,' Sanja said, and her face was soft despite her words when she spoke to me. 'How could I go? Mum and dad and Minja can't make it here without me. I can't leave them. Besides, all the roads are being watched. How could I even get to Rovaniemi, let alone further? I don't have a fake passpod like you.'

'You said you could maybe hack another one,' I reminded her.

'Maybe,' Sanja sighed. 'There are too many maybes in your plan. And if, *if* we could somehow make it to the Lost Lands, and there wasn't any water there after all? It would all be a waste of time.'

'I know there is water there,' I said. 'There must be.'

Sanja would not give in.

'Even if there was,' she said. 'Then what?'

She was right, of course. Even if we did find water – if *I* did, I corrected in my mind – I'd have no way of bringing it to the village. How many villagers would be willing to leave for a strange land only with a vague promise of water? And even if some of them were desperate enough to look for a new place to live, the Lost Lands were forbidden, inaccessible. One or two travellers might be able to make their way there, but the more people making the journey, the more difficult it would be.

It felt insufferable to give up the plan that had been taking shape for weeks and months, but I might perhaps have been ready to try, to bury it under impossibility and quietly let go of it, if that day had taken a different course, if what happened next had not happened.

Sanja switched the past-machine on. The disc began to spin in its nest and a male voice recited the date, which I had already written down earlier. It spoke of research results and weather. I followed my notes, and began scribbling down what he was saying when the recording reached the part we had not listened to before. After half a page or so of new notes, the voice suddenly stopped mid-word. There was a click, then humming, and then a female voice sounded in the loudspeakers. It said, 'Another try. Nils, if you hear this, I'm sorry to record over your log, but this is more important.' She went quiet for a moment.

I glanced at Sanja and saw that she, too, had recognised the voice. I had lately been so concerned with the travel route of the Jansson Expedition that I had nearly forgotten the woman whose tale had been cut short at the end of the first disc. It had not appeared on any other discs. Yet this was undoubtedly the same voice, and excitement wriggled inside me like a fish in a net. The gap between this moment and the Twilight Century had unexpectedly closed. I held my breath, as the woman's next words flowed into the room.

'It's hard to know where to begin,' the woman said on the disc. 'History has no beginning and no end, there are just events that people give the shape of stories in order to understand them better . . . And in order to tell a story one must choose what not to tell.'

She continued to speak, and we listened, and all words that were not hers vanished from us. Outside clouds were covering the sky, and behind them the sky was the colour of deep summer, even if we did not see it. Grass grew, people breathed, the world turned. But inside, in this workshop, in these words everything changed: changed what we knew, changed what we felt, changed like a sea that rises and swallows all streets and houses, will not withdraw, will not give back what it has claimed.

When the disc was finally spinning hollow silence into the room, breath fluttered wildly in my lungs. Something had shifted within me, within us, and when I looked out, it was as if I had opened my eyes for the first time and seen everything more sharply: the jagged stone in the middle of the backyard, the spiky limbs of a dried shrub, a cobweb broken on the hinge of a door.

Once the silent space around a secret is shattered, it cannot be made whole again.

'Do you think it's true?' Sanja asked eventually. Her voice was frail, and the cracked void around us would not withdraw, it rested deep and impossible to banish like the ocean. 'Everything she said?'

'Yes,' I said. 'I think it's true.'

'So do I,' Sanja said.

She switched the past-machine off. The disc slowed down and eventually stopped. Of all silences I had encountered this was the gravest and most inevitable: not the silence of secrets, but of knowing.

That night, when the house was empty and the garden still, and no one was moving on the road, I walked to the spring. The sun was brushing the horizon, but would not drop below it, and the summer night was brighter than a midwinter day.

My lantern cast a glow on the dark rock walls of the

fell. When I lowered it near the surface of the water, I saw what I had already sensed from further away.

The surface had sunk. Not dangerously so, but it was lower than I remembered seeing it before.

The white mark on the rock glinted below the water like a wide, blind eye, clearer than ever.

CHAPTER FIFTEEN

I lifted my insect hood, wiped my brow with a creased rag and drank a sip from a small waterskin. A swarm of dark-winged horseflies bounced about me when I lowered the hood back into place. I whirled the rag in a circle to chase them off. The heavy weather glued the garments to my skin. The summer had reached its sweltering core, and a soggy, molten sun was emanating heat behind layers of clouds. I had only managed one swap so far despite having stood on the village square for several hours. The bulky floor fan had been good enough for the baker, who had in exchange given me two shoulder-strapped sacks of dried bread. I knew the fan was worth more, but this was probably the highest price anyone in the village would pay at the moment. I needed food that was easy to carry and would keep for a long time, so it still wasn't a bad swap.

A short, wide-boned man whose sand-coloured hair had thinned away almost entirely stopped in front of my stall. I could guess his thoughts when he observed with his pale-grey eyes the collection of objects I had gathered from the house: a couple of chairs decorated with woodcuttings, too gaudy for his living room; a handful of past-world books that no one in his house would have time to read; a tea set and a few plates he would find difficult to fill. The only thing he took a longer look at were the sandals – two old pairs that had belonged to my father, one pair that my mother had left behind. The man compared the sizes of the soles with his own well-worn footwear, but seemed to decide that he had no interest in trading those.

'Is that cart for sale?' he asked, pointing at the wagon of the helicycle in which I had placed some of the items on display.

'No, it's the only one I have,' I replied.

'Too bad. I'd have offered blue lotus or pipe-leaf for that,' he said, nodded goodbye and continued on his way.

The atmosphere in the square was almost relaxed today. I had only seen two soldiers when I had arrived, and they had been leaning against a wall at the edge of the square, looking indifferent and drinking amber-coloured liquid from their waterskins. A couple of children were arranging frayed plastic mahjong tiles on the ground, someone was playing an accordion across the uneven puzzle of the stalls, and Ninia's sister Tamara was selling trinkets and hair brooches a short distance away on the other side of the alley. It seemed strange to me that women would still want to decorate their hair. When I had mentioned this to Sanja, she had said, 'People will hold on to what they're used to, for as long as they can. It's the only way to survive.'

I saw a blue uniform flashing among the stalls. It approached, until I discerned a familiar face. Major Bolin saw me as he was turning into the alley where I had set up my own table, and walked right towards me. His heavy boots left deep, sharp-edged patterns in the sand.

Bolin stopped in front of my stall. I bowed to him, and he bowed back.

'Noria,' he said. 'I've been asking the villagers where to find you.' He looked around and lowered his voice. 'I got your message.'

'Would you like some tea, Major Bolin?' I asked.

He nodded. I gestured for him to walk around my stall. I threw a cloth over the sales table to cover the items and left the curtain of the back wall slightly open so I would see if anyone came to trade. Behind the curtain I offered a stool to Bolin and sat down on another one myself. I poured us some warm tea from a waterskin and lit a bitter-smelling incense stick to keep insects away, but horse-flies kept buzzing around us when we lifted our insect hoods to drink.

'How have you been, Noria?' Bolin asked and sipped his tea. His face was paper-dry, his movements slower than I remembered.

'Hanging in there,' I said.

Bolin was quiet, twirling the tea in his ceramic cup, looking sunken in thought. Eventually he said, 'I can help you, but I can't do it for free. Helicarriages are expensive these days, especially if you don't want anyone to start wondering about what you need it for.' He raised his eyes, and I heard an unspoken question behind his words.

'I need it to be able to go and sell chattels outside the village,' I said. 'I know there are more buyers for valuables in Kuusamo and Kuoloyarvi. A skilled seller can make good profit.'

Bolin examined me, and I hoped he was thinking of what I had deliberately left unmentioned: the black market, the rarer items he knew were in the tea master's house, because he had helped my parents acquire some of them.

'Are you sure the risk is worth the price?' he asked.

'There are few tea visitors these days, and even fewer pay as well as they used to.'

Bolin considered this and said then, 'I've heard that the monitoring of the black market is more lenient in Kuoloyarvi than in Kuusamo. Not that such a thing would be of any interest to you, of course.'

'How much?' I asked, congratulating myself on my success.

Bolin leaned forward on his seat and drew a five-figure number in the sand. It was more than I had expected, but I would be able to pay it.

'It's a deal,' I said. 'When do you need the payment?'

'Beforehand,' Bolin replied. 'I can send someone to fetch the money from your house tomorrow.'

'No, it's better if I bring it here,' I said. 'Is that alright?'

Bolin nodded.

'I will see to it that no one makes a connection between the helicarriage and me,' he said quietly. 'I expect you to do the same.'

He drained his tea and placed the cup in the sand next to the leg of the stool. The lines on his face were deep, and they grew deeper as he spoke.

'This is the last thing I can do for you. You know that, don't you?'

'Yes,' I said.

Bolin bowed his head slightly. I bowed back. As he was walking away, a thread of ants climbed up the side of the cup to reach for the drop of liquid left at the bottom. I brushed off the numbers Bolin had drawn on the ground with the tip of my sandal, until there was nothing left but a smooth plane of sand.

* * *

The afternoon stretched towards the evening and little by little people began to collect their stalls and merchandise. I detached the curtain from the supporting poles and folded it. I arranged my items in the cart, lifted the bread sacks among them, and when everything was in place and I had bound straps to hold the load, I steered the helicycle towards the tea master's house. I passed leather-brown, nodding gardens, the medical centre that stared out to the road with blank windows and people returning home from the market. From afar I could see a low, red-brick house and the bright-blue circle on its door. It was the latest house in the village to bear the mark of a water crime. The circle had appeared on the door five weeks earlier. I turned from my route to take a detour so I wouldn't need to drive directly past the marked door.

More than once posters painted on canvas caught my eye on the roadside. They promised rewards to anyone reporting water criminals. The baker's son, who was a year younger than me, was standing in front of one of the posters. I remembered him from the village school. He had been one of the swiftest sprinters in his class, was always impeccably dressed and got mediocre marks. He was wearing a blue uniform and painting a new, raised reward sum on top of the poster. A short distance away was another poster, its wet paint still shining faintly. If he was on military payroll, I thought, that explained how the baker's family could still afford to swap bread for fans.

Back at home I did something I had been avoiding for weeks.

I opened a wooden box I kept on the bookshelf in my room, and took out the message-pod my mother had sent. I had not used it before. In spite of my mother's request, I had written to her a few times on the old message-pod.

I had not mentioned a word about the other, hacked pod, but I had wanted her to know that I was in good health despite the war and the circumstances in the village. I had not received a reply, so I didn't know if my messages had made it to her. Yet now I had to let her know about my decision.

I placed my finger on the screen and waited as the display switched on and Aino Vanamo's name appeared. I wrote in the field, *I've decided to stay in the village until Moonfeast. I will leave for Xinjing the day after the feast and will let you know the date of my arrival. Aino.*

I sent the message, switched off the pod and put it back in the wooden box. I knew the lie I had just told was not the answer she had hoped for.

Early in the following afternoon a young woman dressed in the blue of the army kitchen stopped at my stall.

'Noria Kaitio?' she asked.

I bowed. The woman handed me a sealed letter.

'It's from Major Bolin,' she said. 'He said you'd know what was needed in exchange.'

I pulled a sealed mail pouch containing the money from my bag.

'He also sent a message,' she said, leaned closer and lowered her voice. 'Sunday before midnight.'

'Sunday before midnight,' I repeated. Today was Thursday. The woman nodded, turned on her heels and walked away. When she had gone, I walked behind my stall and looked around to make sure no one was paying attention to me. An old lady was dozing against the wall under the awning of the stall next to me; the two children I had seen the day before were drawing in the sand. I broke the seal and pulled the contents of the envelope out.

202

A map was drawn on a piece of paper and a place outside the village, on the outskirts of the Dead Forest, was marked with a cross.

The messenger had told me when, but now I also knew where.

On Sunday I started walking towards the Dead Forest well before midnight, because the journey was long. The night-glow of the sun floated on the water-coloured sky, but the shadowy chill of the ground seeped into me, climbing my bones and washing me shivery inside. I didn't know what to expect. I had no choice but to trust Bolin.

The village was quiet. I took the long route across the side of the fell because I was worried I might run into soldiers. A smoke-dark haze of insects hovered in the air like clusters of abandoned shadows. They would fall apart for a short while, scatter around me when I walked through them, and clench again into swarming statues dimming the landscape like ancient spirits risen from under stones or buried memories made visible. Stones shuffled under the soles of my walking shoes, grinding faintly against each other.

The Dead Forest had once been called Mosswood, a name that recalled deep-green leaves moving in the wind and verdancy so lush and moist that you could feel it on your skin. Even longer ago, when words for such greenness were not needed yet, because it was a given in these lands, the forest had not had a name at all, so my father had told me. Now its bare trunks and branches twisted towards the sky sand-dry and colourless like a cobweb woven across the landscape, or the empty husks of insects caught in it. Life no longer circulated in them, their veins were brittled and broken, their skins frozen into letters of a forgotten language, near-incomprehensible marks of what had once been. Some trunks had wrung themselves into the ground, where they lay speechless, still.

I followed the path drawn on the map, until I reached the place marked with a cross. I approached it cautiously, unsure of what was waiting for me. I listened.

The only sounds were the slow sinking of the forest, the wind clutching leafless twigs and the faint creaking of the trunks turned towards the earth.

It took me a while to find what I was looking for. The helicarriage was hidden with skill. I would not have seen it, if I had not known where to look. It had been driven into a shallow hole and covered with an earth-coloured, frayed seagrass rug and dry branches. I was content to notice that the road along which it had apparently been brought started some distance away. It meant the carriage was good enough for a more difficult terrain. I lifted the seagrass cover and examined the carriage. I knew little about helicarriages, but this one looked newer and seemed to be in better condition than Jukara's. There were scratches on the sides and the tyres were slightly worn, but the solar panels and seats were unbroken. The start key was in the lock. I pulled the rug back over the carriage. I walked along a narrow path until it joined a slightly wider dirt road, which wound towards the village. The road was closed with a half-rotten beam and large boulders. Seen from the other direction, it looked like it had not been used in years. There were no tracks: Bolin had kept his promise about the carriage being difficult to trace. Yet someone knew it was here, so the sooner I could drive it away, the better.

I had given a lot of thought to where to keep the heli-carriage. The easiest would have been to hide it in the tea master's house, but I didn't want to risk a water patrol discovering it loaded with food and water, obviously equipped for a longer journey. Therefore I had decided to hide it near the plastic grave under an old bridge. The grave was spilling over on the edges with old junk people had left around it, and the mouth of the space under the bridge was nearly blocked by earth and rubbish. From a distance it was impossible to know there was a hollow space inside. Sanja and I had found the place a few years earlier. If someone happened to be passing near the bridge and saw the helicarriage, the discovery would be impossible to connect with anyone. The worst that could happen would be losing the carriage. Transporting food and water to it would be more difficult, but if I took small amounts every day, I could do it.

Once I'd found the gap which had been used to bring the carriage into the forest – it was possible to move the beam, and I managed to pry one of the boulders to the side with a dry branch – I walked back to the carriage. I'd have to wait for the morning, when the nightly curfew would expire, and use the remotest roads possible. The route to the hiding place was difficult, but this meant the risk of being spotted was smaller.

I sat on the crackling dry ground and listened to the stillest essence of the night closing in around me.

I first noticed that the hacked message-pod was missing when I returned to the house in the morning. I opened the wooden box to check if my mother had replied to me, and I saw immediately that the message-pod was not where I had left it, on top of the things I had collected from the plastic grave. The weight of my heart fell into my stomach. I tried to remember when I had last taken the message-pod out and switched it on. The morning before? Or the day before that? I wasn't sure. Several villagers had come to the house to get water in the past few days. The adults didn't usually come any further than the kitchen, but the women had brought their children, who had been wandering around in the rooms as usual. My first thought was that one of them had gone into my room, found my wooden box and taken the message-pod without asking for permission. In theory it was possible. I tried to remember if I could have left the pod somewhere else. I searched in the kitchen. I searched in the living room. I looked behind the bookshelves and under the bed and between the piles of books and in the pockets of my garments, with no success.

I did not want to think about the most frightening possibility: that the message-pod had not been taken by any of the children, and not by mistake.

Sanja came for a visit in the afternoon. I was sweeping the veranda of the teahouse, and was not in the mood for talking.

'I need to talk to you,' she said and looked around.

'There's no one else here,' I told her and placed the broom against the wall of the teahouse. There were things we only spoke of when we were alone, and others we didn't speak of at all. One of them was what the voice of a woman had said on the last silver-coloured disc. I wondered if this was what she wanted to talk about now.

Sanja looked me in the eye.

'I want to go with you,' she said.

'I'm not going to the spring for a few days,' I said and started walking towards the house.

'I don't mean the spring.' Her words sounded unusually heavy. I stopped and turned to look at her. Her face was tense, as if she was holding back grief or excitement. 'I've been thinking,' she said. 'I want to go to the Lost Lands with you. Mum and dad and Minja are alright now that she is better and mum can work again. Can I come?'

I wanted to pull her into my arms, so glad I was that she was stepping into my dreams after all, that we would finally be the real explorers we had played as children. But an unexpected problem was complicating my plans.

'Of course I want you to go with me,' I said. 'But the message-pod my mother sent has gone missing. I don't know where I've put it. I'm afraid someone may have stolen it. I don't have a hacked passpod—'

A flush began to colour Sanja's pale face, and she was moving restlessly.

'Noria,' she said. 'I need to confess something.' She pushed a hand into her bag and pulled out my message-pod. 'I'm sorry I didn't say anything. I wanted to surprise you.' She handed the hacked pod back to me, and I took it without a word. I was relieved, because no one from the village had taken it, and angry, because she had taken it without asking, and a little worried, because she had managed to take it without me realising. I switched the pod on.

'Don't worry, it's every bit the same as it was,' Sanja said. She rummaged in her bag again and pulled out another message-pod, a little older and more battered. 'Look.' She stepped next to me and placed her finger on the display. A paper-white light switched on, and a moment later a name appeared: 'Lumi Vanamo.' The birthplace was recorded as Rovaniemi and the birth date just over a year after Aino Vanamo's birthday.

'You were born in Xinjing,' Sanja said. 'But our parents, Outi and Kai Vanamo, had already decided to return to their homelands near Rovaniemi. They moved there across the continent when you were very small, and I was born only a year later. After our parents drowned in an accident on the seaweed fields, we completed the last three years of school in Kuusamo where we stayed with our relatives. We're now returning to a small village on the outskirts of Rovaniemi to the family home our deceased parents left us.' She raised her eyes from the message-pod and grinned at me.

'Not bad,' I said, impressed. Sanja shrugged.

'I had already thought of two alternative ways that might work for hacking the pod. I needed yours to check which one would do the trick. It didn't take too long in the end.' She switched off her message-pod. 'The most difficult part was to get my hands on another second-hand pod.'

'You're brilliant,' I told her.

'No. Just curious, and I work until my fingers bleed,' she said. 'Well, when are we going?'

Later, when she was checking the settings of the message-pod, I watched the movements of her fingers and the focused expression on her face through which I couldn't see. She had taken the message-pod from my room in secret, but I wanted to block the space suspicion had carved in me. I told her everything about my plan, and the helicarriage, and the places I wanted to go. As if through a dream I could feel the flowing water on my skin, waiting for us clear and relentless, now nearly within my reach. Nothing else mattered.

I didn't ask what had made her change her mind, and she didn't say.

208

CHAPTER SIXTEEN

The residents of the red-brick house were executed the day when everything was ready for our departure, two weeks after I had acquired the helicarriage. I did not see it. I saw the rust-brown stains on the grit of the front yard, and the furniture that had been carried outside. At a glance, some distance away, I saw the door where a plank nailed across the frame split the blue circle in two.

'Don't look,' Sanja said, but I looked anyway, and then wished I hadn't. That was what we did nowadays: tried to avert our gaze from the things that were happening, and failed, and then tried to live on as if we had not seen them. All the while those things stayed with us, made their home under our skin, in the thrumming, dark-red space of the chest, their unbending slivers scratching the soft, wet heart. When I walked on the streets, I could see people carrying these sights within: buried, but not deep enough not to cast an afterthought across their faces, altering them as a slow shift in light.

We were on our way to the plastic grave. The sky was a hazy barrier of white and grey and pale blue, changing like the sea, but whether it was closing into a storm or opening up to a flow of bare light, I could not tell. The silver-coloured discs weighed in my bag.

'We should hide them,' Sanja had said. 'Someplace where no one knows to look, but someone might find them. Those who recorded their story wanted someone to know. They realised that it could change everything people knew about the oil wars and the past-world. We should give the same chance to others. Just in case.'

I knew what she meant. We hadn't said aloud, *if we don't come back*. But I had thought about it, and I was certain she had, too.

We walked across the plastic grave, where the hollow bones of frail junk crunched under the thick soles of our sandals. We reached the carcass of the past-vehicle near the place where I had found the first silver-coloured disc and the past-machine that I suspected had belonged to the Jansson expedition.

I had sealed the discs in the same metal box they had been inside in the spring, and wrapped it in frayed fabric and tattered junk plastic. I pulled the parcel out of my bag. Sanja dug a hole where one of the rear tyres would have been, and we placed the discs in it. I thought of the woman's voice on the discs and I silently thanked her in my mind. She, a tea master's daughter from an unfamiliar time, had gone exploring long before us and shown it to be possible. Without her I might never have found the courage to put my plan into practice. I piled some loose junk on top of the discs, and we covered the whole thing with a ragged cluster of plastic bags. Nothing revealed that there was something important hidden in the place.

Sanja turned to go, but I asked her to wait.

I climbed into the cockpit of the vehicle and pushed my

hand into the hole in the rusted-through dashboard. I took out a round plastic box. It was not heavy, and the items inside moved with a rustle to one side when I tilted it.

'Do you remember this?' I asked.

Sanja's face changed, as if light had suddenly spread across it.

'I'd forgotten!' she exclaimed. 'What did we seal in this one?'

She stepped closer and examined the year we had painted on the lid of the box to mark the planned opening date.

'Still over twenty years away,' I said.

'We had a clause,' she reminded me. 'Not to be opened until the agreed date, except under extreme circumstances.'

'You think this counts as an extreme circumstance?'

She was smiling, but I could see the underlying serious-ness, when she replied, 'If it doesn't, I don't know what will.'

I looked at her. She caught my eye and nodded slightly. She took the box from me and held it. I turned the lid of the box, until the lacquer seal we had carefully melted over its edge cracked and broke. Inside the lid was painted a date from ten years earlier. We had been eight years old when we had collected treasures for this time capsule. We bent our heads to examine the contents together. There was a small, rust-stained metal lock and a key which didn't fit in it, a yellowed page full of small print – I must have torn it from one of my mother's books – a few smooth stones and a pair of old, scratched eyeglasses with one broken stem. The lenses were tinted with different colours: one red, one blue.

'I remember those,' Sanja said. 'The Magic Glasses.'

I too remembered the game we had played with the glasses: as explorer-spies we had taken turns to wear them, look through walls into hidden places and describe to each other what we saw.

'Should we take something with us?' I suggested. 'For luck?'

'Every gram of extra weight will slow us down,' Sanja remarked, and was right, of course. I put the glasses back in the box and was about to close the lid, when she stopped my hand and said, 'Not yet.'

She handed the box to me, untied a worn-thin seagrass bracelet from around her wrist and placed it on top of the other items.

'You too,' she said.

'Have you got your penknife?' I asked.

Sanja searched for the knife in her pocket and handed it to me. I placed the box on the dashboard, drew the thin blade out of its sheath and cut loose a long strand of my hair.

'It's all I've got,' I said and gave the knife back to Sanja.

I twisted the hair into a coil around my fingers, pulled it into a loose knot and placed it inside the seagrass bracelet. The knot loosened and unravelled a little, and settled against the bracelet, within its uneven loop: my dark hair and the dried grass of the sea that Sanja had carried around her wrist, together in an unbroken circle with no beginning and no end. Sanja closed the lid, taking care to fit the broken edges of the seal against each other.

It felt like a precaution against mortality, as if we had cast a spell that could not be undone. If we didn't come back, something would be left of us – even if it was only nameless, childish and without value, but something we had chosen to be preserved, a trace that we had left behind.

That was what I thought.

I believed that was what she thought, too.

I still want to believe this.

* * *

When we left the plastic grave, Sanja said, 'I'll see you tonight.' Her body was narrow and angular inside the rough linen fabric. The shadow of the insect hood was soft on her face. She walked away and did not look behind.

After Sanja had gone, I trudged across the uneven ground to the helicarriage to check once more that everything was in order. The underbelly of the bridge smelled of crumbling earth and decaying rubbish. I went through the contents of the wagon towed behind the helicarriage. I had calculated carefully the amount of food and water and added a little extra to be safe, but not too much. I didn't know how accurate my estimates of our journeying speed would turn out to be, or what the actual condition of the roads might be once we crossed the border. Although my hopes were high, I had not dared to rely completely on finding water, so most of the space was reserved for carrying drinking water.

I moved the sacks of dried fruits, sunflower seeds and almonds in order to make space for one more waterskin, which I had carried on my back. The problem of transporting water had been our biggest headache, because we knew that we would certainly be stopped if we tried to openly carry several weeks' worth of drinking water with us. We had gone through all the devices of water fraud and smuggling plans we had developed over the past weeks when the villagers had been taking water to their homes from the tea master's house. Sanja had made some carefully planned adjustments to the helicarriage, and the result was her masterpiece: she had removed the seats, moulded a lockable empty space under them and concealed it again so meticulously that it was impossible to tell the carriage had been modified. You could fit a week's worth of water-skins under the fake bottom of the cart, and furthermore we had built different secret compartments and containers in the food chests. To cover the cart, we had tightened a double plastic-and-canvas awning over a frame which would protect the contents and under which we could sleep.

One of my worries were the blazeflies. I didn't know how many we would manage to find along the way – those we would take with us when we left the tea master's house would not live until we came back. It was late summer, and daylight still stretched across nearly all hours of the day. Yet in just a few weeks' time the nights would be growing darker again, and before two full moons passed, Moonfeast would turn the year towards winter. While our plan was to return to the village well before that, the fading of the blaze lanterns might become a problem and slow down our journey. The thought of their faded glow also made me uneasy for another reason: I didn't know how deep in the veins of the earth the water was hidden, or what kind of darkness we would need to descend into in order to find it. Sanja had fixed two solar-powered past-torches for us, but their light was dimmer than that of the blaze lanterns, and one of them kept buzzing and hiccupping. 'I couldn't get good enough wires,' Sanja had said, miffed, and we'd had to settle for that.

She hadn't told anyone about our plan, not even her parents. She said she didn't want them to worry. I suspected that she might not have been able to hold on to her decision to go with me if they had asked her to stay.

I spread a cracked plastic tarpaulin to cover the heli-carriage and the wagon and piled dry branches and junk on top of it. When I was happy with the camouflage, I walked out into daylight. We had filled the mouth of the cavernous space with rubbish that was lying around, and I blocked the gap behind me so that it looked closed.

* * *

The sky was the colour of rock and lichen, and fresh bruises. The first drops fell on the linen fabric of my shirt at the edge of the village, spreading into large, uneven stains and soaking their wetness onto my skin. By the time I reached the road leading to the gate of the house, my trouser bottoms were dripping with water and the sand darkened into mud was tarnishing their light fabric. The crisp, wooden scent of wet seagrass floated in the rain-dimmed air.

Out of habit I had carried the rain-containers into the garden in the morning after I had looked at the sky, even if I had no reason to use them. Let the villagers take the rainwater with them when they come tomorrow and find the house empty, I thought. It is the last thing I have to offer them in a while. Jukara would lead them into the cave in the fell before I returned, I was sure of it; I suspected he already went there in secret sometimes, even though I had asked him to avoid it, because a sudden increase in fell trekking among the villagers would not go unnoticed by the soldiers.

I closed my eyes and stood in the rain. I stepped out of my sandals onto the grass. The slippery blades shifted and flattened, drawing latticeworks on the skin of my soles. Water streamed to the back of my neck from my hair, wetting my back and my arms, dripping from the tip of my nose. I shed my clothes like an old skin, and felt raw and fresh and ready.

The wooden gathering-bucket I had placed next to the veranda steps was nearly half-full.

I walked into the house, changed into dry clothes and sat down on the floor.

Until now, I had tried to keep the house at least superficially as it had been in the time of my parents, despite the fact that I noticed how it wished to bend out of shape under change. I still made the effort to do the same, but my reasons were different. I wanted to be sure that when the villagers came here after we had left, nothing in the rooms would tell them that I had gone far and might stay away for a long time. I left clothes on the backs of chairs, as if I had put them down only to pick them up a moment later. There was an open book lying face down on the living room sofa that I had no intention of taking with me. Half of my morning tea was still left in the cup on the kitchen table; I didn't clean it away. I wanted to leave behind a still frame of a life in progress: the illusion of unchanging quality would conceal the big change. I wished to delay the suspicions of the villagers for as long as I could.

Until the night, or another morning.

Everything was ready.

I locked the door and swept the stone slabs that formed the path to the teahouse. The rain-soaked leaves and blades of grass clung to the bristles of the broom. I placed it against the wall on the teahouse veranda.

I walked to the edge of the rock garden where the three tea plants grew. The rain had stopped, and water drops glistened on their narrow leaves. My father's grave was covered by grass, and nothing distinguished its outline from the rest of the lawn now. I wanted to say something to him, but my mouth held only silence.

The sand of the rock garden was ragged with rain. I picked up the rake from the ground and raked it until it was neat. The traces of the metal teeth undulated among the boulders like water that flows in the darkness of the earth without slowing or quickening its pace.

The notebooks weighed in my bag, and in the garden the shadows were thickening, when I closed the gate behind me.

When I reached the bridge, everything seemed as it should. The blocked opening was covered in junk, and there was nothing to suggest that the place had been visited after I had left it earlier in the day. I thought she had not made it there yet. I moved a broken armchair and a roll of useless cable to the side in order to manoeuvre myself into the hiding place.

I didn't immediately understand what I saw. It took a while before my eyes adjusted to the dim space under the bridge, and it took longer before I could comprehend what they were telling me.

The helicarriage and the four-wheeler with their contents were gone.

Breath caught in my chest, and a heavy lump formed at the back of my belly. I felt as if I had swallowed a large, sharp block of ice.

I sent a message to Sanja's message-pod, then to her family's pod. There was no reply. Not knowing what else to do, I began walking towards her house. I took a shortcut across the plastic grave, where my feet slipped over the rain-soaked surfaces and dark crannies opening into the very core of the buried past. I passed a few people who had been drawing mud-stained water from the small brook near the edge of the grave. Some of them were trying to catch rain from the sky into their skins and buckets. I passed houses, and saw people letting the water falling from clouds wash over their thirsty faces and bodies and hands.

I turned to the street where Sanja's family lived and stopped.

There were soldiers in blue uniforms outside Sanja's house.

The door was open, and I'm certain of this: there was no blue circle on it, only the washed-out grey colour that it always wore. I didn't see Sanja or her parents, but the soldiers kept coming and going out of the door, and I saw two of them walking towards the backyard and Sanja's workshop.

One tall soldier was standing in the front yard, and when he turned his head, I recognised him despite the distance. It was Muromäki, Taro's blond-haired second in command.

I turned around and forced myself not to run. My feet swelled heavy on the mud-tainted road, and the clouds hung low, brushing the dark fell-tops and bursting with the weight of their water.

In this landscape where everything had shifted and the world had fallen out of joint, I walked back into the tea master's house, and I waited.

No one moved on the narrow road. The lights of my message-pods did not switch on. The world did not spin slower or faster.

After midnight I went into my room and lay in bed in the grey-blue dusk of the sunless night, and I couldn't sleep, and I couldn't move. Near the morning I fell asleep for a short while, and when I woke up, it was difficult to breathe. I went to the veranda for some fresh air.

The clouds had withdrawn. The brightness of the morning slashed my eyes. I walked over the moist grass to the gathering-pool that rested in the middle of the garden. When I bent down to drink from it, I saw my own reflection on the surface of the water briefly before it shattered.

I heard the door close itself slowly with creaking hinges.

I turned to go back inside.

The blue circle on the door was still glistening moist with paint, shining in the luminous morning like a ring cut from the sky.

PART THREE

The Blue Circle

'A circle only knows its own shape. If you ask where it begins and where it ends, it will stay silent, yet unbroken.'

Wei Wulong, 'The Path of Tea'
7th century of Old Qian time

CHAPTER SEVENTEEN

Water is the most versatile of all elements. It isn't afraid to burn in fire or fade into the sky, it doesn't hesitate to shatter against sharp rocks in rainfall or drown into the dark shroud of the earth. It exists beyond all beginnings and ends. On the surface nothing will shift, but deep in underground silence, water will hide and with soft fingers coax a new channel for itself, until stone gives in and slowly settles around the secret space.

Death is water's close companion, and neither of them can be separated from us, for we are made of the versatility of water and the closeness of death. Water doesn't belong to us, but we belong to water: when it has passed through our fingers and pores and bodies, nothing separates us from earth.

I see it clearly now, the dark and narrow figure standing next to the rock garden, by the tea plants, or walking among the trees. The face is patient, and not unfamiliar. It has been the same face from the beginning. I think it may have been waiting for me all along, even when I did not understand it yet.

I can feel water wanting to leave me. I can feel the weight of my own dust.

A few days passed before I understood my situation.

That first morning, after I turned and saw the blue circle on the front door of the house, I stood still for a long while. The rainwater I had drunk from the gathering-pool trickled down my chin and neck, seeped inside the collar of my tunic. I wiped it on the back of my hand. Tree leaves fluttered in the light wind, and I thought of the wings of blazeflies brushing against the glass walls of a lantern. I stared at the endless loop of the circle, which provided no way out. The ground was still steady under my feet and the sky where it should be. The world carried on with life beyond the invisible barrier that had been raised around me: people were thinking their thoughts, walking on the roads, talking to those they loved. For a moment reality wavered around me unclear, crumbling on the edges and split in two. Some part of me is still walking outside these boundaries, I thought, living the life that was to be. She is on her way to the Lost Lands, and she is nearly as real as I am, in some moments more real, perhaps, but she is looking the other way, and she is not coming back.

The thought broke and blurred and slipped away.

I was here, and nothing could change what I saw.

Branches were swinging in the breeze; light coloured the dense, dark-green mesh of the grass, where stalks knotted into uneven tangles. The only shadow cast on the ground was mine, and in the quiet of the morning I could discern no sounds of footsteps or breathing, no words carried in the wind. I walked to the door and touched the circle. Some paint came off to my fingertips. I wiped the sticky colour on my trousers, and the fabric was stained by three blue streaks. I knew they would be impossible to wash off. The thought left me indifferent.

The floorboards creaked when I stepped into the house. My throat was sand-dry; it hurt to swallow. I stopped in the kitchen, turned the tap on and remembered at once that I had gone to the fell to close the pipe two days earlier. There wouldn't be any water.

There was water.

I filled a teacup and drained it. I drank another cupful, then one more. The water didn't stop running. I recognised the taste: it was coming from the spring in the fell. I turned the tap off, then turned it on again. There was still water.

The metal was cold and even under my fingers. I turned the tap off, sat down on the kitchen floor with my legs bent and pressed my forehead into my knees.

I listened to my own breathing. I listened to the movement of blood in my veins. I listened to the silence of the house and tried to understand what had happened.

Faces of villagers surfaced in my mind, requests and words of gratitude on cracked lips, hands lifting full waterskins, their bones ashen fans under the taut skin. Their footsteps heavy-pressed on the ground, when they carried the weight under their clothes that the life of their children or spouses or parents depended on. One of them had entered my house, sat in my kitchen and taken home my water – only water, I corrected in my mind, not *my* water. Upon returning to the village, they had looked at the posters along the streets, the award sum painted on them. And after days or weeks, footsteps steady or staggering, they had walked to the guard on the street. Said, I've got something to tell that might interest you.

How long had the military known?

Had they been following my movements and my travel preparations, did they know about the helicarriage and the fake passpods? Maybe they had known about the spring for weeks already, but had found out somehow that I was going to leave the village, and they had waited. Perhaps they had been keeping watch on the hiding place of the helicarriage, monitoring how Sanja and I carried food and water there. And yesterday, when Sanja had walked along the edge of the plastic grave to wait for me, they had stepped out in the open, three soldiers in their heavy boots and blue uniforms, perhaps only two – just one would have sufficed, because Sanja was not of large build. I could see them blocking her way at the entrance of the underbelly of the bridge below the dark-hanging sky and drawing their sabres from their sheaths. Rain blurred the blades into a blistering mirror surface. One of the soldiers tied her hands behind her back while the other strode into the space under the bridge, where the heli-carriage was waiting, ready to go. They took the carriage and the food and water laden into the cart, and drove her away, and she had no way of escaping or contacting me.

I tried not to imagine what had happened to Sanja.

Under all my thoughts I knew that there was another possibility. That she had not been captured. That the soldiers had not needed to come to her.

But I couldn't think of this. It would not fit within my bounds without shattering them.

I thought of everything I knew about the events at other water crime houses in the village. There wasn't much: rumours, hearsay. Uncertain glimpses of prisoners, distant and quiet as ghosts. Dried blood on the sand of the garden path.

There was an instant of hollow terror when I realised

224

I might not be able to leave the house, but then I remembered I had already been outside with no consequences. I had no idea how far from the house I could stray. And what would happen when I reached this invisible boundary drawn around my life? Would I be shot dead on the spot, or would a warning be enough?

There was only one way to find out.

My legs were shaking when I stepped out to the veranda.

The path from the front door of the house to the gate was as familiar and commonplace to me as the back of my own hand. I had walked the route countless times, on most days of my life, and I could have described its shape with my eyes closed. Yet now the journey across the grass was strange and new, the arch of each step bright-cut and each movement of the centre of my body as heavy as an uprooted rock. I saw a moth caught in a cobweb under the eaves where I hadn't seen it the day before. I saw the ripples of the stone slabs, the unevenly slated shape of their edges, the metal-dark layers of the mineral, squeezed against each other by time. I saw my own foot, made of brittle bone and thin skin, which spread pale and vulnerable on the shield of stone in the soft frame of grass-stalks.

Breath passed in me hastily, raggedly, and on each step I expected to feel somewhere in my body – what, exactly? I had seen bullet wounds, bandages tarnished by dry blood and sticky, yellow liquid around them, but I had never seen a bullet find its way to its victim. I had not seen the pain on the face of a person, when metal penetrated their skin and tore their tissues apart and sank into bone. I imagined a stinging, burning agony, like a small explosion in my flesh, and then I tried to imagine the same pain hundredfold, because I was certain my first thought was nowhere near reality. How much would I realise? Would

I have time to follow as life slowly left me, or would it all be over so quickly that the screeching pain caused by the wound would barely cut to my consciousness?

Blood weighed in my feet as I forced myself to take one step after another. Grass-stalks fell back under the soles of my shoes and straightened towards the sky again as my feet rose from them.

Something rustled in the direction of the forest. I didn't see movement among the trees. I realised I had stopped. My breathing sang, stuck in my tense throat. I relaxed my muscles and let the air out of my lungs into the crisp morning that smelled of last night's rain. The gate wasn't far away now. A step: in a few long strides I would reach it. A step, another one and another: I could touch the night-chilled metal of the gate if I reached out my arm. A final step: I was standing right in front of the gate.

Leaves swished against each other and wind tugged at the branches. Shadows changed on the sand of the road. The windchime hanging from the pine tree tinkled softly behind me.

I took a breath, closed my eyes and opened the gate.

Nothing happened.

I looked around and still didn't see anything suggesting another person's presence.

I took a step through the gate.

Then a second one.

On the third step a sharp but surprisingly faint bang cut the air, as if a thick plank had been split in two with one metallic stroke. A fistful of sand shot into the air only a couple of finger-widths away from my toes. I froze. The echo of the bang faded into the landscape.

As a child I would wrap myself inside a curtain in the corner of my mother's study and hide in there during thunderstorms, in the soothing, soft dusk where light sieved through the texture of the fabric. I would wait until the menacing cracks in the world sealed and faded away, and it was safe again to walk in the house without the shelter provided by the curtain. Now the same impulse struck through me. Every fibre in my body screamed that I should turn around and run into the house as fast as my feet would take me, curl into the corner inside the curtain, until the cracks of the world would be closed again, and I couldn't slip through them into the tight-entwined darkness or too-white, all-scorching light. But the curtain had frayed on the edges ages ago, the corner was full of cobwebs and knotted dust, and there was no place left in the house or garden or fell where I could have escaped the cracked-open, glass-edged crevices of the world.

I stepped forward again.

The sound tore through the air and sand spilled on my foot where the bullet reached the ground. I raised my eyes and saw movement perhaps ten metres away: a strip of blue among the tree-trunks, the stabbing glint of metal where sunrays hit it.

My third attempt confirmed what I had begun to suspect. Sand scattered again, just close enough to be an effective warning, but purposefully beyond my outlines. These soldiers knew how to shoot, and they wanted me to know my limits. Nevertheless it seemed that for some reason it wasn't their intention to hurt me.

A suffocating silence weighed on the landscape, when I slowly backed into the garden through the gate.

When the sun turned to afternoon, I had discovered the boundaries of my captivity. They followed the garden fence everywhere except behind the teahouse, where there was no fence. The invisible wall had been raised approximately ten steps away from the back wall of the teahouse, but I was free to go into the teahouse itself. I concluded that there must be several crackshots in the immediate surroundings of the house, constantly following my movements.

After returning into the house I locked the door and drew all the curtains in every window. I understood now why the windows of the other houses marked with a blue circle had always been covered. When life is chained within narrow limits, the slightest illusion of freedom is valuable. The weathered wood of the door and the fragile glass of the windows would not keep away those who were threatening me, but if I could still hide one small slice of my life from them, make it mine alone, I would not give up this shred of privacy, possibly the last one I had.

I remembered the message-pods. One of them was still where I had packed it in order to take it to the Lost Lands. The other one I had left in the wooden box in my room. I pulled the hacked pod from my bag, placed my finger on the screen and waited for the light to switch on. A row of dots flashed on the display: the device was looking for a connection to a pod network. Eventually the message *No network* appeared on the screen. I chose the option *Search again* under it. A minute later the same message reappeared. I walked into my room and dug up the other message-pod. Its screen told me likewise that there was no network in the house. Those keeping me captive had seen to it that I had no way of communicating with the outer world.

Towards the evening I began to get worried about food. I had water, at least for now. I'd filled all my skins from the kitchen tap in case the supply would be cut. There wasn't much in the way of eating, however. Looking forward to the journey, I had laden the helicarriage with everything that would last longer than a day. In the kitchen cupboard I found a few amaranth crackers and ate one of them with weak tea. I was grateful for the garden; the berries, vegetables and fruits were ripening. However, most of them wouldn't be edible until several weeks from now. I had enough porridge flakes maybe for a week, if I used them sparingly.

When the sun had dropped as low as it would tonight, I searched the kitchen drawers for a thick-bladed knife. I stood in front of the closed front door. A long time ago, a two-forked metal coat rack had been nailed to the door. I usually hung my insect hood from it. I moved the hood to the shelf on the wall and placed the tip of the knife against the wood, which was painted white. I discerned in the paint brush-strokes, the movement of my mother's hand: she had scraped off the old paint, made the door look shiny and new again. Over ten years had passed since, and the paint was cracked.

I pressed the blade hard against the door and drew one vertical line on the wood, on my side, the reverse of the blue circle. The paint peeled away under the cut. There was still plenty of space for other lines.

Back in my room I pushed the knife under my pillow. I lay with the light of late summer on my face, the message-pods dark and mute on the table next to my bed.

In the morning I drew another vertical line next to the first one. The air in the house seemed suffocating and stuffy. When I opened the door, I saw a trayful of food had been left on the veranda steps. There wasn't a lot of it: half a loaf of bread, a handful of dried figs, a small pouch of beans. I placed them to soak in a bowl of water and divided the food carefully into rations, because I didn't know how many days I would need to survive on it. The empty tray I left where I had found it.

I thought of the water running from the kitchen pipe when it shouldn't have been, and of the crackshots who deliberately aimed their shots right next to me, but missed. I thought of the food left on the veranda. I began to feel certain of what I couldn't understand: somebody wanted to keep me alive, at least for the time being.

They also wanted me to be afraid.

The following night I kept watch at the window in order to see if anyone came into the garden. The soldier arrived a little after six o'clock in the morning. He was carrying a tray with a portion of food on it. When he placed it on the veranda steps, I got up despite the tiredness weighing my limbs. He raised his gaze when I opened the door.

'Why is my house marked?' I asked.

The soldier picked up the empty tray and didn't answer. He turned around and started walking away. I went after him. I understood it was not a safe thing to do, but I had to try.

'What am I being accused of?' I asked. 'Couldn't I speak to somebody?'

The soldier continued to walk without a word. I made a sprint to overtake him and blocked his way. He stopped and placed a hand on the hilt of his sabre. I only realised now that he was the baker's son I had gone to school with and seen in the village painting posters.

'Let me speak to somebody,' I said. 'If I must live in captivity, I want to know what I'm being accused of, at least.'

He stood there, tense, and I waited for the cold-burning cut of the sabre on my skin. He still didn't speak.

'Please,' I said and hated my own pleading tone of voice. When he didn't reply, I asked, 'Why are you doing this?'

His hand remained on the hilt when he said, 'You're not permitted to talk to anyone, and I don't have the answers to your questions. I'm only doing my job.' He went quiet and observed me, and for a moment I saw in him the boy I had seen running fast on the schoolyard between the classes for years, never paying much thought to him.

'I should slash your face,' he continued, 'but I'll let it go this once. The other guards may not be as kind. It would be wiser to stay in the house when the food is being brought.'

He started towards the gate again. I stood in my place, because his voice and expression had turned my tongue into stone and rooted my feet into the ground. I had seen a darkness behind his eyes that frightened me: a darkness born not only of things one has had to see despite wanting to look away, but a denser, more pungent one.

A darkness born when one does things from which others want to look away.

I knew with utter certainty that if I followed him or spoke to him again, he would slash me with his sabre and leave me bleeding until I would move no more. I watched him disappear through the gate between the trees, and only many moments later my blood flowed light enough that I could return into the house.

On the evening of the third day I was standing by the rock garden, when I saw movement on the road coming from the village. From the distance I could tell the figure was moving on foot and not wearing a blue uniform. She seemed too short to be Sanja. The figure moved closer, blended with the shadows of the trees, and no one stepped out to cut her way. As she drew nearer to the gate, I recognised her as Mai Harmaja. Approximately ten metres outside the gate she stopped in her tracks and stared at the house. Her eyes shifted and hit me, then her head turned towards the house again, and I knew her gaze was fixed on the door. A moment later she looked around her, turned and started walking back towards the village with hasty footsteps.

As her short figure drew away, I knew I wouldn't see any more villagers on the road among the trees surrounding the house.

CHAPTER EIGHTEEN

The blade scratched the paint and revealed a light wooden surface below. The line I had just scraped down started the sixth row of marks. I pushed the knife into a sheath that didn't fit, but was still better than no sheath at all, and placed it in my pocket, just like I had done each morning for the past five weeks.

I had not spoken to anyone after the day when the baker's son had turned his back on me and walked out of the gate without looking back. Each morning I had found the tray on the steps, and occasionally I had seen a glimpse of a blue uniform, but I hadn't had the courage to speak again to the soldiers.

Only when the boundaries of life are fragile and close, the aching need to hold on to them becomes clear.

Every morning and evening I would still switch both message-pods on. There is nothing more persistent than hope: even after I imagined I had completely banished the wish that the light on one of them would be flashing, it would flicker in me, and again I had to shove it into the darkness where it would have no space to live or breathe.

Every time the lights of the message-pods remained off, my heart would beat a little heavier. But it only lasted a moment, and then my captivity was again opaque mist in which I took one step at a time, not knowing when the view would grow clear or what I would find ahead.

My days were filled with trying to find food in the garden and storing what water I could. The taps in the house had turned unpredictable: sometimes there was water, sometimes there wasn't. When I wasn't digging up root vegetables or filling skins and pots, I was making futile guesses of what might be happening in the outside world. I didn't know what was going on in the village, where around the continent battles were taking place or if the routes to Xinjing were clear. For all I knew, Xinjing might have burned to ground, and the news wouldn't have reached me. Maybe even the village wasn't there any longer. Perhaps all that remained were this house and garden, the trees bowing in the wind and the sand road flowing towards the village, the coarse sides of the fells and the sky beyond.

Maybe my mother was there no more. Maybe there was no more Sanja.

There were moments when the muteness of the house, the stillness of my life enclosed within its walls threatened to lock my footsteps entirely, until I felt as if I was turning into stone. First my feet would lose their flexibility, their skin would little by little be tinted rain-grey and harden, until they would no longer bend in the knees or ankles, and I'd have no strength to lift them. Unable to take a step, I would watch the porous substance of rock spread its way in me, disease-like, solidifying my hips and sides and chest, dripping leaden into my fingertips and palms, chaining my wrists and elbows into place. The last to petrify would be my face: the eyelids would remain open, and I would feel my eyes slowly grow dry without being able to blink, listening to the echo of my heart within its shell of stone, until even that would eventually fade.

I had to evade the thoughts that had the power to freeze me. I could not stop, not yet.

I went to pick up the food tray of the day from the steps and brought it into the kitchen, where I emptied the food onto the table. The supply was modest today: a handful of amaranth, a pouch of sunflower seeds. The soldiers had taken notice that the crop in the garden was ripening. After a scanty breakfast I took the tray back to the veranda and went to the bathroom to wash. I got undressed and stepped under the shower. Instead of a burst of cold water, only a few drops leaked from the shower head. I waited a short while, turned off the tap and turned it on again. The water pipe wheezed for a moment and a low, metallic screech sounded from somewhere deep, as if the pipe was turning over. Eventually water gushed forth. I applied foaming soapwort all over myself quickly, because I was already used to the water supply in the house being irregular these days. I thought of the surface of the spring and the white mark which had loomed right below it when I had gone to the fell for the last time, but I felt my blood turning heavy again and banished the thought. At least I still had water at my disposal. Even as a marked criminal I didn't need to walk in dirty clothes or spend weeks without bathing. Even in my captivity I had more than most villagers in their freedom.

I still didn't understand the reason for this.

After getting dressed I went to sweep the stone slabs leading to the teahouse. The night dew that clung to the grass brushed my feet through the lattices of my sandals.

The day was cloud-wrapped, but did not ooze with the humidity of rain. I collected the leaves fallen on the path into a pile by the corner of the teahouse, selected a handful to scatter on the stones and carried the rest into the compost behind the hut, taking care not to go too close to the border of my invisible prison.

The berries were red-veined and plump on the gooseberry bushes by now, pulling the branches low with their weight. I picked up a bowl from the veranda. Gooseberries pattered against the plastic, calming as rain; their juice burst sweet into my mouth and their seeds crunched between my teeth. As I was carrying my hoard of berries towards the house, my fingers tender from the prickling bushes, I saw a helicarriage approaching on the road. At first I didn't pay much attention to it. Soldiers would come and go around the house, mostly by foot, but occasionally a helicarriage would bring them and take them away. The change of guard was usually unnoticeable: some moments I could almost pretend that there was nothing out of the ordinary going on in my life, because the soldiers kept their presence mostly invisible as long as I didn't try to cross the line.

This helicarriage, however, stopped under the seagrass shelter for visitors' vehicles, which none of the previous ones had done. I put the berry bowl down on the edge of the veranda. A tall man stepped from the carriage. He walked through the gate into the garden, stopped in front of me and bowed.

I did not bow back.

'Commander Taro,' I said. 'What have I done to deserve this unexpected honour?'

Taro stepped closer, so close I could see my own reflection in his hard, black eyes despite the mesh of his insect hood. My muscles stirred, wanting to step back, but I forced myself to stand still. He was measuring me with his gaze. I did not lower mine.

'I can see you haven't changed since our last meeting, Miss Kaitio,' Taro said. The corners of his mouth twisted into a smile that made me think of knives and sabres and something even sharper. 'What do you think of our hospitality?' He waved his hand, as if catching the house and garden in his fist. 'I think we have been extraordinarily kind: there is plenty of space for exercise, food and water are regularly delivered. Few prisoners enjoy such luxury.'

'I can't deny I have wondered why I've been given such privileges,' I replied. 'I presume you have come to enlighten me.'

Taro seemed amused, but the expression was like a thin mask placed over his features. Nothing moved behind his eyes.

'It would be a shame to let your special skills go unused, Miss – I mean *Master* Kaitio,' he said. 'So I'm suggesting we have this conversation over a cup of tea. Would you be so kind and perform a ceremony to honour my visit?'

Despite his formally polite tone I knew it was not a request.

'Give me fifteen minutes, Commander Taro, so I can prepare everything. There are no sweets,' I remarked without trying to soften the tone of my voice. 'You will accept my apologies for that, I expect.'

'As you wish, Master Kaitio,' he replied.

I left him on the lawn and walked into the house. After making sure that the curtains were tightly closed, I took the tea master's ceremony outfit from my wardrobe and put it on. It was softer and more familiar than it had been one distant Moonfeast day that now belonged to another age and life, when I had first worn it. Yet there was still something alien about it, as if I was wearing a skin that wasn't my own, but merely borrowed. Dressing up in the master's outfit was an irrational and pointless thing to do: I knew Taro didn't expect it from me. But the unchanged form of the tea ceremony bound to the unbroken chain of masters was the only tangible bridge I could build between my own vulnerability and the inviolability of a tea master. The outfit offered a shield behind which I could take cover.

There were several tea sets in the teahouse, and I had swept and aired the hut daily, even washed the floors a few times, so I only needed to carry the water. Ten minutes later I stepped out of the house wearing my outfit and holding a waterskin I had filled from the kitchen tap.

I did not see Taro right away. Then I noticed that he was standing outside the teahouse and sprinkling water on the lawn from the stone basin in front of it. Moistening the grass with water marked a symbolic purification of the teahouse and its surroundings, and no one besides tea masters and their apprentices was permitted to do it. Anger rose bitter in my throat and behind my eyes. The soles of my sandals slapped softly on the stone slabs as I walked to the hut.

'I'm afraid you will have to crawl through the visitors' entrance again,' I said. 'We didn't change its height when we repaired the teahouse.'

Taro wiped his moist hands on the thick fabric of his trousers and smiled his sharpened smile. The look in his black eyes shifted like a movement flickering in a mirror in a dark room.

'I thought so,' he replied.

Neither of us bowed. I walked around the teahouse to the master's entrance.

When I had started the fire, poured the water into the cauldron to heat up and placed the tea set on a tray, I slid the door of the visitors' entrance slightly open. A moment later Taro entered on his knees. He had left his insect hood outside. Without any thought, directed by my muscle memory, I bowed to him. A smile spread on his face again, and he bowed back. It seemed to me that he exaggerated the gesture with scorn, but so slightly that I couldn't tell for certain. Blood rushed to my cheeks. I took a deep breath and thought of water: water that carried and chained me, water that separated me from dust, water that had not deserted me, not yet.

There were ten bubbles at the bottom of the cauldron.

I prepared the tea and offered the cup to Taro. He took it unhurriedly, blew into it, did not sip, because the tea was still too hot, and placed it down on the floor.

He was watching me steadily, and I knew I was being assessed. The weight and coldness of his intent terrified me. He had come here with a goal in his mind. I did not know what it was, but as he was sitting there, unmoving and soundless, I knew nothing could disrupt it, nothing break or even scratch its glistening, hard surface. He was not in a hurry. He could wait and look for my weak spot until he found it.

Eventually, after a long silence, he said, 'You're not afraid of me, Noria. Why not?'

I noticed that he had dropped the titles and used my first name, which was a deliberate breach of etiquette, a disrespectful way of addressing the tea master during the ceremony. I did not reply, and he did not take his eyes off me.

'You do realise I could hurt you if I wanted to?' he continued. His expression did not change. 'Or I could order someone else to do it, and watch.'

I understood it, of course. Everyone knew of the things taking place in darkness, those from which it was easier to avert your eyes. I had thought of them, maybe too much. Of my mother, the walls around her, perhaps thicker and closer than those that held me; of unbending metal that might be grazing her delicate, fragile skin. Of Sanja. I pushed her from my mind, again, because my boundaries began to shake and crumble, and I couldn't let this happen, not now.

'Yet you speak defiantly and do not bow to me,' Taro said. 'Why?'

I said the only thing I knew to say in that situation, and as the words left my mouth, I realised they were true.

'You can no longer do anything to me that matters.'

Taro lifted the cup to his lips, blew into it again and took a drink.

'Nothing at all?' he asked. The same evaluating look remained in the blackness of his eyes. 'What if I said I can give you your life back?'

'I wouldn't believe you,' I replied.

'I know about the spring,' Taro said. 'But I'm sure you had guessed that already. It would have been wise to tell about it. I understand your father was stubborn in the matter, and transferred the same stubbornness to you. The worn-out traditions of tea masters are tedious from my point of view. But of course it was only a matter of time when my suspicions would be confirmed.' Taro ran his finger along the round rim of the teacup. My mother had taught me to sound a drinking glass using the same movement: when you brushed the rim with a moistened finger, it created a strange, high-pitched sound which echoed and filled me with restlessness like an escaping thought I couldn't catch. My mother had told me that if you played the glass for too long, it would break. I hadn't dared to brush out the sound from a single glass since.

'Even most tea masters have forgotten this,' Taro continued, 'because they have been living in cities for many generations now, but the hidden core of the profession pertains that tea masters were once guardians of springs. Your father trusted his luck too much. A backwater village tea master who has been able to resist the temptation of the cities, whose garden is flourishing and whose tea tastes better than the tea of those who buy the best-quality water? It was obvious which secret he was guarding.'

Taro's fingers stopped on the rim of the cup. I had listened to him speak with growing restlessness, and I couldn't contain myself.

'What do you know about the alliance of tea masters and water?' I asked, more hotly than I had meant.

Taro's smile was like the sound of ringing glass.

'There's no need for you to look so worried. Your father was not lying when he told you it was hidden knowledge,' he said. 'It's true. Only those who have been trained as tea masters know.'

I nearly asked how many of them he had tortured in order to gain this secret information, but words stopped in my mouth and something in my memory stirred.

From the beginning, there had been a distinct deliberateness about Taro's way of breaching the etiquette of the ceremony. I had met tea guests who made mistakes because they were not familiar with the etiquette, or because they had forgotten part of it. Their errors were coloured either by confusion or ignorance: they were embarrassed that their unlearned background was revealed in their mistakes, or they didn't even know there was an exact etiquette to be followed, and cared little. Taro, however, had already on his first visit given the impression that had he wished to, he could have followed the etiquette perfectly, but breached it on purpose just because he had the power to do so. He was familiar with the tea ceremony down to every detail as much as I was, and because of this, he knew precisely how to offend the tea master and other guests.

Every memory I had of him revealed itself in new light: how he turned his first tea visit into a cross-examination, how he ordered the teahouse to be taken apart, knowing that rebuilding it in the same way would not be possible, how he had the tea masters' books confiscated from the house although he must have known no tea master would leave a written record of a secret spring behind. How he had sprinkled water on the grass despite the fact that it was the task of the tea master and apprentice alone, and would mean contaminating the ceremony if performed by anyone else.

He watched me, and waited. Waited for me to understand.

'You are a tea master,' I said.

Taro turned his head slightly. I couldn't read his expression.

'I was,' he replied. 'Or to be more accurate, I was supposed to be. I learned from my father, who was a watcher of water, one of the last. He despised the masters of the cities, regarded them as traitors to the profession.'

The humidity rising from the cauldron floated in the air of the teahouse, concentrating on the window and my face.

'But you're not practising,' I said.

Taro drained his cup, placed it down on the floor and pushed it towards me. I filled it.

'Not after I revealed the location of my father's spring to the military,' he said. 'I also let them know that I might be interested in an army career. They were very favourable towards me after that. But we are woolgathering,' he said. 'As I said, I can give you your life back, if you want.' He lifted the cup to his lips, but the liquid was still too hot, and he placed it down again. 'Maybe not exactly as it was, but a large enough part.'

I kept my hands on my knees, although I wanted to wipe the humidity from my brow, and said nothing.

'You haven't heard, have you? About your mother.'

I knew I shouldn't have agreed to trading with him, but I had been staring at the blank screen of the message-pod for too many days, and my thoughts had built too many stories I did not want to follow to the end. I had no power to stop my words.

'What do you know about my mother?'

Taro's expression did not change.

'There was a rebellion in Xinjing. Your mother has been missing for a month,' he said. 'She is believed to be dead.'

I had been fearing this knowledge, and yet now, faced with it, I felt nothing. Grief would come later, but now it simply poured off me and dissipated and left an emptiness behind.

'It's not in my power to bring back the dead,' Taro said. 'But what about those who are still alive?'

He saw me startle and I read contentment on his face.

'Isn't there someone else you would save if you could?'

My breathing clung to my throat and my heart beat faster.

'Where is she?' I asked.

Taro tilted his head and his expression steadied into contemplation.

'She asked me to deliver a message. She asked you to accept my offer.'

I swallowed.

'What's the offer?'

'You can both have your freedom back and you may continue your lives just until now, in peace, protected by the military. You could even use the spring more freely than the rest of the villagers.'

I thought of the weeks when the spring had been ours alone. The corners of Taro's mouth twitched, and I knew he had seen the change on my face. I forced myself to look him directly in the eye.

'On what condition?'

'You only need to consent to the spring belonging to the military from now on, and to both of you working for me.' He paused, letting the words sink in. 'You made some crucial mistakes, of course, but you also showed intellect and cunning. I nearly believed for a while that there was no spring. Muromäki had to spy on you for a long time and make a lot of enquiries before he found out where the water was coming from and how it was being smuggled to the village. We could use spies with your skills.'

For the second time during our conversation images shifted in my memory and their details were laid out in a new manner. Muromäki's tea visit on the wrong day, him stopping at the gate of Sanja's house and his conversation with Sanja. And a memory that was almost lost, but surfaced now, clear amidst others: the blond-haired guest at my father's funeral, the face that had seemed familiar but I had been unable to name. All this time I had not understood how the net was closing in around me.

Everything was still in the room, and I couldn't see the

path ahead of me due to the mist rising from past weeks and their incomprehensibility, the cracks of the world, a dark mirror in which I couldn't discern my own face.

'And Sanja asked me to accept that?'

'She said she would, if it meant you could see each other again.'

I thought of Sanja, and I could feel myself turning towards the thought. I was weary. 'Yes' was an easy word in my mouth, and the image behind my eyes impossible to turn away: her hand in mine in the spring, where the restless current pressed against our outlines, our mark forever in the memory of the world and water.

I closed my eyes and drew in a breath.

'She believed it would be worth it,' Taro continued softly. 'That's why she came to us.'

I opened my eyes. Words slipped away, and images, and all that I could not make true even if I wanted to.

'You are lying,' I said.

Taro's face twisted into an expression that wasn't quite a smile, and something fell off, a mask, a carefully woven plan – I wasn't sure which. I just saw that a crack had appeared in his solid intent, and before he had arranged his face into an unmoving blank canvas again, I knew I was right.

'I could admit that I am,' Taro said. 'But you don't know that. You only have my word, and you don't trust me.' He went quiet. We gazed at each other, and the only things moving in the room were our breathing and our thoughts. 'What if I told you that Sanja didn't come to us because of you, but because she wanted to protect her family? Would you find that easier to believe?'

Shadows wrapped Sanja and carried her further from me, until I could no longer see her. I did not raise my hand. I did not speak a word to forestall her. She walked away and did not look back.

I was alone, and I said the only thing I could.

'Nothing will make me accept your offer.'

Taro lifted the teacup to his lips, drained it slowly, wiped his mouth and placed the cup on the floor.

'Is that your final word?' he asked. 'Think carefully. There won't be another chance.'

'It is.'

Taro nodded. The finality of the gesture echoed in the walls of the narrow room. He got to his feet and his shadow fell over me. For a moment it merged with me as if it was my own.

I moved across the floor to the visitors' entrance and opened it slightly for Taro. He kneeled down again and was just about to crawl out to the veranda, but stopped and turned towards me.

'I'm curious,' he said, and for the first time I saw something in him that resembled genuine interest. 'Why? Do you believe that there is some reward waiting for you, in another life or afterlife, if you do what you imagine is the right thing?'

'No,' I said. 'I believe that we must make hard choices every day despite knowing that there is no reward.'

'Why?' he repeated.

'Because if this is all there is, it's the only way to leave a mark of your life that makes any difference.'

Taro did not nod, did not smile, did not sneer. He just looked, and turned again to go.

'I'm curious too,' I said, and he stopped. 'If you don't believe in rewards, if you know even your power will fade, why do you keep hoarding it and doing things you know to be wrong?'

Taro did not stir at my question. He was quiet. I heard his breathing in the humid air of the hut, and I imagined there was a nearly unnoticeable quiver in his expression, but I was probably wrong. He was looking away, and when he turned his face towards me again, it was only cold glass and stone I saw.

'Because if this is all there is,' he finally said, 'I might as well enjoy it while it lasts.'

We sat still on our knees, turned towards each other, and nothing separated us, and nothing held us together. His choices could have been mine; all shadows share the same colour, and they all disappear in the dark.

'Goodbye, Commander Taro,' I said eventually. 'There's nothing more I can do for you.'

I did not bow farewell. Yet Taro bowed to me, and this time I did not see contempt or jeer in his gesture, although I did not see respect, either. I waited until he had crawled out of the hut and I could no longer hear the steps of his boots on the veranda or on the stones of the path.

That evening I counted the lines I had drawn on the door, and I counted the days I knew had passed in other water-crime houses between the appearance of the blue circle and the execution of the inhabitants.

When I went out to fill my night lantern with blazeflies, I saw a dark, narrow figure by the corner of the teahouse, where the shadows were thickening. I couldn't see the face, not yet, but I sensed that the figure was looking directly at me before turning around and vanishing behind the teahouse, beyond the boundaries that I had been granted.

CHAPTER NINETEEN

It was still dusky outside when I rose to make my morning tea. The water pipe was acting up, as it had been nearly every day for the past three weeks: first the water burst out into the pot in a rushing fall, then waned into drops and eventually settled into a narrow trickle. The metal of the pipes stretched and the sound ebbed away in the innards of the house. I placed the teapot under the dripping water.

There wasn't much time left now.

While the teapot was filling, I went to draw a new line on the door. It was the sixth of the seventh row. Just over a week had passed since Taro's visit. My arm felt heavy, and the blade was reluctant to move and break the painted surface; but even if I stopped the movement, left the seventh row blank, I wouldn't be able to hold the hours running out around me.

I returned to the kitchen and saw that the trickle of water had drained completely. I peered into the teapot: it wasn't even half-full. I emptied the remaining drop of water into it from the next-to-last skin that still had something in it. I'd need to try to fill the skin later, if the pipe would consent to working. I didn't turn the tap off, but put a large pot under it. I would hear if the water started to run again. My ears had had time to grow sensitive to the sound which had previously been so commonplace that I hadn't paid any attention to it.

I buttoned up my cardigan, pulled woollen socks on my feet and picked up my shawl from the rack on the wall at the entrance. The morning was cold, much colder than most mornings of the eighth month of the year. I opened the door and drew in the scent of the garden recovering from its night-rawness. My breathing clouded in the outside air.

As I bent down to pick up the food tray from the step, I saw the water-glow of a swelling half moon over the fell. Moonfeast was drawing near. Soon the villagers would be baking sweet, sticky feastcakes and hanging blaze lanterns painted in myriad colours from the eaves of their houses. The Dragon had been built ready for the parade, and the plastic grave would be bustling, as people were looking for accessories for the feast decorations and children's fancy dresses. This year there probably wouldn't be fireworks; they would be considered too dangerous, with no water to spare for putting the sparks out. Light would have to be found in other fires. Perhaps on Moonfeast night Ocean-Dragons would wander again and cast their glowing reflections across the dark vault of the sky.

Perhaps someone would sit on the Beak and watch them. Perhaps there would be someone sitting next to her, placing a hand on her arm, and nothing would need to be different.

A sound from the direction of the gate caught my attention. Someone was speaking softly. I turned to look, but only saw a stretch of blue disappearing into the copse. Yet the voices were still floating in the dawn: two soldiers were talking. One of them laughed.

They would walk into the village later this afternoon, or whenever their watch ended. They would polish their boots and buy bread or perhaps blue lotus at the market, and they would sleep through the night or stay awake without counting the hours of their lives. Wind would tug at their insect hoods and the sun would shine on their knuckles, and they wouldn't even notice the refreshing coolness or soothing warmth.

I didn't know their names, or where they came from, or how they looked, and I had never hated anyone like I hated them at that moment.

The tray was light. There was nothing on it except a handful of dried beans in a small earthenware bowl. My steps were only slightly shaky when I carried it inside and closed the door behind me.

I was surprised at the strength of the anger that gripped me. I was surprised at the movement of my arm, and at the sound the bowl made when it crashed and broke against the wall.

The fabric of reality rearranged itself around me in a way from which I could not avert my gaze. Threads of life wove their way across and around each other, they intertwined and grew apart again, forming a web that held existence together. I could see the cracks in it clearly, the strands coming loose and slipping away from me. The world still grew and throbbed with stories, but I no longer had a foothold in them.

And behind it all was a void I could almost touch now: a cold space of silence and nothingness, a place we reach when we vanish from the memory of the world.

The place where we truly die.

I wanted to turn away, but I was held still by the chain of events that had brought me here, the past that lay behind me set in stone and would never give in, never break, never shift its shape. I would be looking towards it until I would no longer be looking at anything at all. Stories about it might bend this way and that, but the truth behind them could not be transformed. It bowed to no power but its own.

The burn rose from somewhere deeper than my throat and chest, and broke from my mouth in a heavy, ragged sob. My breath clutched and my whole body curled around anger and grief, and then the sobs were dragged from me in such rapid succession that I couldn't withhold them any more. I collapsed against the door and let them come.

Dust floated quietly in a shaft of light against the grey dusk of the house. My limbs were heavy. I was lying on the floor. Tight, salty streaks were drying on my cheeks and in the corners of my eyes, and I tasted hot metal in my mouth.

I could stay here, I thought. The soldiers will come tomorrow. The skins are nearly empty. I could stay here until my water flows away.

Silence thickened on my skin. I wanted to give in to it. I closed my eyes.

Something moved in the dead, bone-dry hush.

If only that fly would stop buzzing, I thought. Then I could sleep.

But it didn't: it kept thumping against the glass, unable to understand why it couldn't break into the free air outside. I opened my eyes and saw its shadow bouncing in the narrow space between the window and the curtains covering it.

Something stirred deep in my memory: another fly, its heavy body glistening green and black, its wings whirring as it sought its way up and down a tight mesh wall, looking for an opening.

I turned my head and saw my seagrass bag, which I had left leaning against the wall below the clothes rack. Through its woven surface I discerned the rectangle of my notebook.

The memory unfolded further. The fly gave up on the mesh wall and landed on a table covered with tools and pieces of cable. The surface of the silver-coloured disc spilled with light as Sanja placed it in the dent of the past-machine and pressed the lid closed. The loudspeakers rustled. A stream of words that would not leave me alone drifted in the hot, still air.

My mind was trying to grasp something, an invisible strand that ran through years and ages and lives.

The memory shifted: a leather-covered book was heavy in my hands, and on its pages words were building a bridge to the past that would have been lost otherwise. Characters drawn by the hand of a long-gone tea master pulled me in, and somehow he was still there, alive between those covers, because of what he had left behind. The sentences caught me and dragged me back from the shrouding silence.

This is my last story, and after I have recorded it on these pages, my water may run dry freely.

There are just events that people give the shape of stories in order to understand them better.

Too many stories are lost, and too few of those that remain are true.

Despite the chill emanating from the gap under the door, the wooden floor felt warm when I pressed my palms against it and slowly pushed myself up. It was like struggling against a strong wind: I had to force myself to stay in the sitting position and not give in to the fatigue that weighed on me, trying to pull me back down. The bag was only a metre or so away. I lifted my hand and reached for it, fumbled for the shoulder strap and nearly lost my balance. Eventually I managed to get a grasp of the tightly woven fabric and pull the bag towards myself. I took the tea master's book out of the bag. The leather of the cover was soft against my fingertips.

My handwriting ran across the pages, slanted and narrow. The entries described dutifully the ceremonies and teaware used, weather, how the guests were dressed and how they behaved. Yet most of the space was taken by the log of the Jansson expedition, which I had written down from the silver-coloured discs: fragmentary, incomplete, but still true at its core. I kept turning the pages and arrived at the contents of the final disc I had listened to with Sanja one cloudy summer afternoon.

It was an account of ruin and devastation, of oceans reaching towards the centres of the continents, swallowing land and fresh water. Millions fleeing their homes, wars fought over fuel resources revealed under the melting ice, until the veins of the earth ran dry. People wounding their world until they lost it.

Then it turned into a tale of truths forged and lies told and history changed for ever: a story of books crumbling into shreds of paper mist at the bottom of the sea and replaced with the easily modifiable pod-books, until any event could be erased with a few pushes of buttons from the memory of the world, until responsibility for wars or accidents or lost winters no longer belonged to anyone.

It was a story those holding power in New Qian had

sought to destroy, just like they had destroyed almost everything else about the past-world. And yet I was holding it in my hands: not the whole truth, because the whole truth never survives, but something that was not entirely lost.

I stared at the sentences on the pages and I began to understand what I needed to do.

I could stay put and wait until dust defeated water. I could let someone else tell my tale, if it would be told at all: someone who would twist it and make it unrecognisable and perhaps harness it to their own purposes. If I left my story to those who had drawn the blue circle on my door, it would no longer be mine. I would no longer be in it. I would no longer be anywhere.

I could let that happen. Or I could try to leave my mark on the world, give it my own shape.

The final third of the tea master's book was still blank.

My legs barely carried me when I got to my feet.

Thick curtains were covering the window of my room. In the twilight I opened the tea master's book on a new, blank page, sat down on the bed and moved the blaze lantern on the nightstand so that it cast enough light across the pages.

Ink glistened at the tip of my pen and left a star-shaped stain on the paper as I started work.

The words were slow to come at first, faint and wan in the darkness where they'd been stowed away for a long time. But as I reached for them, they began to flicker and flash and float towards me, and their shapes grew clearer. When they finally burst to the surface, bright and bold, I caught what I could and let them pour out of me.

I wrote about the hidden spring that no one else had

ever written about before. I wrote about the fishfires that wavered in the sky-ocean like wide shoals of fish flashing their scales and in which you could see the forms of dragons if you knew how to look. I wrote about the plastic grave, the secrets drowned in its layers, the crushed past-objects that had once belonged to somebody and meant something, each one of them.

The sentences on the paper broke the circle of place and time. Water ran to the house from the fell again, and my father was walking in the rooms. I saw the way he would stretch his fingers after raking the rock garden and placing the rake against the railing of the veranda, and the way he would knit his eyebrows whenever he bent his head over the cauldron to count the bubbles at the bottom. My mother was sitting in her study, and I saw her stroking back her hair, lost in thought, and tilting her head as she tried to remember where she had left her pen. I smelled the lavender and mint scent of her homemade soap, and the onion stew my father would sometimes cook. I heard their footsteps: one slow and steady pair, the other more emphatic and impatient. Their voices filled the kitchen again and floated in the garden, and I wasn't alone anymore.

I wrote about Sanja. The glow that would take over her face when she was picking out pieces one by one from the guts of a past-machine in her workshop, memorising their order and placing them neatly on the table. The way one corner of her mouth would rise a bit higher than the other when she smiled, and how she always knew what to say or not say to make me feel better. Her habit of pulling her dark hair back with a scarf, the outlines of her hands, the cracks and torn skin of her fingertips. The way her limbs looked through dark water where daylight did not reach.

Outside the sky changed and dimmed down, but inside the room it was as if shadows shrank and curled, and the book cast its own sheen, fuller and brighter than the blaze lantern. The slice of blank pages at the end grew slimmer. I summoned the spirits surrounding me and caught them between the covers with all other things lost, until I had scribbled across every last inch of paper and my wrist ached.

When I finally put the pen down and rested my forehead against the leather of the back cover, night was already diminishing outside the curtains. My body felt like an empty husk: light enough for any breeze to carry away, free of the weight of water and words.

I put on my tea master's outfit. It was loose and soft on my skin, and I felt the unwashed scent of my own sweat on it. My socks were slippery against the wooden floor when I walked to the kitchen with the notebook in my hand. The lightweight fabric pouch was in the kitchen cupboard where I had left it. I loosened the string holding it closed and looked inside. A few spoonfuls of tea remained at the bottom, the same one I had chosen at the Kuoloyarvi market for my graduation ceremony. The scent was fainter than back then, but I could still sense the same flow in it: the moistness reviving the dust of the earth, the wind shaking the branches of all things that grew, the light wavering on water.

I lifted the final waterskin from the floor. Its small weight sloshed quietly. I placed the mouth of the skin against the metal of the tap. I spoke to it in pretty words and ugly words, and I may have even screamed and wept, but water doesn't care for human sorrows. It flows without slowing or quickening its pace in the darkness of the earth, where only stones will hear.

There are seven times seven vertical lines on the door of my house, and the paint of the blue circle outside has dried a long time ago.

Everything is ready now.

This morning the world is the way we left it, and yet I did not recognise it immediately when I opened the door and stepped into the garden. Not only the colour was different, but also the scent, and the silence: I know many silences, but this one was unfamiliar.

For a moment I thought I had been born again.

I wrapped the shawl tighter and pulled the sleeve ends of my cardigan to cover my hands. I could have stepped down from the veranda with my shoes and socks on, but I wanted to know how the icy grass would feel under my bare feet. The stalks rustled and their paper-crisp coldness cut through me when I walked to the rock garden.

The sun came out from behind the cloud and I was dazzled. I had imagined the brightness of past-world winters, but this brightness was different. A delicate layer of snow rested on the branches of the tea plants and on the grass and in the folds of the sand of the rock garden, and on tree leaves and the roof of the teahouse. When the light fell on it, my eyes watered, and I had to close them.

All waterskins on the veranda were empty. White frost covered their scratched sides. I carried the final skin from the kitchen to the veranda of the teahouse, picked up the broomstick and swept from the stone slabs the white-veined ghosts of leaves that were slowly beginning to get soggy in the sun. I selected a handful to be scattered on the stones again, so the path wouldn't look too much like it had been swept. That was one of the things my father always insisted on.

The visitors' entrance was narrow and angular around me as I crawled through it into the teahouse, pushing the waterskin ahead of me. I emptied the water into the cauldron and went to get some dried peat from the shed. In the water room I pulled the tea master's book from under my cardigan and placed it on the floor under a shelf reserved for the teaware. I put a large metal pot, a smaller earthenware pot and a single teacup next to each other on a tray. I carried the tray to the edge of the hearth, sprinkled the remaining leaves from the pouch into the earthenware pot and started a fire under the cauldron.

I thought of my father, who was only in my blood and bones, and of my mother, of whom nothing remained but me.

I thought of Sanja.

I knew, like in a dream you know that the other person in the room is familiar, even if you don't know their face, or like you know you love.

Steam began to rise from the cauldron, and I waited until I could count ten small bubbles at the bottom of it.

I filled the metal pot with hot water, prepared the mild tea in the earthenware pot and used it to warm the cup. Then I filled the small teapot again and poured the tea from the cup over it, until the brown, porous sides were wet. My movements flowed unforced, supple as a tree bending in the wind or a wave crossing the oceanbed.

The tea was clear and pale in the cup, its scent soft around me.

I slid the door open for the one who was coming, and settled in the middle of the teahouse floor, so I could see through the doorframe the trees arching over the path and the light sprinkled by the sun on the smooth, moist stones.

This is not the ending I imagined for myself. Yet it is

the only one I have. Or that may not be entirely true: I suppose I could run through the gate and continue running until I heard a bang cutting through the air and felt a sharp burn somewhere in my body. Perhaps that would be quicker than waiting for the soldiers who must be drawing closer now, the blades of their sabres, the blood I will not see drying on the stone slabs. But it would only change the journey, not the outcome. There is no way out. Yet I have decided to keep breathing for as long as I can. I may end here, but there will be others who will carry the story forward. Perhaps some small stretch of the world will be more whole after them.

The ceremony is over when there is no more water.

I can't see beyond this garden. I don't know if cities have crumbled down, and I don't know who calls the land their own today. I don't know who is trying to confine the water and sky without realising that they belong to everyone and no one at all. There are no man-made chains that will hold them.

I don't need to see beyond this garden, not anymore.

Very soon now, as long as I'm still alone in the teahouse, I will go into the water room, push my hand under the shelf and feel around until I find a small dent in the floorboard resting in the corner. It's one of the boards from the old teahouse, darker than others. I will push my finger into the dent and lift the board, which is not nailed in place. I will wedge my other hand carefully under it, until I manage to move the board aside. Under it there is a dark niche which emanates the coldness of the earth.

The leather cover of the book is soft and warm, almost like a living thing under my touch. No one will see me place the book carefully into the niche through the hole and push it a little to the side, under the solid floorboards, so the fingers or eyes of a seeker would not catch it.

The visitor is opening the gate right now, stepping into the garden through it, looking for the path that leads to the teahouse. Her feet don't leave marks in the thin snow. A wind rises and the tea plants shake shimmering dust from their branches. Luminous flakes float into the ground, where snow is already melting into flowing water, threading its narrow brook in light. I follow them as they take their place, deep, deep in the stream, where there is no beginning and no end.

The aftertaste of the tea is sweet in my mouth.

I have tried not to think about Sanja, but she bleeds into my thoughts, and I wonder: do I bleed into hers, into what may be left of her?

This image emerges before my eyes uninvited, and emerges again, and will not vanish: she is standing in the fell cave by the pond. She is looking into the foaming water, and I would like to think she is coming to me. Yet I see another her, turning away from me, and she is not coming back. I don't know which one of them is real and which one is a reflection in clear water, so sharp that one might almost mistake it for real.

I can pick my own ending, the one I want.

The day outside is burning bright, and in the frame of the doorway I see her as she steps closer to me.

I reach my hand out to her.

EPILOGUE

She steps through the doorway.

'What's your business, miss?' asks a blue-clad porter sitting in his glass-walled lodge. The entrance of the university building is quiet this early in the day.

'I'm here to see Lecturer Kaitio,' the girl says. She looks weary and narrow in the dim artificial light of the foyer, no older than twenty. 'I haven't arranged an appointment, but could you let her know I'm here, please?'

'May I see your passpod?' the porter asks and slides open a small window in the glass wall. The girl hands the pod to him. He reads the ID information on the screen, lifts the receiver of the internal phone off its hook and dials a short number. 'Lecturer Kaitio?' he says into the speaker. 'There's a young lady here who is asking to see you. Miss Vanamo.' He measures the girl with his gaze, and something resembling a smile surfaces on his face. 'All right, then.' He places the receiver down. 'She will come to meet you here.' He hands the message-pod back to her.

The girl notices Lian Kaitio's expression freeze for a passing moment when she arrives in the foyer. The porter is not looking at them, because he is busy fiddling with his mahjong game, and there is no one else in the hallway.

'Please, follow me,' Lian says, and the girl does.

When they enter Lian's office, she pulls the door closed behind her, turns the key in the lock, seizes the girl's shoulders and asks, 'Where is Noria? Is she alright?'

She reads the answer in Sanja's expression and pulls her into her arms, and all words are lost to them.

Sanja tells her everything, later.

She tells how the village was crushed in the grip of the military, and water was taken from people, and the spring became a shared secret.

She tells how Noria wanted to search for water in the Lost Lands and how it was their plan to go together.

She tells how she saw a water patrol behind her family home the same day when they were meant to leave, how she ran for the hiding place of the helicarriage and drove the carriage into the Dead Forest where she hid for weeks. She sent Noria one message after another, but each one of them bounced back. Eventually she crept into the village in secret, only to find out that her family had been taken away by soldiers and that there was a blue circle on the door of the tea master's house.

She tells how she decided to travel across the continent to Xinjing, because she had no other place to go.

When she has told everything, a silence falls into the room, and Lian is crushing a wet handkerchief in her hand.

'I don't know what you want to do, Mrs Kaitio,' Sanja says at length. 'But I know what I need to do.' She goes quiet for a moment. 'I brought you something.' She takes a threadbare roll of fabric from her bag and places it on the desk. She unfolds the knot.

Seven silver-coloured discs are glistening on top of the worn cloth.

This morning the world is dust and ashes, but not devoid of hope.

ACKNOWLEDGEMENTS

No novel sees the light of day without an enormous amount of support and faith, and I am grateful to those who helped this one become more than just a pile of paper buried in a drawer:

Emma Coode for believing in this book.

Silja Hiidenheimo, Jussi Tiihonen and everyone else at my Finnish publisher Teos for being consistently fantastic.

My agent Elina Ahlbäck for working so hard to bring this book to audiences outside Finland.

Patricia Debney for being the first one to see a novel between the lines of those early pages and for acting as a midwife along the way.

Nancy Gaffield, Nancy Fulton, Jeremy Scott, Craig Ferguson and Mark Wilson for discussion, insight and encouragement.

Todd McEwen and Lucy Ellman for their generosity and kindness.

Marika Riikonen and Päivi Haanpää for friendship, feedback and being the official godmothers to this book.

Mari Paavola for being there when everything changed.